THE AVENGER'S APPRENTICE

David Roy

THE AVENGER'S APPRENTICE

Previously Published in 2022
by
Hobart Books, Oxfordshire, England

The Lost Man 2

~ § ~

The Avenger's Apprentice

By David Roy

Prologue

'What can you see?'

'Nothing.'

'Keep looking.'

Ted strained his eyes to see better in the dark… but it was the dark that was the problem: impenetrable, complete. Not one ray of light made it into the room and Ted just shook his head at the sheer impossibility of his task. They had practically admitted they didn't know what they were doing; now he knew for sure that they hadn't been lying. If anything, they had underplayed their lack of… what was it… competence? Experience, maybe? He wondered if they actually knew anything more than he did.

'Just keep looking,' said the voice. 'Let me know when you see something.'

Ted could still see nothing. He had never known such unadulterated blackness as that in which he now stood. But he could smell something. Burning? Smouldering perhaps, like a dry cloth carelessly dropped onto a light bulb, or dust on a seldom-used heater. Whatever produced the smell emitted no light. But he could hear something; a low hum from somewhere, like the sound of an electrical transformer. He connected the smell to the sound, which achieved nothing of course; they wanted him to *see.*

'Can you see *anything*?' asked the voice. Did he detect a trace of despair displacing the quiet optimism of only a few minutes ago?

'Nothing. Just blackness.'

'Can you see the outline of any shapes? Even slightly?'

'Nothing,' said Ted. His small reserves of patience suddenly ran out like the last grains of sand in an egg timer. 'Why don't you just put the bloody light on?,' he asked, facetiously. There was no reply but a moment later the light did indeed come on. Ted shielded his eyes. 'I think I can see something now,' he said.

He heard a voice on the other side of the plywood wall, someone uncharitably calling him a cheeky bastard. He smiled, quite uncaring of the insult.

His vision was just returning when he heard the door creak open. A staff sergeant poked his head in.

'Visitor,' he said and indicated that Ted should follow him. Ted smiled nastily at the civilian technician in charge of running the experiment as he made his way from the studio. The man frowned, camply. He was an emaciated character who looked perpetually damp, but not from washing. His hair was dark and lank. In fact, he looked like someone who smelled, but Ted never got close enough to put the man's malodorous qualifications to the test.

'What were you up to in there?,' asked the staff sergeant as they strode towards the exterior door. Ted knew he wasn't allowed to discuss the experiment. He wondered if his discretion was being tested and *then* he wondered if he even cared one way of the other. Perhaps the senior NCO was just making conversation. The staff sergeant looked like a right dumb bastard, he decided – a lifer; twenty-two years in the army with no chance of parole.

'I was testing pills that help you to see in the dark,' he said casually.

'Really?' said the NCO, enthusiastically. *Yeah, a dumb bastard*, thought Ted.

'Aye,' said Ted, keeping his voice matter-of-fact. He stepped through the door held open by the other man. The light outside was fading and thin clouds began to take on a pinkish hue. He wondered just how gullible the other man was. Was it a deep-seated, profound gullibility or something more superficial, like minor daftness?

'And did they work?'

'Yeah. It was amazing really,' lied Ted. 'It wasn't like broad daylight or anything but it was pretty clear.' The NCO shook his head in wonderment. Ted had his answer on the question of gullibility.

'Blimey,' he said. 'Right, you've to wait here until you're called in,' he added, suddenly getting back to business.

To his left, Ted could see a twin-engine plane parked on the runway. It looked like a civilian aircraft decked out in wartime camouflage. An RAF corporal with a side-arm stood guard, as if plane theft were a big problem round here. Perhaps it was. It needed a special kind of thief to steal a plane, thought Ted – one who could fly for starters.

He smirked. He didn't really know where he was but they were looking after him, so he had no complaints. The staff sergeant returned looking faintly excited. It was repressed excitement, the sort you experienced when you had thrilling news to impart but wanted to keep it for the right moment, like the birth of an illegitimate child two doors down; you'd save that for tea time when the whole family was there to choke on their spuds.

'When you go in, salute and just call him 'sir',' he said. He was almost – but not quite – hopping from foot to foot as if he needed the toilet.

'Call who 'sir'?'

'You'll get it in a minute. You must be bloody important whoever you are,' said the staff sergeant, gushing. He ushered Ted towards the door and after a brief pause, Ted made his way inside. The room was well-lit but spartan, nothing more than a few folding tables and canvas-backed chairs. A group of men stood in a huddle chatting amiably. One of the men was in the uniform of a field marshal, one was dressed as a brigadier and the other wore a suit and overcoat.

'Ah, Dexter,' said Brigadier Murray. 'Come over here.' His tone was light, as if he had just finished laughing. 'You've met the PM already. This gentleman,' he pointed at the field marshal, 'is the King.' Ted had closed the distance between them and the man had turned by this time. Ted stopped and saluted.

'Close your mouth, Dexter,' said Murray, kindly as the King returned the salute. 'King George has come to award you your medal.' Ted made no reply, his vocal cords paralysed with shock. *Boy from Belfast meets King*, went the headline in his mind.

'I couldn't invite you to the palace unfortunately, Corporal Dexter. I am given to understand that you no longer exist,' said the King, with a chuckle. Churchill beamed like a proud father. It was the PM's cue to speak.

'Corporal Dexter is my secret weapon, Your Majesty. He is going to wreak havoc on the Nazi war machine,' he said. 'Brigadier Murray is my avenger-in-chief,' he pointed to the officer who bowed his head modestly. 'And young Dexter is his… well… I suppose, his apprentice. Would you say so, brigadier?'

Ted blanched. He hated any mention of his new role. So long as he remained in this place (wherever it was) like a prized prisoner, he could blot out any thoughts of the danger in which he might soon find himself. He didn't want any reminders. He didn't want to be heroic. He didn't want to be *considered* heroic. He didn't want any words with heroic connotations used in the same sentence as his name.

Murray smiled. 'Nicely put, sir,' he said, obsequiously.

They could all turn it on, these officers. Ted imagined the staff sergeant outside practically crapping himself with excitement. He'd be going home tonight to his badger-faced wife bursting with the news. She probably wouldn't believe him… which was funny.

'So how is your training going?,' asked the King, with what appeared to be genuine interest. Ted decided to lie.

'Very well, sir,' he said. Now was not the time to mention the dark room and the night vision tablets that did no good, or the unarmed combat classes led by an alleged Spanish Civil War veteran from Manchester who'd been arrested by the police on a charge of burglary just three days into their training. He'd also been trained to use a variety of German weapons only one of which subsequently worked when they took it to the range for test firing. He wouldn't mention that either.

'Good,' said the King, happily. 'Well, Brigadier Murray has told me all about you and about the radio equipment you brought back from France; a quite remarkable story. This medal is well deserved,' he said reaching for a small box. 'Unfortunately, you can't wear it, I understand. That's one of the problems with not existing.' The PM and Murray laughed politely. 'But well done anyway. When we have won this wretched war, I expect that your exploits will be famous. You might even have a few more medals to wear by then. I am sure we shall meet again.'

I hope not, thought Ted. He wasn't averse to receiving a medal for his exploits, rather, he didn't really fancy doing anything which required further gallantry awards to be made. *Maybe if he were to meet the King socially, rather than for the presentation of a medal…*

***

'He's not what I expected,' said the King, after Ted had left. They were seated in a comfortable ante room, a decanter and cigars within easy reach. Murray looked on at the two men whose power, influence and privilege created a distance between themselves and himself that could never be bridged, irrespective of any promotions that might come his way in the ensuing years. They didn't deliberately exclude him from their conversation; they didn't have to. Some indefinable cultural barrier existed that kept Murray in his narrow band of society, just as the King and PM had to remain in theirs.

'That's part of the appeal, Your Majesty. Who needs an agent who draws attention to himself?' said Churchill. He helped himself to a cigar and passed one to the King. 'Cigar, brigadier?' he asked, inadvertently emphasizing the gulf that existed between them. The King's cigar was an unalienable right whereas his was an afterthought, a gift to a deserving underling. Well, so be it. He had his job to do and he would try his best.

Chapter One

'We have a job for you,' said Murray. 'Are you ready for it?' The room in which they sat was cold and uncomfortable. The grate was laid out with newspapers and logs ready to light but no match had been applied. Ted's chair was like a relic from another era; rescued from an Edwardian drawing room and stored badly since. It was lumpy as if it had been stuffed with gravel and it creaked every time he moved. He tried not to move. The brigadier at least had a desk with a few sparse accessories to play with during the awkward silences between the two men. Ted shrugged his reply unhappily and then spoke.

'I don't know if I am, sir,' he said. 'If you have a job for me then I suppose I've just got to be ready.'

'You don't think it's gone well, do you? The training, I mean.' The officer waited for Ted's reply. He felt disinclined to argue with Murray's assessment of his training so far; it had been uniformly hopeless. However, he was also disinclined to say anything which meant someone else getting into trouble. It was a part of his personal code that he, generally speaking, raised few complaints.

'Well,' he began. He shifted in his seat and it groaned like an old drunk stirring in his sleep. 'Some of it has been okay, I suppose…'

'Which bits?,' interjected the officer quickly. He smiled slightly, hoping that the NCO wouldn't feel too intimidated. He wanted the truth from him.

'Em. Well… It's hard to say, sir because I don't really know what I'm going to have to do.' Ted's fingers interlocked and he rubbed his thumbs together, wishing that he were somewhere else. There had been times – not many, but a few – when a prisoner of war camp, where he had so nearly ended up, had looked like a nice, safe place to be and an acceptable alternative to his new regime. Life spent staring at a ceiling with nothing to do seemed like quite an attractive proposition. This – this new strange life – was safe too but it wouldn't remain so. His day was coming. He had a date with destiny, one that he would happily forgo. In the meantime, he remained isolated and forlorn.

'It's been three weeks since you got back. That's not much time to turn someone into an agent, saboteur, spy… whatever you are.'

'Whatever I am,' concurred Ted. He scratched his head as if to visually reinforce his doubts. Murray smiled, enigmatically.

'The problem is that we are all amateurs at this game. The PM wants hordes of men in Europe causing mayhem – 'setting Europe ablaze' – is his current phrase. You are just the first member of an underground army he wants to be established to keep us demonstrably in the war. He wants us to take the war to Hitler and not just sit tight defending ourselves. But we know nothing about this business. We make it up as we go along, gathering in whatever talent we can find, hence our unarmed combat expert now languishing in jail.'

Ted nodded.

'Was he any good, by the way?'

'I think so, sir.'

'Yes, he had a number of talents we could have exploited. If he hadn't got caught by Scotland Yard he might have made a more compelling case for his continued employment with us.' The brigadier paused, thoughtfully. 'What I am trying to say is that I know your training hasn't been ideal but that's only because we are all learning. There is no real precedent for this. Nevertheless, we have a job for you – something quite straightforward.'

Ted said nothing but regarded the officer with a serious look.

'We want you to go back to France and find the officer who gunned down Miglorine's platoon.' The brigadier paused, letting the words sink in. Ted still said nothing. 'Can I get you anything? A coffee or tea?' Ted shook his head.

'No thanks, sir. Back to France? I wasn't expecting that.'

'Well, we need you to fight the Germans. The Germans are in France,' he replied simply.

'Yes of course. It's just… I've only just escaped…'

'As I said it's quite straightforward. Find him and, er… kill him, I suppose.' Ted wondered how much consideration had actually been given to this plan. Not a great deal by the sound of it. 'I suppose you could try to get him back to Britain where he could stand some sort of trial but that's not exactly practical is it? You must have lots of questions but I think I can probably pre-empt and answer most of them. Firstly, we do know *who* he is. Secondly, we do know *where* he is. Really you just have to get in close and dispose of him.'

Ted smiled to himself. Brigadier Murray made it all seem so easy, reasonable and tidy. His words were clean, soft words, untainted by blood and gore.

'You're smiling?'

'When do I go?' he replied, ignoring the implicit question.

'Soon. You'll be going whether you think you're ready or not. The point is that *I* think you're ready. You're certainly ready for *this*. It's nothing you haven't done before. A simple in and out type of job.'

'So, it's all planned, sir?'

'We're working on it. It's quite straightforward. I think we'll be giving you a bit of language training – French and German – then more weapons training, and we've got another chap coming in to take over the unarmed combat.'

'And how do I get there?'

'Parachute?'

'Mmmm. And getting back? How do you plan to get me back out, sir?'

'As I said Corporal Dexter, we're working on it. I must say you do a very good job of keeping your enthusiasm in check.' He gave Ted a wry smile as he spoke.

'It just seems to come naturally, sir,' explained Ted.

***

Ted thought about 'the plan' as he lay in his bed that night. He shook his head as he reached for his cigarettes. It wasn't really a plan at all. The only 'plan' he was interested in would have some provision for his return to Britain as a bare minimum. He wasn't keen on the idea of parachuting either. He pictured himself jumping out of a perfectly good aeroplane, plummeting to earth, his parachute not opening, and wondered what noise his body would make as it hit the ground at high speed. He put a cigarette in his mouth thoughtfully, his eyes darting round the room as if subconsciously looking for an escape route. The first match he struck broke and he imagined it to be one of his legs smashing like a brittle twig as he landed… and that was with an opened parachute!

How had Murray come by the information about this man he would be sent to kill, he wondered? Perhaps he'd ask about that, although from what he had seen so far, he doubted if an answer would be forthcoming.

Ted sat up and removed his boots. New boots. New socks. New everything, in fact… but still the same old Ted Dexter. He was his own weak link. His confidence had been adequate, if not exactly sky high, following his safe return from France. On the back of a miraculous escape and a visit to see the PM, anything had seemed possible. Weeks later and reality had taken its toll, eroding his confidence, making him doubt if he was really the man, they – Churchill, the King, General Brooke and Brigadier Murray – thought he was.

He questioned his own motives at every turn. He had killed the enemy – commendable in the circumstances – but had he done so merely for reasons of self-preservation? Just how much of a patriot was he? How heroic? In one of his increasingly frequent periods of self-doubt he had confided in Murray that he questioned his own suitability to the role of agent. The nature of his new role was vague but not *so* vague that he couldn't match his actual capabilities to the likely demands of being an agent.

'I'm just an ordinary man,' he had once told the brigadier. Virtually the only person with whom he had any regular contact, he had become a confidante of sorts. Murray wasn't totally comfortable with that role. He wondered if he had become Dexter's *de facto* guardian.

'And that's part of the reason you'll be so good. But I don't think that you should underestimate your abilities. You did volunteer, if you recall.'

Ted perched his cigarette on the edge of his bedside locker and scrabbled through his drawer for the medal.

'Something else to polish,' he muttered. *Mind you*, he thought, *a DCM. One below a VC. He was Corporal Ted Dexter, DCM now*. He smiled, slipped the ribbon onto the medal and held it up, imagining it pinned to his chest. Then he snorted, dismissively.

A moment later his optimism evaporated, hope supplanted by fear, and his thoughts strayed to his parents. In his mind, he pictured them in that tiny front room, somehow diminished by their loss. They were grey, aged overnight, overcome with a grief so overwhelming that there was no room for pride in his peculiar achievements. He wanted to see them. He wanted to sit and talk about inconsequential things. He wanted his mum to scurry about tidying up, baking, fussing. These were the things that defined her.

If they – his new lords and masters – ever gave him leave, where would he go, he wondered?

***

His training continued the following morning. He wondered why, with his new status, he couldn't be supplied with PT kit that fitted him? The white singlet slipped off his shoulders, making him look like someone dragged from the sea following a sinking. The blue shorts flapped around his knees. The plimsolls – gutties, he called them – were two huge black canoes. He felt as if he had been kitted out for clown school, rather than being put into… well, what exactly was it? Secret agent training? That sounded more than faintly absurd. So here he stood like an extra from *'The Marx Brothers go to the Gymnasium,'* with cold Arctic winds blowing up his shorts and one skinny goose-bumped shoulder protruding from his PT top like a piece of chicken.

The physical training instructor looked like a circus strongman, his face curiously devoid of expression behind an enormous moustache. Perks of the job; his kit fitted him and actually imbued him with a look of physical fitness. Ted's looked like a badly applied shroud falling off someone who'd died of starvation. The PTI never asked his name or what he was doing there. If he wondered why he had been taken from the depot where he turned the nation's malnourished youth into strapping soldiers, then he never showed any inclination to ask. Luckily for Ted, his own shapeless PT kit disguised a young man in fairly good shape. He managed the press-ups, sit-ups, burpees, the runs. He milled with the PTI and acquitted himself reasonably well. The PTI grew to like Ted, especially since his natural fitness made his own job rather easy.

'You don't really need me,' he said one day.

Ted shrugged. He said, 'it's okay, sergeant. I might be glad of all this fitness training soon.' *When I need to run like hell*, he thought.

Another unarmed combat instructor was found. Ted never knew much about him but he looked like a boxer or a street fighter. His face was marked. His eyebrows had been beaten off and his right ear looked as if it had been tenderised by an artless butcher. When he smiled, he displayed an incongruously full set of gleaming white teeth. And he smiled often, especially when he was about to throw Ted on his backside for what seemed like the hundredth time. He too came to like and respect the Ulsterman. Ted swiftly regained his feet after each throw and stood poised and ready. More and more he foiled his instructor's attempts to up-end him. He blocked the slaps that came his way and began to fight back using the few simple techniques he'd been taught.

After three weeks he could gouge eyes, snap necks, fend off punches. He could trip and foil, duck and push. He was able to punch at weak spots and defend himself with alacrity. It was dirty fighting but he was a natural. Now he just needed someone to try it out on. He could think of a few candidates.

Ted learned to speak French and to understand some words of German. He would never pass for a Frenchman though. French spoken through the mouth of an Ulsterman somehow lost its lyrical quality, like the poems of Wordsworth translated into Dutch. He had initially been eager to meet Madame Prunier, imagining a graceful, elegant creature like Geneviève Boutin. He had been disappointed. She was neither graceful nor elegant… a creature maybe, he thought uncharitably. She seemed to resent him and the task that she had been given. He wondered if her bitterness was borne of French defeat, or was she just a miserable old cow? Perhaps she simply didn't like him, he mused. That was entirely possible.

'Her charms aren't always immediately apparent,' explained Murray at one of their meetings. One day, when Ted was an officer, he would recognise a euphemism when he heard one, but for now he matched her distaste with charm and seeming enthusiasm for the subject. If nothing else this would leave her perplexed, he thought.

Over time, her teaching did have the desired effect. He could say hello, goodbye, count to one hundred. He could ask for things, give directions and knew some useful technical terms. He still struggled to comprehend what was said to him but Madame Prunier grudgingly reassured him that this skill too would come with time and practice.

More weapon training was organised, this time with a selection of German small arms that actually functioned. He became proficient with a Mauser rifle, realising that it was an inferior weapon to the Lee Enfield he had previously been issued. The Mauser was beautifully made in the German fashion, but the pull on the bolt was too long, meaning that each time a new round was shoved into the breech, the firer had to move his head from the sights, upsetting his aim.

He enjoyed using the MP38, erroneously described as the Schmeisser. He fired the odd-looking Luger pistol and the compact Walther PP, hoping that he might be equipped with the latter when he finally returned to France.

'Do you know what to do with this?' said the sergeant major, handing him a German 'potato-masher' grenade. Ted nodded, remembering the men he had killed in France, having taken exactly this type of weapon from the personal equipment of a sleeping solider. He also remembered meeting Miglorine for the first time and his astonishment that the Germans had seemingly exploded before his eyes. They hadn't really, of course, but that was Mig's perfectly reasonable explanation for what he saw as he came over a hill on his motorbike.

'Go on then,' urged the CSM.

'Use it, sir?'

'Aye.'

Ted unscrewed the base cap and let the little ceramic ball fall into his hand. The sergeant major looked on, his face impassive, then Ted pulled on the cord and hefted the grenade down range. Both men ducked behind the revetment. The resultant explosion was more muffled than he remembered it, absorbed by earthen banks.

'Not bad,' said the sergeant major, moderately impressed.

***

The obstacle course was a favourite with the PTI, but Ted wondered when he might really be required to surmount a twelve-foot wall or swing across a swampy gap on the end of a rope. Nor could he readily envisage a time when he would climb a scramble net, vault over the top and descend once more, but if he needed to, he could. Not the twelve-foot wall, though. He wasn't really expected to get over it by himself but there was only him on the course.

His instructor enjoyed watching his doomed attempts, each of which consisted of Ted throwing himself into the brick work and then falling on his backside in the dust. He needed at least one other person to help him but he was alone.

One morning he completed the course to find the brigadier waiting for him. He gave Ted a few moments to get his breath back.

'I have some good news for you, Corporal Dexter,' he said as Ted straightened.

'Leave?'

'Parachute training.'

Ted wondered how this divergence on the meaning of 'good news' had come about.

Chapter Two

'Have you seen one of these before?' asked the flight lieutenant.

'I haven't actually seen one but I know what it is. A Westland Lysander,' said John.

'Right. This is your new mount, so to speak.'

John was disappointed. This was the only front-line aircraft he could think of which was slower, more underpowered and more vulnerable than the Fairey Battles he had flown previously, and he considered himself lucky to have survived *that* experience. The Lysander crews, flying in the army cooperation role, had suffered terribly in France – not as badly as Battle crews but not far off either.

'You don't look too thrilled, Flight,' said the officer.

'Should I be, sir?'

The officer looked on, concerned. The man to whom he spoke was Flight Sergeant John Guy VC; he'd earned the right not to be too thrilled if that's what he wanted. He had been briefed not to ask about the medal and so his curiosity remained unsated. *A VC, though.* They weren't handed out for nothing and more often than not the recipient didn't survive the deed that earned them this highest award. Guy didn't look heroic. He looked… ordinary. He didn't swagger or appear to have the level of arrogance he might have expected from such a man. Perhaps people who acted that way didn't win the VC very often, he supposed.

'Have you been told the purpose of the squadron? It's all new stuff. We're pioneers.' He tried to convey the enthusiasm which he personally felt without sounding like an over-eager school boy. He felt very keenly his lack of combat experience and was keen to get started. He needed a fund of stories for his later years when he would be asked what he had done in the war.

But for now, who was he to try to sell the idea of this new unit to the holder of the VC, a veteran of the French campaign and reputedly the only surviving pilot from his squadron?

'What did you fly before, sir?'

'Gladiators.'

'A good aircraft,' stated John, plainly. Despite its antiquated appearance the Gladiator biplane probably gave a pilot a better chance of survival than the seemingly more modern Fairey Battle. Not only that but if you shot down a Gladiator only one crew member was lost; the Battle had a crew of three.

'You flew Battles?'

'Yes, sir.'

'I understand you're a bit of an expert on night flying too?'

'Well, it's a skill I picked up quickly, shall we say,' said John, enigmatically. He also knew not to discuss his recent experiences. It was pretty clear to him that this secrecy stemmed from the nature of the equipment they had recovered from France: coding equipment and a Fieseler

Storch aeroplane. *Very hush-hush*, they liked to say. The phrase had begun to grate.

'Well, that must be why you've been posted here. Night flying is most definitely going to be our game and this aeroplane is the best there is for the sort of work we have to do. Basically, we are going to be running agents into France, dropping supplies off, collecting parcels, that sort of thing. All under cover of darkness. This is the best aircraft in the world for taking off and landing in short distances.' John cast a glance at the ungainly looking Westland. It was certainly odd-looking enough for the job but he doubted if it really qualified as the best. The German Fieseler he'd flown recently must surely hold that title. Its handling characteristics were nothing short of remarkable. The Fieseler could take off and land in spaces that were too small to even park some other aircraft.

'Are you sure we aren't restricting ourselves to night flying simply because it's so bloody ugly we don't want anyone to see it?,' quipped John, sardonically. The officer smiled awkwardly. How was he supposed to answer? *Perhaps when he had been blooded, he could give the sort of reply that the comment warranted.*

He decided to press on. 'So, this is the Westland Lysander. It's a short field, army cooperation aircraft, hence its sturdy appearance.' He cast a sidewards glance at John as he spoke. He had translated John's 'ugly' into the more acceptable 'sturdy.' He smiled. He had to 'sell' this new plane to his war-weary NCO. 'It's well-armed: four machine guns, one in each wheel spat and two in the rear cockpit. It can carry a small bomb load, but I doubt if we'll be using that. This is the MKII with a 905 HP Bristol

Perseus.' He pointed at the big radial engine. 'Top speed of 212 mph.'

'Slow,' commented John. It was a statement of fact rather than an outright criticism.

'Yes, quite slow but its main advantage is its short take-off and landing run. Besides which, how fast do you want to be going at night?' He smiled defensively, his enthusiasm dented somewhat. John detected the other man's waning fervour and regretted his obtuseness.

'Well, I should be pleased really,' said Guy. 'I thought I was going to be posted to a bomber squadron.'

'Didn't fancy it?'

'I want to live.'

The officer nodded but didn't comment. 'I expect you'll want to take her up, get the feel of her?,' said the officer. Nothing was further from the truth, but since it appeared that his continued participation in the war was required then he'd better get the hang of this aeroplane. The VC, he supposed, caused people to over-estimate his enthusiasm for armed conflict. Perhaps it was normally awarded to war-mongering loons, but he doubted it.

***

The controls were easy enough to use and the system of flaps much more straightforward than those in the Fieseler. He flew with the flight lieutenant in the back seat and they did a series of circuits and bumps, trying to reduce the take-off run each time. Compared to its German equivalent, the Lysander felt heavy and ungainly but also more powerful, faster and stronger. It flew well and with a degree of agility he didn't expect. The officer in the back said little until they landed.

'What did you think?,' he asked. They climbed out and John removed his flying helmet and undid his jacket. The sun beat down on the airfield.

'It flies better than it looks,' he replied, grudgingly. The officer assumed that this might have to suffice for the boundless enthusiasm he would normally have expected from his pilots.

'Well, that's good! Do you think you'll like it here, then?' he asked, capitalising on John's good humour. John cast a glance round the stark airfield. A squat control tower, two Nissen huts and a third one being put up, a grass runway, a windsock, a few dispirited erks standing in a smoky huddle and one aeroplane that looked like it had been drawn by Walt Disney on an off day.

John couldn't think of a single reason why he would like it here. He cast his glance around once more before answering.

'I think so, sir,' he lied.

Flight Lieutenant Embury beamed. 'That's the spirit!,' he said. 'Jolly good!'

Chapter Three

'There'll be a car waiting to take you to Ringway in the morning. If you report to the guardroom you can sign out. You should be gone for about a week.'

'Right, sir,' said Ted. 'Supposing I can't do it?'

'Can't do it?'

'Jump out of an aeroplane, sir.'

'Is there any reason to think that you can't?'

'Well it's not natural, sir, is it? A perfectly good aeroplane and jumping out, that is.'

'We have to get you there somehow. We can't land at an aerodrome and have a car waiting for you in France. This is going to be enemy territory. We could get you there by sea but if you needed to be inland then you have too far to travel. Parachuting is much less hazardous in the long run.' The brigadier smiled in what he hoped would be an encouraging way. The truth was he wouldn't have fancied it any more than Dexter. He looked at the young corporal before him and wondered if he really was the man that Churchill needed him to be. The PM expected such a lot from people. Corporal Dexter was just a young soldier and had never pretended to be anything else. He almost felt sorry for him. 'Look, have a go, Corporal Dexter. We'll play it by ear and see how it works out, okay?'

Ted nodded, unhappily.

***

It no longer suited Ted to be alone with his thoughts. Solitude was fine, but solitude laced with anxiety was almost more than he could bear. The car was noisy and draughty. The driver was a spotty private from the RASC with a ragged haircut. His jug ears sat out from his head like display boards for acne and he sniffed throughout their journey as if he were onto the scent of their new destination. His one saving grace was that he made Ted feel slightly more heroic than he had done for some time. Everything was relative. The two men barely spoke, which suited Ted fine.

The roads were virtually empty: a smattering of small black cars on vital business and unimpressive looking convoys with unhappy looking soldiers crammed into trucks. Overhead the Battle of Britain raged, with the destiny of Europe at stake, but Ted's world was an insular odyssey staged in secret. He felt divorced from the struggle, a remote, isolated figure pushed to the side lines with a new vague purpose that might never be realised. That should have been a comfort and yet everything he did, every morsel of training, every briefing felt like a prelude to doom. Ted's confidence attenuated gradually with each chilly mile spent in the car.

Where was Ringway, he wondered? Not that it really mattered; since he didn't know where his journey had begun, he couldn't possibly gauge how far he had to go to arrive at another place, the location of which was also a mystery. In fact, he really knew little about the geography of his country. Growing up in Belfast had given him an intimate knowledge of an area encompassing maybe twenty streets radiating out from his parent's house – the centre of his tiny universe. It was all he had needed back then. A rolling map in his head told him exact whereabouts at any given moment, signposted by street corners and shops, doorsteps and dustbins. Now and again they went as a family to Bangor but other than that his world was bounded by the comfortable dangers of Egmont Street, where the fearsome Steele family lived, or Barnard Avenue on which loomed the terrifying edifice known as 'the Chapel.'

The Chapel was the local Roman Catholic church and as such was a place to be feared and avoided. It exuded menace from on high, its soot blackened walls reminiscent of some gate lodge at the entrance to hell, or so it seemed to the younger Ted.

He was a Protestant; Northern Ireland was their 'promised land' and Belfast its cultural centrepiece, a showcase to the rest of the world. The Ulster Scots were the chosen people and lived a life of privilege… but it was a relative term for they were all, in fact, dirt-poor, their *privilege* being an esoteric thing of no direct financial worth. His stomach knotted at the thought that he might never see his modest homeland again. It was a dump but it was *his* dump.

The sun was high in the sky when they arrived at the guardroom. The little car turned in slowly as if the driver was afraid of what lay beyond the manned barrier. An RAF Police corporal approached and briefly studied a letter handed over by the driver. He looked as if he couldn't read but was not yet ready to share that secret with his employers. Regardless of the truth, the barrier lifted and they drove through, following the road to the left and continuing past a series of accommodation blocks until they arrived at what looked like a detached house.

'This is it, mate,' said the driver, tonelessly. They both climbed out and stretched their legs for a few moments before the driver collected Ted's case. Their pleasantries were terse, more like orders, and soon Ted found himself standing alone by the side of the road with his suitcase and a stomach full of apprehension. The car pulled away, but a tang of petrol fumes remained in the air. When he looked at his suitcase he was reminded of the Belgian refugees he had seen, their entire lives contained in one or two pathetic bags. *What had happened to them, he wondered? Were they safe? Were they alive? Had their lives taken on some vestige of normality once more?*

Ted raised his eyes to watch an unfamiliar plane fly overhead, a slab-sided monoplane with twin engines and a curious nose-down attitude. It looked like the aeronautical equivalent of a potting shed, devoid of aesthetics, aerodynamics and...

'A Whitley,' said a voice from behind. Ted spun on his heel to find an older RAF officer standing there. His uniform sported two rows of medals from the Great War. The man smiled and held out his hand. Ted hastily saluted and then shook hands. 'You must be Corporal Dexter,' said the officer. Ted felt a moment of panic. If he no longer existed then how could he be Corporal Dexter?

'It's all right,' said the officer, correctly discerning the nature of Ted's worries. 'I'm in on the secret you might say. Brigadier Murray and I are old friends and colleagues. I'm just making sure that you are looked after and that no awkward questions are asked. I'll show you to your new home,' he said and together they made their way up a short path and into the house.

The house was a three-bedroomed affair, like any wartime home but tidier perhaps and more austere. Its homely touches looked as if they had been added by a teenager reading a dull manual called 'Turn a House into a Home.' It had unconvincing comfort. There was a small living room with a radio, an open grate and three chairs that looked as if they might be comfortable for people with spinal deformities. Books lined a shelf: Pickwick Papers, Bleak House. *How apt*, thought Ted. A low table created a space for newspapers and some old magazines. A final touch was a rug with a garish pattern that matched no décor the world had ever seen, swirling, garish patterns of nightmare creatures.

'There are three bedrooms upstairs, so just pick whichever one you like best. They're all much the same to be honest. There is a fully stocked bathroom.' Ted thought of the bathroom at Geneviève Boutin's farmhouse. 'And a kitchen. We have a lady coming in to cook and clean for you. She'll do your washing and ironing.' Ted looked around at his new surroundings. His appreciation was grudging but appreciation nevertheless. This was better than a bunk in a billet. *If only they didn't also expect him to jump out of a bloody aeroplane,* he thought.

'So, will it do?,' asked the officer. He smiled encouragingly. They both knew that it would have to do.

'Very nice, sir.'

'This lady I told you about has been briefed not to ask about you. The point is that you mustn't discuss your reasons for being here with her – but I'm sure you're aware of that.' Ted nodded. 'You'll be kept separate from the other trainees also. No one is to ask about you and you are to keep yourself to yourself. You're barred from the

NAAFI but your housekeeper might be able to supply you with a bottle of beer or two if you ask her nicely… although I strongly recommend that you avoid drinking too much. There will be a car at 08.30 hours each morning to take you over to the hangars and you'll have your own instructor assigned to you. When you finally do your parachute drops, you'll be by yourself. Well, there will be a crew in the aeroplane of course and a dispatcher.' Ted nodded again, greatly discouraged.

'Is there anything you would like to ask about?'

'Not really, sir,' said Ted. He felt empty as if someone had drained him of all emotion.

'Well, if you think of anything ask me. I am Group Captain Murray.'

Ted frowned. 'Are you…?'

'Yes. His brother. It's a rather incestuous world you have entered.'

***

Only when he'd left did Ted realise that he had a question for his new guardian. 'What the fuck does incestuous mean?' he muttered.

He spent a few minutes just touring the house and picking a bedroom. Each room was as featureless as the last, the homely touches adding to the overall sense of despair rather than dispelling it. Ted picked up a hideous glazed ornament of a boy sitting next to a girl in some sort of bucolic idyll. He examined the base. '*Made In Germany*,' it said. Ted gave a dismissive snort. *Terrific.*

***

The following day Ted began his training. He looked at his new equipment with disdain. It seemed complicated, dangerous even – dangerous to the user that was. The quartermaster handed him a padded helmet.

'This'll make you look like a complete arse,' he said, laughing at an oft-told joke. Ted didn't doubt it. It was an utterly unfetching item, rather like something given to a mental patient to prevent them from harming themselves. 'Your parachute comes from the parachute room. I believe that one is going to be brought to you.' Ted nodded, unenthusiastically. He supposed that if he was going to jump out of an aeroplane, then the parachute would come in handy and yet…

The officer looked as if he was about to ask him a question and then thought better of it. It was a look of stifled curiosity that Ted had seen many times recently. He was the object of that curiosity, in fact he wondered if he *was* a curiosity and nothing more. *How odd that a single man of unremarkable appearance and lowly rank should be treated so well, kept from his peers and clothed in complete secrecy.* 'I'll help you carry it out to the car,' said the QM as if to emphasize the specialness of his single charge.

A WAAF corporal assisted Ted with his parachute, showed him how it fitted and the basic precautions he should take with it. She smiled reassuringly, correctly interpreting his blank looks as fear, which she had seen often.

'Don't worry about it… or try not to. It's very easy apparently,' she said, making it clear that she had no first-hand experience of parachuting. Her voice was soft, kindly. She sounded well-educated but with no particular accent and certainly not posh – to Ted's ears she was just English.

'I'll bear that in mind,' he replied, uneasily but with an attempt at good humour. He glanced around the room. There were just the two of them and hundreds of parachutes laid out on tables ready to be packed. He was reminded of a mortuary or somewhere that dead bodies were put into shrouds on an industrial scale. Mass embalming or… He shuddered, involuntarily. Suspended from the ceiling with wire was a huge sign saying, *Remember - a man's life is in your hands.* He hoped that the girls would always remember and wondered if any incidents of chutes failing to open were traced back to the packer. What a thing to live with, if so.

She was a pretty girl; petite, auburn hair, nice smile. 'We have all sorts coming through here,' she said. 'The one thing that they all have in common is that they look terrified.' She laughed as she spoke, unsure whether or not this man with the strange but compelling accent was reassured by her words. He certainly listened intently almost as if she held the secret to his survival.

'I'm surprised you haven't been instructed not to talk to me,' said Ted looking down at the bulky parachute on the table which separated them. It sat there like a fat, inanimate chaperone. He suddenly felt the urge to tell someone who he was, what he was. It would be like a confession – a Protestant one, unheard of.

'I've been told not to ask you any questions but I haven't been told not to talk,' she smiled again and Ted felt his mouth run dry; he was really out of practice at this sort of thing. 'So, if you ever want to talk… well, you can talk to me and I promise I won't ask who you are.' She gave another little laugh.

Ted sighed. *Why did his life have to be so complicated, when, having ceased to exist, it should have been so simple?*

He said wistfully, 'that would be nice. I don't get to meet many people nowadays.' He didn't add that the only people he *did* meet wanted him to kill Germans.

'My name is Jean,' said the WAAF holding out her hand.

'I'm… oh, I'm not allowed to say who I am,' he replied with a rueful laugh.

'You could give me your first name and I still wouldn't *really* know who you were,' suggested Jean. Behind Ted, a door opened and his driver poked his head in.

'Ready?' he asked.

'Ready. Just coming.'

He grasped Jean's hand in his. 'Ted. I'm called Ted.'

Chapter Four

John allowed his gaze to follow the aircraft as they slowly circuited the airfield: three black-painted Lysanders, like fat old crows, escorted by the altogether more elegant Anson, a twin-engine light bomber/aircrew trainer.

'Things are really taking off,' said Embury with relish. 'If you'll forgive the pun.' John acknowledged the other man's great humour with a tiny smile. He noticed that the officer danced lightly from foot to foot as he watched his new planes being brought in. He was either excited or needed the toilet.

John's doubts assailed him now, as they did on occasion. He wondered for how long his nerve would hold.

'We'll get this other one painted up as well,' Embury said, pointing to their original camouflaged aeroplane. 'Looks like we'll be taking the rear guns out too. We need more room for the passenger.'

'What about pilots?' asked John. He wondered if he could light a cigarette. Talking to officers sometimes made him uncomfortable and being uncomfortable made him crave tobacco.

'Ah well. Just you and me for the meantime. All the new pilots are being posted to fighter squadrons for obvious reasons, so we'll probably have to wait until things have settled.'

'I wouldn't be surprised if we didn't get seconded. Especially you, sir. You are a fighter pilot after all.' Embury looked uncomfortable. News of fighter command's losses filtered through to the other squadrons with stark, unembellished reality. Volunteers from bomber squadrons were being sought and the length of time spent on training each new pilot was being compressed terribly, much to the chagrin of the pre-war regulars who ran the RAF. Even the Fleet Air Arm was helping out with pilots, and foreign volunteers were increasingly pressed into squadron service.

'We'll have to see,' he said, uncertainly. 'This is considered important too, don't forget, Flight.'

The first of the Lysanders touched down, the ATS pilot not bothering to attempt a particularly truncated landing. As it taxied to the hard standing, the next two planes dumped themselves unceremoniously on the grass, followed by the Anson. The latter kept its engines running and the three female pilots disappeared into its fuselage with the briefest of waves. Moments later the Anson spun around and trundled off down the runway, lifting into the air and slowly gaining height. The turret gunner swung his single Vickers gun to and fro as if to ward off predators from the Luftwaffe.

'I thought they'd stay longer. Hand over the aircraft properly, that sort of thing,' said Embury. He sounded disappointed, as if this were a deliberate slight designed to remind him of his lowly place in the establishment. For the time being, his little unit was not the RAF's greatest priority.

'All the paperwork will be on the pilots' seats, sir. Just get the mechanics to check them over and that's it done.' He smiled at his new boss. He wasn't an expert in reassurance and did not feel any urge to become one.

'Oh, okay. Well, pick an aeroplane, Flight Sergeant Guy. When you're ready, take her up. Stay inland of course and try to keep her low. But basically, just get a bit of practice in. We'll start our take-off and landing training properly tomorrow and then try to get some night flying in.'

'Will we have ammo for our forward firing guns?'

'Might be a good idea, just in case we meet the Hun,' said Embury. 'I'll speak to the armourers.'

John shuddered.

***

In the event they both took an LAC with them to operate the rear guns too. Neither was a trained gunner, but so long as they didn't shoot their own tail planes off, they would offer a degree of protection from opportunist Luftwaffe fighters. Embury's Lysander scrabbled into the air first and John followed, deciding to make his own way cross country, avoiding any RAF fighter bases.

'Just keep an eye out for 109s,' he said to his gunner. There was no reply and John looked down at his lap to see that his intercom wasn't connected. He reprimanded himself. 'Silly bugger.'

'Say again, Flight,' said the aircraftsman.

'I said 'silly bugger.' I wasn't talking to you. just keep an eye out for 109s.'

'Roger.'

At five hundred feet he levelled off and began cruising at 170 knots. This was the sort of flying he liked. Here he could be at peace with the world and even the deafening thrum of the big radial engine became just an aural backdrop, as he delicately adjusted the controls by increments to guide the big plane through the clear, warm air. It wasn't too bad to fly really, considering its rotund appearance. It lacked even the *apparent* grace of the old Battle he'd flown and yet it displayed a surprising amount of agility.

'How are you doing back there?'

'Fine Flight. Just keeping an eye out.'

'Good man. Shouldn't get any trouble but you never know.'

John spotted a flat, grey lace below them and identified it as the A303. Two brown ambulances traversed its length in a tiny convoy and he remembered his fateful meeting with Ted and Miglorine in France. He smiled at the memory. They'd probably saved his life or at least spared him the ordeal of capture. *And now here he was free to fight on.* You can't have everything, he supposed.

Far to his right he saw a fighter station, a flight of interceptors taking to the air like purposeful insects.

'Middle Wallop,' he said to his gunner. 'We'll steer clear of there, I think.'

'Good idea, Flight. They might not have seen a plane quite like this one before.'

It was a good point, realised John. Their fat, black, winged-cigar was unlike anything else in the skies. They might shoot them down and ask questions later.

'We're a bit conspicuous, I suppose,' he agreed. He adjusted his course eastwards and dropped his height to about four hundred feet. He supposed that he would be doing a lot of low-level flying in his new role, going in to enemy territory under the radar screen. The tactics involved would be quite different from those required for flying the Battle into combat. They had always been sitting ducks, flying straight and level in the hope of getting their bombs on the target. With hindsight it had been a hopeless way of doing things.

So low down, the ground was a rush of colour, a blurred blend of hues merging as one yellowy-green carpet blanched of depth or defining features. He kept the Lysander virtually level, following the gentle undulations of the ground. He made slight corrections, almost imperceptibly moving his feet on the pedals. It required little thought.

In the distance, far to the east, he saw the foreshortened outline of a town and the hairline fracture of a railway line leading to its centre. Cows stood in fields, unconcerned by the events that shaped their owner's futures. Their futures were bleaker; for them there was no hope.

A few minutes passed and John decided to take the Lysander higher, climbing slowly to six thousand feet. The world below looked so much different from this lofty perspective, picked out in minute details that had been lost at lower altitudes. He scanned the skies, looking for signs of the epic battle that was being fought daily. But they were alone.

John took the plane down again and turned for home. They'd been flying for forty minutes and he still had three quarters of a tank left. He knew he had a feel for the Lysander now. He felt a degree of confidence; *perhaps this wouldn't be a bad way to take part in the war*, he thought. John glanced at the instrument panel, mentally ran through the function of each dial and switch, and then glanced from left to right, surveying the broad corridor of air before him. He looked above but saw only endless acres of blue sky.

The pilot of a Lysander certainly had a good field of view, so good in fact, that he could quite clearly determine the look of astonishment on the German pilot's face as he sped past just one hundred yards away. He'd come from nowhere, perhaps escaping pursuit in the great battle into which he had been drawn. Their closing speed was about five hundred knots but their brief encounter was sufficiently long for both men to reach a decision about their immediate future.

'Holy…' said his gunner. John heard the guns being cocked.

'Time to earn some medals,' said John. There was no reply. He took the Lysander into a shallow dive and watched the airspeed indicator wind round to an indicated 220. He pictured the Bf 109 pilot pulling a tight turn, eager to bag such an easy kill. The fighter was a bird of prey, the Lysander, well, there was no analogy to be made. 'He'll be with us soon. Try not to shoot the tail off.'

'Roger,' said the aircraftsman. He sounded calm. *Maybe*, thought John, *he knows what he's doing.* He'd certainly have to learn quickly if that wasn't the case.

John glanced skywards and was alarmed to see a squadron of Heinkel bombers far above him. To his left and right but at greater altitude he saw the darting outlines of fighters: Hurricanes and Bf 109s, duelling to the death. One of the German bombers exploded, filling the air with debris which tumbled to earth. A parachute deployed to his extreme right and drifted to earth like an ethereal life raft.

'Here he comes,' said the gunner and John felt the vibrations of the twin Vickers guns being fired. The battle was joined but it didn't feel like *his* battle at all. He wanted somehow to excuse himself and bow out. *Just a training flight. Terribly sorry chaps – I'll get out of your way.*

It was all happening too soon after those desperate air battles over France.

Cannon rounds sliced through the air on his port side and then the same thing to starboard. None of them hit. The gunner kept firing. Short, disciplined bursts. *Good man*, thought John. He was now south of the main fray but the Messerschmitt was still behind them in dogged pursuit. This was too easy a prize to let it escape.

John jinked to the left, then the right and lost more height. 240 knots from a plane that only did 212! Suddenly and unaccountably he felt exhilarated. He knew – without knowing how he knew – that they were going to make it.

And then, without any prior warning, the German aircraft exploded, the shock waves rocking the Lysander.

Chapter Five

'Eyes front, you lot,' said the RAF sergeant to his charges. They had turned to gawp at Ted as he was led through the hall to the most distant set of apparatus. They were recruits for the newly formed Parachute Regiment. Tough-looking men, hoping for adventure, they regarded Ted as an oddity; a corporal who belonged to no regiment, who spoke to no one, who lived in a house on the base and who never went to the cookhouse or the NAAFI. They trained in platoons, he trained by himself. They ran or marched everywhere, whilst he had a car and driver. 'You'd better learn to concentrate or you'll be RTU'd in a bloody shroud,' the sergeant warned them.

Ted was presented to a smiling sergeant who was to be his jump instructor.

'Sergeant Davis. How do you feel about this? Nervous?' He held out his hand and Ted shook it.

'Yes. Nervous,' confirmed Ted. He found it hard to replicate the sergeant's nonchalance. 'Terrified really. Don't think I'm too good with heights.'

'Well, try to relax. This is the easy part. All we're going to do is practise landing and that sort of thing. When you've got the hang of it and I think you're ready, you'll jump out of the tower, then out of a balloon and then out of a plane. Then we'll send you back to wherever you came from.' Ted nodded. The training was designed to make parachuting seem as natural as breathing. It was a lot to ask in the circumstances, when one activity was essential to life whilst the other seemed likely to end it prematurely.

The NCO, whom he took to be a Geordie, exuded confidence, as if Ted's parachute qualification was a formality. He showed him how to wear his parachute and check the fastenings and how to attach it to the static line inside the aircraft so that it would deploy correctly. He ran through the procedures for landing and Ted practised the slow, deliberate tumble on a rubber mat. His confidence grew by degrees, only taking a knock when he accidentally spied the tower from the corner of his eye; he couldn't quite picture himself jumping from it. Only then did the entire undertaking seem impossible again.

Ted anticipated the lurch of his stomach as he fell through the air, breaching the huge distance to the ground, tumbling through a void. He seriously doubted if he would ever jump.

'Everyone feels like that,' said the sergeant, quietly. He smiled but not unpleasantly.

'Like what?'

'Like they can't jump. But you will. Hardly anyone refuses.'

'And those that do, do you throw them out?' He didn't specify if he meant 'out of the plane' or 'out of the course.'

'Not usually. Like I said, don't worry about all that yet. When the time comes, you'll do it.' Sergeant Davis seemed as if he was about to add something but he stopped short and looked over Ted's shoulder, then came to attention.

'Sorry to interrupt, Sergeant, but I need a word with your pupil. I'll send him back when I've finished.' It was Group Captain Murray who spoke.

'Fine, sir. I'll go and have a brew.'

Ted followed the RAF officer from the hangar. This time the other trainee paratroopers didn't look at him. Outside, the sun was bright, infusing the world with vivid colours. The air stirred up smells of summer. Murray scanned the skies as if looking out for enemy planes. Ted felt himself to be on the periphery of the war. It suited him fine.

'This way,' he said and the two men walked briskly to a prefabricated building at the edge of one of the giant runways. 'What do you know about one Captain Pomeroy?,' asked Murray.

'Captain Pomeroy? He was one of my officers, sir.'

'Well, we have a chap here who wants to talk to you about him. Take as long as you like. I'll have drinks sent through.'

The man was dressed in civilian clothes and looked to Ted's untutored eye rather like a policeman. It was the suit that did it… and the overcoat, the appraising look in his eye as if everyone was guilty of something, a suspect in a crime.

'Take a seat, Ted,' said the man, indicating a wooden chair. 'Is it alright to call you Ted?'

Ted shrugged, wondering how many other people knew his name. He was more in demand since ceasing to exist than he ever had been previously. A moment later, drinks and plain biscuits were brought in by an orderly. Ted was on his guard, suddenly suspicious.

'I need to ask you about Captain Pomeroy. I believe he was second in command of your company.'

'Who told you about me?'

'You're right to be wary Ted, but Brigadier Murray has told me a little bit about you and the need for secrecy. However, you are better acquainted with Pomeroy than most people – at least in the terms of my investigation.'

'You're in the police?'

'Inspector Eric Doyle. You can trust me, Ted. I just need to know about Pomeroy.' Ted remembered that for any dealings between the police and a soldier an officer's presence was normally required. He had always assumed that this precaution was deemed necessary lest the hapless soldier in question admitted to a crime he hadn't committed or antagonised his interrogators in some way. He supposed that in this case everything had been cleared in advance.

'Is he in trouble?,' asked Ted, suddenly interested. If he could assist in Pomeroy's downfall, then it would be churlish to be obstructive. He hated the man.

'I don't know exactly. He might be. But whatever your loyalties to him, you have to tell me the truth – you understand that.' The policeman looked Ted in the eye as he spoke.

'I don't have any loyalties to that bastard, believe me,' said Ted vehemently.

Doyle smiled.

'Well that might make things a bit easier for us. I need to know about your dealings with him when you were in France.'

'Specifically?'

'Specifically, anything he did which you thought was odd.'

'Odd?'

'Odd.'

'Pomeroy singled me out. There was one time he got me and three others to stay behind to delay the Germans while the battalion withdrew.'

'Four of you to cover the withdrawal of an entire battalion? Odd.'

'Odd. There wasn't much we could really do to hold up the Germans.'

'Did it feel like he was trying to get rid of you?' It was a leading question of course but Ted did not recognise it as such.

'Yeah, I suppose it did. There was no love lost between us.'

The detective sat forward. 'Why was that?' This, for him, seemed to be the crux of the matter.

'I don't know. He just didn't like me.'

'But was there anything that made him dislike you?'

'I don't know really. He just wasn't very nice. He was a stuck-up bastard. I just wasn't his cup of tea. He probably thought I was a bit cheeky. When I was promoted to lance corporal he was against it and tried to get the promotion stopped, but the OC went ahead with it anyway.' Ted scrutinised the policeman's face as he spoke. He could tell by his frown that this wasn't quite what he wanted to hear.

'Typical officer?' suggested Doyle.

'They weren't all like him. Some of them were decent enough but Pomeroy…' Ted shrugged. 'What's he done?'

Doyle seemed to ignore the question.

He said, 'cigarette?' Ted shook his head. 'Just supposing he *was* trying to get rid of you. Why? Did you know something about *him*? Had you seen him do something? Did you have some sort of hold over him, something that would get him in trouble?'

Ted pulled a face.

'No. There's nothing like that.'

'Are you covering up for him?' asked Doyle, suspiciously.

'Not at all. I don't like the man – I told you. I don't care if he gets in trouble but I don't know anything about…'

'But he sent you off by yourself to do something that was virtually impossible.'

'He did it twice.'

'Twice?'

'Yeah. There was the first time at the canal. He left the four of us there but we withdrew of our own accord.' Ted inadvertently made it sound as if they had run away from battle. He couldn't be bothered supplying the details. 'Then when we caught up with the battalion, he sent us out again on a recce patrol.'

'Recce patrol? Why you? What did he expect you to find?' Ted shrugged again.

'Look, he *definitely* wanted us out of the way. By rights he should have sent an entire section or even a platoon to hold up the Germans if that's what he wanted us to do. The recce patrol? Well, he could have used anyone but the truth was we knew where the Germans were anyway, so it was pointless. But as to why he did it, I couldn't say.'

'Did you think it was a strange way to get on?'

'Not for him. Like I said before, he was a bastard.' Ted shrugged again. 'The other fellas reckoned that he had it in for me. It always annoyed them because whatever he did to get back at me involved them too.' It pained him to recall that his men were all dead – Whitey, Snowball and Dinger. He blamed Pomeroy for their deaths but only when he had time to think of anything other than his own safety. But people died in wars, with or without someone to pin the blame on.

Ted didn't feel that he could add much to this vague investigation. Nevertheless, he was intrigued. 'If you tell me what you think I've seen then I can tell you if I have or not. It might be something that I didn't even think about at the time.'

Ted studied the policeman. Doyle pursed his lips. Clearly, he was reaching a decision. He opened his mouth to speak but then changed his mind.

'No. I could be barking up the wrong tree. I don't want to be accused of planting an idea in your head,' he said finally. He talked with a sigh in his voice. His regret was obvious. 'If you'd seen this thing happening, then you'd remember it. If you'd seen it then I think the rest would make sense.' He put a hand over his mouth and then rubbed his chin in a subconscious gesture. 'And I can't ask the other men, can I?'

'Not unless you can commune with the dead. They didn't make it home. Maybe Pomeroy just *thinks* I've seen it – whatever it is that he's done,' suggested Ted. The policeman nodded.

'Maybe,' he said. 'I'll leave it for now but I'll probably be in touch again.'

The two men parted. Ted was baffled, Doyle dissatisfied.

Chapter Six

Jean brought two bottles of ale with her. Ted glanced up and down the road like an inept robber's lookout, as he ushered her into the house.

'You looked very guilty doing that, you know. Have they actually told you that you can't have visitors?' she asked. She perched on the edge of an upright chair, looking prim and proper. She smiled and held out the drinks as if she were presenting a modest prize. 'Best I could do,' she said.

'No. It's fine. I don't have a drink very often. I'm just glad you made it.'

'It's not every day I get asked out by a handsome stranger.'

'Handsome?'

'Oh yes. Handsome. And mysterious. For all I know you're not even called Ted,' she said, archly.

'Well, I am, that much I can confirm. If I was going to invent a name for myself it would be something more dramatic than Ted.'

'Ted's a nice name.'

'Nice but not very exciting. Errol. That's a better name.'

'Like Errol Flynn? You don't look like an Errol. Do you have a bottle opener, by the way?'

Ted raised an eyebrow as if *not* having a bottle opener was an impossibility and then made his way to the kitchen.

Jean shouted through while Ted rooted around the half empty drawers for the bottle opener.

'Very cosy here. You must be a VIP.'

He appeared in the doorway, brandishing a brass implement.

'VIP? Never thought of it like that.'

'You are intriguing, Ted. You look so lost and so worried all the time and yet someone has faith in you as if you are expected to do great things.' Jean smiled at him as he prized the lids off their beer bottles. 'You are being looked after personally by the group captain for one thing. And you get lots of important visitors…'

'Are you talking about that man in a suit who came today?' he asked. Jean nodded. 'He was a copper, asking me about one of my old officers. He didn't give me many details really.' Ted decided to change the subject. 'I bet you don't normally drink beer, do you?,' asked Ted. Jean shook her head.

'I don't usually drink at all. A glass of sherry now and again. Lots of the girls drink but I don't usually bother much. Some of the girls are a bit rough and ready but they're okay. They all do their job, so no one has any complaints. We all rub along.'

'So, you pack parachutes?'

'Yes, that's about it. I train the new girls as well. It's a big responsibility. If they're not packed right, they won't open,' she said matter-of-factly. Ted shuddered involuntarily.

'I'd rather not think about that,' he said, moving his chair closer to Jean's. 'I'd like to talk about you – where you're from and what you like. I want to talk about things other than this war, other than parachuting.'

Jean smiled and for a fleeting moment Ted wondered how many times she had sat in some sheltered corner, comforting a scared soldier. He realised that he was jealous, knowing that in a few weeks he would be gone and that he'd never see her again. He was jealous of men he'd never met, who might not actually exist in fact. He envied other men their lives. No life seemed as dangerous as his. No one faced the same hazards…

'What are you thinking, Ted?'

'I don't know. I'm scared, I think.'

'Scared of what?' Jean put her drink down and stood up, urging Ted to do the same.

'Scared of everything,' he said with a despairing laugh.

'Come here. Don't be scared. You're a brave man, I can tell. I'll stay with you tonight if you want.'

Ted nodded.

***

He woke to the sound of Mrs Torrance shutting the front door. He heard her walk through the tiled hall and into the kitchen, her shoes click-clacking on the hard floor. He was already familiar with the sounds of her morning routine: the tap running, the kettle filling, the gas being lit, the first brew of the day and the first cigarette… The bed was empty, or rather it would be when he got up. He sniffed at the pillow, taking in its last trace of perfume, almost drawing it out from the fabric, and then smiled.

Ted shivered against the early morning cold and made his way to the bathroom for a wash and shave. Never before had he known the luxury of a sink and mirror all to himself. He had his own toilet and bath, too. The house even had heating!

'Morning, Mrs Torrance,' said Ted as he came downstairs. Life felt slightly less bleak this morning.

'Good morning,' she replied, cheerfully. That she didn't use his name always jarred. *Good morning* sounded wrong. By extension, *Good morning, Ted* sounded right. But then he supposed she didn't know his name or, if she did, felt obliged to not use it.

How did you talk to someone who didn't exist?

He wondered if he could ask her to call him Ted or was that just a liberty?

'Tea or coffee?' she asked.

'Coffee?'

'Yes, indeed. From America. Someone wants you looked after very well.'

'Well, I'll have a coffee please in that case. Will you join me?' he asked.

'Don't mind if I do.' Again, it jarred. *Don't mind if I do, Ted…*

'Do you know my name, Mrs Torrance?' he asked suddenly. He saw her pause, tense.

'Well…' she stirred their drinks briskly, seemingly formulating her answer. 'I do know your name – Ted – but I think I heard it by accident. I'm not supposed to know it. I'm not supposed to know anything about you.' She turned round with a nervous smile. She was a very attractive lady, thought Ted.

'Well, since you know I'm called Ted, then I don't mind you calling me Ted. I won't tell anyone.' Mrs Torrance smiled, sadly.

'You're still an enigma though, Ted.'

'Yeah, that's me,' he said wearily. 'The coffee's good by the way. I'm being spoiled.'

'I'm called Ivy.'

They chatted for a few minutes. Ted found her easy to talk to – caring without being a mother hen type.

'How did you get this job, Ivy?' asked Ted. Ivy stood and made her way over to the oven to start his breakfast. She fussed about with a pan and eggs and bread. She retrieved some bacon from the larder.

'My husband is a sergeant in the RAF. He flew Whitleys. That's the sort they have here. Anyway, he was shot down over Bremen. Dropping leaflets of all things.' She paused again as if the retelling of her story had drained her of energy. More than that, she seemed temporarily bereft of will. She had stopped talking as if unwilling to continue but it felt important to ask.

'Was he captured?' ventured Ted.

'Well, that's the thing, Ted. I don't know. It was three weeks ago and I haven't heard anything. Apparently, the

Germans send word through via the Red Cross – if they have a prisoner of war, I mean. But I haven't heard a thing.'

'That doesn't mean you should give up, though. How long does it normally take?'

Ivy shrugged and sighed. She said, 'I don't know but every day that passes and I don't hear anything makes it more unlikely that I'll see him again.'

'I'm sorry.'

'Just one of those things. I'm not the first and I won't be the last. The worst bit is just not knowing but that's how it is and I just have to get on with my life.' She wiped a restrained tear from her eye. 'It's strange, but having hope just makes it worse.'

There was no trace of melodrama about what she said or the manner in which she said it, but this was real life, not the pictures. No violins played. There were hundreds of women just like her. Presumably there would be hundreds more. Ted wished he could do something to help her. But what could anyone do? The war would roll on until some sort of conclusion was reached. Then it would be over, and then… who knew? No one could predict the future, less so now than ever.

Chapter Seven

'What the hell happened there?,' asked John. He pushed the canopy back as the prop shuddered to a halt. Ground crew approached from either side like stealthy sightseers. John released his straps but remained seated, regaining his strength, letting his heart rate settle and allowing the trembling of his hands to desist. 'Did you hit him?'

'No idea, Flight. Didn't think I had hit him but someone sure got him!' said the gunner. 'But I didn't see anyone else around.' Escaping death made him breathless but he got his words out. He tried to keep the tremulous note from his speech. Adrenaline charged round his body like an express train.

'Well, unless one of the fighter boys claims him, you've just shot down your first Jerry!' said John. 'That's quite a claim to fame. You'll be debriefed about it, so just say what happened.' He stood and stretched before beginning the long climb to the ground.

They stood under the aeroplane's high-mounted wing. John clapped the other man on the shoulder. 'That's a good morning's work. Mind you, I don't fancy our chances if we had to do that every day.' John's cheer was partly forced, partly born of survival and, not for the first time, he wondered how long he could keep going. Each encounter with the enemy seemed to deplete his resolve. What would they call it when it finally happened? Lack of moral fibre? What was the penalty? He could choose between death and disgrace? If it was the latter, could he use his VC as part payment towards clemency, he wondered.

***

The sergeants and officers shared a mess, such was their paucity of numbers, and as the only two pilots on the little base, John and Embury felt obliged to dine together. There remained between them a divide that would not close easily; they shared a profession but nothing else. Embury's commission and his obviously privileged background kept them apart, but it was more than that. Their lack of shared experience was the biggest contributor to their divergent views. Embury had yet to be tested in combat and, although he would never say so, craved John's experience for himself. What made it worse was having a subordinate whose very presence seemed to undermine everything that Embury stood for. He desperately wanted to take the war to the Hun and to be seen to do so but he didn't really know what doing so might involve. By contrast, Flight Sergeant Guy knew all about war and was as eager to distance himself from combat as Embury was to join the fray.

This was a time for leadership and determination; he hadn't earned the luxury of disillusionment. That would come later – if he lived long enough.

'I hear you had a bit of a tangle with Jerry this morning, Flight,' said the officer, taking a bite from a sandwich. A glass of lemonade sat on the table untouched. Normal conversations about normal things predominated, providing a reassuring background burble to their discussion. 'Did young Aircraftsman Brown bag his first 109?'

'We don't know for sure yet, sir. We're just waiting to see if anyone else claims it. If they don't, it looks like it was his.'

'Does *he* think he got it?'

'He's not convinced, sir.'

'Good flying though. Well done,' said Embury, hoping to win round this laconic Londoner.

John smiled. He wanted to get up from the table and leave the officer to his idiotic enthusiasms. 'I was just trying to save our skins,' he said after a pause. 'That's what people forget about so-called heroes. Most people are fairly brave when it comes to self-preservation.' He sighed and reached for his enamel mug. He really didn't want this or any other conversation. John had the luxury of disillusion but it was not something in which he revelled.

At the same time, he almost pitied Embury for his lack of guile. He was a prisoner to enthusiasm and War Office directives. He was obliged to chivvy the men and keep their morale up. John stood. 'Can I get you a brew, sir?,' he asked. Embury shook his head and John made his way to the urn which stood on the counter. He chatted to the cook sergeant for a minute or two then reclaimed his seat.

'I'll do my job, sir. Don't fret about that. But I can't promise to like it.' It sounded like a confessional.

'I understand, Flight. I know that you've had a tough time… well, I'm glad you're here,' he said with embarrassment.

A tough time? Images of dead pilots came to mind like a cast of ghosts. He was eager to dispel that line of thought. 'When do we start our take-off and landing practice?'

'This afternoon? Or we can start tomorrow if you want to take it easy.'

'This afternoon, sir. Get back on the horse, so to speak.' That was as close as he could bring himself to enthusiasm. It would have to do.

***

The two Lysanders stood next to one another, their engines running. Through the prop's grey disc, he could see the ambulance that Embury had placed to one side of the runway a few hundred yards away. The arrangement was that they would try to leave the ground before getting that far. *And if we don't manage it, having an ambulance standing by will come in very handy*, thought John. He looked above him for signs of the great aerial battle that was absorbing the rest of the air force. The sky was clear at present but things changed quickly, as he had discovered this morning when a brief jaunt to familiarise himself with a new kite had become a fight for life. He had stumbled upon the climactic battle which would decide his country's future, and retrieving himself from that battle hadn't been easy.

Embury gave him the thumbs up and they trundled forwards, the engines racing, eager to pluck them from the inconvenient earth. The object of the exercise was to have as short a take-off run as possible. Within a few seconds, Embury's plane was beginning to lift, its tail wheel unsticking from the grass as the force beneath the wings equalised and then exceeded that holding the plane on the ground.

John recalled his one and only flight in the little Fieseler he'd used to escape from France. Almost by trial and error, or some hitherto unrealised pilot's instinct, he'd lifted off in just a few feet and climbed away into the black skies over the Channel to the safety of British shores.

Now, as then, the plane was snatched from the earth and continued to climb in a manner which would have been alarming in another type. He grinned, unaccountably pleased with this small victory. Ahead and to starboard, he saw the officer glance round and then give him another thumbs up. Now all he had to do was land. Large mechanical objects shrugged off momentum with as much difficulty as they gathered it…

At four hundred feet, he wheeled slowly round and retraced his course to their base. He let Embury get ahead so that he could land first. He knew that the officer must have practised this before his arrival – that's exactly what anyone would do – and he didn't begrudge him his evident expertise. It would be politic in any case to let the officer have his moment, to let him show off a little. Also it meant he knew what he had to beat.

John flew a slow circuit as the other plane touched down and glided to an abrupt halt well short of the ambulance. *Fair enough*, he thought.

He made his own approach, descending steadily, losing speed. The grass became an extended blur, just feet below the Lysander's spatted wheels. They touched, one tiny bounce and then they seemed to stick as the plane once more became a clumsy earthbound thing. John throttled back and came to a halt beside Embury. He killed the engine and, as silence enveloped the scene, he glanced over at the other pilot.

Thumbs up. Praise indeed.

Chapter Eight

'I see you rang the bell!' said Jean, through tears of laughter. Ted shook his head in mock exasperation.

'I thought I'd get some sympathy,' he said mock sternly. Jean reached out and touched the enormous bruise that described a thick mottled line across his cheek. At first, he backed off but then succumbed to her gentle touch.

'My poor dear. You're not the first, not by a long chalk. Would you like me to kiss it better?'

'Go on. If you think it'll help.' Ted stepped forward gallantly and let her kiss his cheek. She slipped an arm around his waist and then kissed him on the lips. 'Do you think this counts as preferential treatment?' he joked.

'Well, I certainly don't do this for all the young men that pass through here.'

Ted sighed happily and stepped back to look at her better.

'So, this happens a lot, then?'

'Ringing the bell? It happens more often than not. It didn't used to be so bad because the parachutists jumped from the back of the plane where the rear turret usually is. It's when they changed to jumping 'out of the hole' that people started banging their faces.' She kissed him again. 'At least you've done it.'

'Do I look a mess?' he asked, shyly.

'No Ted, still beautiful,' she replied. Ted laughed at her description of him. 'So, you'll only have another few jumps…' she said sadly, not really wanting to finish the sentence, as if the omission could postpone his departure.

'I suppose so. Then I'll go back to my own base.'

'Your mysterious base.'

'Even I don't know where it is,' he said, truthfully. Jean laughed. 'It's true,' he assured her, also laughing.

'Who are you Ted?' she asked, suddenly serious.

'I'm Ted.'

'But I don't know anything about you.'

'What do you need to know?' She leaned against the wooden locker which held spares for the parachutes she maintained and looked at him as if she'd never laid eyes on him before.

'You know I've fallen for you? My mystery man. Why did I have to fall for someone who I can never really know?'

'It's war, corny as it sounds.' Ted approached her, held her as if his very existence depended on it. 'We still have time together.'

'But then we'll never see each other again.'

'Don't say that. Who knows what will happen?'

'What if I volunteer for the same thing that you do?'

'Oh no. Not that. Anything but that.'

'It's too dangerous? Too dangerous for a woman?'

'I don't mean that. But yes, it is too dangerous. It's too dangerous for anyone, not just women.'

'But you do it.'

'Well, that's different. I wish I wasn't bloody doing it either.' He paused. 'I feel like we're having an argument.'

'We're not arguing. I just worry. I'll miss you.'

'But don't volunteer. Stick to this – you'll be safe. No point both of us taking risks. I love you, Jean.'

'My God, Ted. I thought you'd never say it.' They held each other tight.

***

It had been a hard week and Ted's relief at putting it behind him was tempered by the fact that it brought him closer to his departure from Ringway and Jean. Worse still, it brought him closer to his new mission. If they managed to drop him in the right part of France, then assassinating the officer would be easy, but there was a lot to be done before that had been achieved.

Monday had seen his first jump from the tower. Tuesday was more of the same. Wednesday, he jumped from a balloon. Thursday and Friday, he jumped from the Whitley. It was the second of these jumps that did the damage but at least he had managed to land properly. Two men had already died and fifteen injured so seriously that they couldn't carry on, since these courses had come into operation. Thirty men had refused to jump. But that was out of several hundred men who'd volunteered so far.

Ted was relatively unscathed. That was if you didn't count hurt feelings from the numerous insults thrown at him, as Sergeant Davis tried to pry him through the hole in the Whitley's fuselage where once had been found a retractable gun turret. Strangely, Ted had been more reluctant to jump on the second occasion than the first. He supposed it was a case of ignorance having been bliss. Knowing what to expect really didn't help.

He had thought about courage a lot recently and came to a few conclusions. For instance, doing something that required courage was much easier when you weren't aware of the fact that courage was required. He recalled an apocryphal story of a soldier awarded a medal for rescuing his comrades from a minefield. Asked about it afterwards he admitted, 'if I'd known it was a minefield, I wouldn't have done it.'

'You've done it once. Now fucking get out!,' Davis had shouted above the roar of the engines and the typhoon of air blasting past his exit point. Below was a wall of cloud that obscured the ground far below. That didn't help for some reason. The problem was not the proximity of the ground, it was the sudden lurching acceleration as he fell that affected Ted so badly. Once the 'chute opened it was relatively straightforward. The thought of having to go through all that and then carry out a mission in occupied territory held little appeal for Ted, terrified him in fact. He liked his dangers in isolation, one at a time, or better still, not at all.

It wasn't just the obvious risk involved in parachuting, but also the fact that no one else, as far as he knew, had ever done what was planned for him. It all seemed to be untested, experimental almost, and he wasn't keen on being part of an experiment. Nor was he convinced that anyone really cared what happened to him in the event of the experiment going wrong.

Everyone talked about parachuting in such breezy, dismissive terms. Ted wondered if he was alone in experiencing paralysing dread.

Chapter Nine

'Do you feel ready?' asked Murray. Ted didn't. He felt anything but, in fact.

'Yes, sir,' he replied, without feeling.

'Did the parachuting go well?'

'I suppose so,' said Ted. He had hated every single minute of it. Only his time spent with Jean made it worthwhile.

'Well, we had very good reports about you from Sergeant Davis. Said you were a natural.' Ted suspected that Murray knew this to be a lie. There was a twinkle in his eye as he spoke. Ted nodded. 'All we need to do now is to brief you and send you off.'

'What about getting me back, sir? Have you given any thought to that?' asked Ted. He looked away as if a question about his own well-being, his safe return, was impertinent in the circumstances. At times like these perhaps the ultimate sacrifice was the only suitable choice. Death or glory – or death *and* glory – the precise composition didn't matter too much. Perhaps he was a disposable commodity, like a bullet, or a tin of processed meat from a ration pack.

'Naturally, Corporal Dexter. We want you to come back.' There was a knock at the door and they paused as an orderly brought in drinks and biscuits. Ted felt as if he existed in a different world, one which looked like the old world but which was slightly more comfortable in small ways. Biscuits for one thing, even plain things like these were an unimaginable luxury. 'We're going to get you out by plane. Parachute in – fly out. We even have an old friend of yours lined up to extract you – Flight Sergeant Guy.'

Ted grinned. 'It'll be great to see him again, sir.'

'Especially when he's at the controls of your lift home. He has a good track record in that department! That's another thing we have to plan and practice. Anyway, let's have a look at the map.'

The two men stood, Ted gathering up a plain biscuit as he did so in case someone took them away again while his attention was elsewhere. 'This is northern France. You are familiar with this region of course – the Pas de Calais. We intend to drop you here,' said the brigadier, jabbing a finger at the map. Ted moved in closer. He was looking at the city of Lille near the border with Belgium.

'And that's where he is?'

'That's where he is – Lille,' confirmed the officer. He stood back for a moment as if his job was done. 'We know all about him: his regiment, the barracks he is stationed in, the block number for the officer's mess. We know which platoon he's in charge of, his name, his age. We even know quite a bit about his regular movements.' He made it sound as if he was talking about his *bowel* movements. Ted nodded, impressed. 'You'll have to learn it all off by heart of course.'

'When do we start?'

'After lunch.'

Ted thought of the grim little room in which he sat alone to eat his meals; his life was like solitary confinement but without the opportunities for relaxation.

'We've thought about getting you a house down here and a housekeeper for you. Have you any thoughts on the matter?'

'Sounds fine, sir. Mrs Torrance?' ventured Ted. He'd grown to like and trust the pilot's wife.

'Oh good. That's exactly who we had in mind. She's willing to move down here. Seems you made a good impression with her and we know that she's discreet.'

***

'This is him,' said the brigadier. The screen showed a grainy black and white image of a young Wehrmacht officer sitting in the back of an angular field car. He had a full Germanic face which seemed to exude a conqueror's arrogance, even from a distance. 'Leutnant Karl Feldhus. He's from a town called Herford. Twenty-three years of age. Five years in the army, two of those spent in the ranks where he reached the rank of corporal before being commissioned. He's a member of 712 Pionier Bataillon. Not exactly the cream of the German army, but professional soldiers nevertheless.'

'That might explain what they did,' offered Ted. The officer looked confused. 'If they're not the cream of the German army… killing Miglorine's platoon like that.'

'Yes, I see what you mean. It's not typical of the Germans to behave that way. Not that we need have a high opinion of them, of course, but they do tend to take prisoners rather than kill captured soldiers out of hand.'

'How do you know all this, sir?'

'We have people in place, French men and women who will continue the fight. It's all very early days.' Ted frowned as Murray explained. It sounded like a lie. 'They don't have much in the way of weaponry and many of them have no military training but hopefully they are the cadre for some sort of... um, *resistance* to the occupying forces. For now, they can get us intelligence. We might eventually get a network of safe houses for the likes of you and a cadre of local people who will assist generally.' He smiled, with a hint of weariness. 'It's my job to try and set these things in motion.' He smiled again, if anything even more wearily. 'I'm going to be busy,' he added ruefully. Ted nodded. He felt as if the war would never end and that he would never rest.

'So, I parachute in, find him and kill him?'

'It sounds easy enough when you put it like that. The trick will be to make your escape. This isn't a suicide mission. We're using you to test out the basic principles for covert warfare – what works and what doesn't. You're no use to us if you can't get back.'

'Won't the Germans take it out on the locals, though? When this man is killed, they're hardly going to assume that it is the work of the British. They're bound to think that it was a Frenchman.'

'That's the sort of thing we need to find out, isn't it?'

'There's another thing, sir.'

'Yes?'

'Well, if you're taking me out by plane, then why not put me *in* that way? Fly me in instead of parachuting.' Ted hoped that he was making a reasonable case for this alteration to the plan.

'But we've trained you to parachute!' exclaimed the brigadier. It was his turn to frown. He didn't like to think of their efforts having been wasted.

'But if I break my leg then I won't be much use. Land me in a plane, then at least I *start* the mission uninjured.'

'You might have a point. I'll give it some thought. Anything else?'

'A gun.'

'What would you like?'

'Walther PP.'

'Okay. Is that it?'

'What if I don't get him, sir?'

'You come back.'

'You don't want me to do something else?'

'Like what? A consolation prize?'

'Kill someone else? Sabotage? Make some contacts?' As he spoke, he wondered why he was even suggesting these alternative courses of action.

'A secondary mission would be a good idea,' conceded the brigadier. 'But I wasn't going to suggest it.' Ted pulled a face to show that he didn't quite understand. 'Well, Corporal Dexter, to be honest, you didn't seem all that keen. I was trying to keep it simple. Not too hazardous. The main thing is that we get you in and then back out. But since you have to go, I might as well make sure that the trip is worth the risk...' His words tailed off through lack of belief in what he was saying. 'If that's what you want?'

Ted shrugged, assailed by new doubts about the mission and his ability to carry it out.

Murray looked at him doubtfully. 'It's very commendable of you to suggest it but I don't want you to overstretch yourself. We're both trying to find our feet, so to speak.' His mind was made up – keep it simple.

Relieved, Ted studied the map again as if he could picture the ground by studying the names of the towns and villages. 'By the way, Corporal Dexter, what is the story with this Captain Pomeroy fellow? He must have been a naughty boy.'

'I suppose so but I wasn't able to help that policeman very much.'

'But Captain Pomeroy left you stranded, did he not?'

'He did, sir. Twice in fact. And the inspector wanted to know why. But I didn't know why.' Ted shrugged. The muscles in his shoulders were developing nicely from all the shrugging he had done recently.

'That's a pity. If we had some dirt on him, we could coerce him into doing some nasty jobs for us.' Ted looked at the brigadier, waiting for the punch line. As ever there wasn't one. Ted realised that, whilst Brigadier Murray might be championing him now, he didn't want to fall foul of him in the future. His outwardly affable nature disguised a ruthless core. He had a job to do and he would do it at whatever cost. People like Murray helped win wars, he supposed, and men who won wars accepted the need for great risks and possible casualties.

Before he left, the brigadier handed Ted his identity documents with the recommendation that he should learn everything there was to know about his new self. Ted was now Maurice Grima, recently discharged from the 12th Infantry Regiment. He sighed. The documents looked very impressive.

He really was lost, he thought. Not just lost but replaced. Would Ted Dexter ever see the light of day again?

Chapter Ten

A gentle wind blew wispy clouds from left to right across the screen of fingers Ted held up to his eyes. His battledress tunic lay neatly folded on the grass and his shirt sleeves were rolled up. Earlier in the day he'd watched a strange-looking fighter make an emergency landing on the grass runway. It looked a bit like a Hurricane from the front but had a turret with four guns wedged in behind the cockpit like a hastily added defensive measure. Its fuselage left a deep furrow in the ground as it slithered groaningly to a halt just twenty yards from where he sat. At once the smoking plane was assaulted by a team of firemen and medics and the two crewmen were released in seconds. Each was led away, plainly uninjured. Aside from that, little had happened.

The base was a sleepy backwater in the midst of the giant air battle being fought high above. A crane and a flatbed lorry arrived and a team of erks began dismantling the aeroplane so that it could be taken away and repaired or scrapped. The men worked steadily in the hot sun, occasionally looking over at the single, slacker soldier who sat on the grass smoking, or, on occasions, not smoking. Ted wondered how he could eke out his idle time, grab more peace from the all-consuming war and bundle it all together into something that required no effort whatsoever and provided no risk. He wondered if he had finally found his niche, the one thing that really set him apart from other men – the gift of idleness. Here, in the sun, on the grass, he excelled. When nothing was required of him, he rose to the challenge in a way that few others could ever hope to match. He sighed happily and shut the door in his mind to the awful reality that queued up for entry in little lurid packets of despair.

To his far left he saw a hangar door being rolled open by two airmen. Some others wheeled out a little training biplane, conspicuously painted yellow. Ted pondered the wisdom of flying such a delicate, fragile little aeroplane in the sometime presence of Luftwaffe hordes clawing at Britain's straitened defences. The air was a lethal place to be. In their wake he heard the familiar rasp of a bass broom being wielded. Its rhythm was discordant but evocative of the life of a serviceman; nothing could ever be clean enough, even in war.

He knew from experience that the rough bristles of the broom lifted the top layer from the concrete floor, creating dust that had to be swept away. It was like a self-fulfilling prophesy, or more aptly, a self-perpetuating task. In short there would have been less dust had the floor not been swept.

To his right he saw another airman checking under the bonnets of a small fleet of trucks: refuellers, ambulances and tenders. It looked to him like a classic skiving activity; *the sergeant major makes work for idle hands* – obviously as pertinent in the RAF as in the army.

Life was good. Well, it was okay, and better than some of the alternatives. If only this peaceful respite could last. He thought again of his little family back in Belfast and wondered for the… well, he'd lost count of how many times… why the hell he had volunteered for this. This espionage lark wasn't really a Ted Dexter type thing at all.

He wondered again what he was. Was he a spy, an agent, or something else? Did it have a name or was that too one of the details they were working out? But it took more guts to back out than to carry on… and he just didn't have that type of courage. At times, his reserves of fortitude were dangerously low, his morale brittle.

Lying there, at peace and in the sun, he had finally decided that he was an assassin, and was thinking how absurdly appropriate that title was, when his reverie was disturbed by a voice.

'You look like a man pondering the mysteries of life.'

Ted looked up at the figure that stood over him.

'Jean!' he said, scrambling to his feet. They embraced and he heard some of the airmen snigger. 'What are you doing here?'

'Got a posting down south. I'm a driver now. No more packing parachutes for me,' she said, sounding relieved.

'Did you come here because of me?' asked Ted, hopefully.

'No, not really.' He looked crestfallen. For a moment he looked like a little boy with a disappointing present. 'Course I did, you silly bugger.'

'I'm waiting for a plane. Some practice flying exercise.'

'I know,' she said.

'How did you manage to get a move?' He held her hand, strictly against regulations though it was.

'I went to Group Captain Murray and told him everything. About us, I mean. I told him that I didn't want to know what you were being trained for but thought that you would be better off with some company.'

‘And he fell for it?’ said Ted, incredulously.

‘Not at first but eventually he called me in and said I’d been posted down here… and here I am. I must say you’re looking very well.’

‘Beautiful?’

‘Yes, beautiful,’ she said laughing. ‘So, can I see you tonight? There’s a pub called the Old Oak about two miles from here. If you can get a lift…’

‘Eight?’

‘Eight,’ she agreed. And just then his other lift – the airborne one – swung into view.

‘Here’s my personal pilot now,’ he said with feigned nonchalance.

‘My mysterious man,’ she said with *faux* drama. She clasped her hands together like a silent film heroine who had just been rescued by the dashing adventurer. ‘I’d better be off. Don’t want to find out any secrets.’

They kissed and she trotted away. He watched her appreciatively as she disappeared from view. He noticed how well her uniform fitted. *As one door shuts*, he thought.

***

Moments later the chunky Lysander taxied to a halt, the engine stilled and the canopy was drawn backwards with gusto.

‘Taxi for Dexter!’ shouted the pilot. John was in uncharacteristically bullish mood.

Ted waved, startled and pleased in equal measure for he had no idea that his pilot would be John Guy. This was the man who had snatched him and Miglorine from the beach in France when all seemed lost. Rarely was he so pleased to see a senior NCO.

'I can't talk to you, you know.'

'No?' queried Ted.

'You don't exist, do you? Hush-hush, need to know and all that.'

'Yeah, of course, I get it now. If we spoke, I'd have to kill you.'

'And I'd have to kill you, too.' He clapped Ted on the shoulder.

'So, this is your new plane? Better than the old one?,' asked Ted. They began to walk round the Lysander as if on a brief tour of inspection. John surprised himself by feeling quite proprietorial about his new machine. It was as if some new found interest in his job was asserting itself. Either that, or he was starting to recover from a type of chronic professional malaise. That his previous interest in flying had waned was hardly surprising, given that it seemed to offer only the prospect of a grisly death.

The commencement of operations in France with the ill-fated Fairey Battle had quickly disabused him of any interest in the aeroplane as a machine. His childhood passion had been snuffed out in an instant. The comics and magazines about aviation's so-called 'Golden Age' which he had avidly collected and read over and over again, hadn't really touched on the dangers of flying in war time. No one wanted to know about that sort of thing back then.

'Yes, it's better in terms of… well, it's better at its job than the old Battle was at *its* job, put it that way.' He stopped short of patting it affectionately; it wasn't *that* good. 'I'll be taking you to France in this. At night. Much safer that way but a bit tricky for landings.'

'Do you know where in France?'

John shook his head. 'I'll be shown today. Night flying, landing in a field somewhere, that's what we have to practice and then we'll be off.'

'And then you'll come and get me?'

'Then I'll come and get you,' he assured Ted. 'It'll all be fine.'

'They were going to make me parachute, you know. I've done the course and everything. I suggested this and thankfully they listened. I thought you'd be in a Hurricane shooting down German bombers.'

'Not yet. That might come when they start running out of pilots but at the minute it's this – dropping agents in France.'

'And how many *have* you dropped in France?' asked Ted. John scratched his chin and looked to the skies as if seeking a blank canvas upon which to do this mighty mental calculation.

He sniffed and then said, 'None. You're the first.'

John led the agent to the back seat of the Lysander.

The rear cockpit was quite roomy. Ted could imagine himself and Miglorine fitting in here quite comfortably for their escape from France. He remembered the little Londoner and smiled, particularly at his discovery of General Rommel's suitcase and its bounty of women's underwear.

'It can take off and land in short distances,' said John.

'Like the thing you flew last time?'

'Yeah. Not quite as good but it does the job.' He pointed into the rear cockpit. 'That thing is where the machine guns were mounted but we've taken those out to give you more room. All you really have to do is sit there until I come to a halt, slide this canopy open and jump out.' He pointed to the catch which released the rear canopy. 'I'll keep the engine running and when you are clear, I'll spin round and take off again. Dead simple, except it'll be dark. I expect you'll be disorientated at first. You'll have to find your way to the town and remember how to get back to the same landing site when it's time to go home. You don't have any means of making contact with us so you've got to be there for the pick-up or you're stuck. And, by the way, I'm under instructions to stay on the ground for no more than thirty seconds. If you don't appear then I'm off.'

Ted nodded. He climbed aboard and John did likewise, starting the engine moments later. The plane rolled forwards for a few feet and then the engine note changed to a more insistent buzz that pulled the big aircraft forward with urgency. It felt as if they were propelled into the air by an under-arm slap from an unseen giant, and Ted's stomach lurched unpleasantly. Through the headphones he heard John say, 'howzat?' and then bank the Lysander round in preparation for their landing. Ted glanced out of the window at the ground which rushed past beneath them. The wings straightened and they plunged sickeningly.

Ted heard the engine note change, felt the wheels bump on the grass, the engine note change again, and then they pulled up short as if they had flown into a huge mattress that had absorbed the impact of the heavy aeroplane.

'Easy,' said John through the mic.

'Easy,' confirmed Ted, although with slightly less conviction. In reality this would be the moment when his troubles *really* started.

'I'll do it again and then you can practice getting out and taking cover. Will you have a case with you?'

'I'm not sure yet.'

'We should really practice it with the case but we still have time for that. Once we get the hang of it, we'll do it at night.'

John wound up the revs in the big engine but then let them die down again. 'Don't forget that when you get out you have to run at ninety degrees to the aeroplane. If you run in any other direction, you'll hit the tail or the undercarriage. You might even run into the prop.'

'Got it,' said Ted. They took off and went round again.

***

Mrs Torrance had made tea for John and Ted, a very palatable steak pie with vegetables and boiled potatoes and then they had returned to the airfield to practice their night flying. As far as Ted could gather, John was able to replicate the same quality of flying in the dark as he had managed in broad daylight. He only had the uncomfortable lurch in his stomach – like he was in a dinghy in a heavy swell – to gauge things by of course, that and the fact that they didn't crash. The moon was a bright, thin slice but obviously gave John sufficient light for his needs. Ted, on the other hand, found himself almost completely disoriented as he staggered away – ninety degrees, as ordered – from the Lysander.

This was where he would take cover and wait for his friend to pull away again into the cold, night air. He would have no safe house to go to, no transport and no friends to assist him. He'd be lost, effectively. Literally even.

The practice assured him that, together, they could pull off his insertion to rural France, and he had faith in John to fly safely and take them to the correct spot. He had less faith in himself to carry out his mission from that point onwards however. There was so much that could go wrong. It wasn't hard to imagine the Germans being alerted to the fact that a plane had landed in their newly acquired territory and then taken off again. Why would it do that, if not to drop off an agent?

***

'Tomorrow night,' he said. Jean didn't speak at first but held him closely in the dark. He doubted if he was going to sleep well. She began to run her fingers through his hair.

'And when are you due back?'

'Thursday. I've got three nights there to do the job.'

'I know you're going to France, Ted,' she said, quietly.

'How do you know?'

'Where else? Besides which, that particular plane couldn't get you any further afield than that.'

'Oh, I see. I suppose it wouldn't, really.'

'I can hardly stop myself from figuring some of it out, can I?' she said.

'No, but I can't tell you anything.'

'I know that. Probably better that I don't know – I'd only worry. Is it dangerous?'

'Dead simple.'

'That doesn't answer the question exactly.'

'It's not dangerous,' he said.

'Liar,' replied Jean. Ted didn't bother to argue. He felt the weight of his responsibilities terribly. So much expected of him, time and money spent on his training, preparation for a mission which would lead to the development and refinement of the procedures used in future operations. But there was so much danger and uncertainty. He was only Ted Dexter. He was nothing special – nothing special at all.

'You'll be okay, though,' said Jean from the darkness. She squeezed his shoulder as if she needed reassurance that he was still there.

'That's good,' he replied, suspending his terror just for a moment. 'How do you know?'

'Because you're brave and resourceful and lucky.' He wondered which of those attributes he would need most. Luck, he decided, would have to be his main defence against capture or death. There were too many aspects of his mission over which he seemed to have no control for it to be otherwise.

'I'm lucky to have *you,'* he said, at once acknowledging and evading her evaluation of him. She squeezed him again, wishing she could save him from his own obdurate sense of duty, but then again, she reasoned, would he be the same man if she did?

'It's like you're all alone in the world, Ted. As if, even with those people around you, you are still an outsider, completely different from them.' He didn't speak and she wondered if he understood what he was trying to say. 'You're a man apart, a lost soul.'

'A lost man,' he added by way of qualification. 'As far as anyone knows I'm a lost man.'

'What do you mean?' she asked, sitting up slightly. The blankets and sheet slipped from her shoulder. He wondered if he was straying into territory better left unexplored.

'Well,' he began. 'I was in France with the BEF but *officially* I never came back. So, when everyone else evacuated from Dunkirk, I stayed behind. That bit is actually true enough – but I got home by other means.' He swallowed as if overwhelmed by the enormity of his problems: past, present and future. 'I'm not on any prisoner of war lists, so as far as anyone knows I'm probably dead.'

'But what about your parents?'

'They think I'm dead. My brother too. He thinks I'm dead. The best they can hope for is that I'm just missing in action, but it's late in the day for that to be a realistic hope.'

'God, Ted that's terrible. It's awful for them. *It's awful for you.'* Beside her Ted sighed mightily. She ran her fingers through his hair again. 'I don't know how you stand it.'

'Well, I've got you…'

'You have. I'll always wait for you.'

He could tell she was crying. Whether it was her fear for him or as a result of the sad tale he'd told he could not say.

'And I'll always come back, Jean. I'm lucky, don't forget.'

Chapter Eleven

'Good luck, Ted,' said Murray. 'Get him there in one piece, John,' he added, turning to the pilot. Ted was shocked at the officer's use of their Christian names. Was it a final show of affection because he didn't expect to see them again?

'I'll see you in a few days, sir,' said the corporal assassin.

'Indeed. There might even be a few drinks lined up for you both.'

Ted laughed, unconvincingly. His stomach gurgled as his intestines tied themselves in knots. He hadn't eaten and his mouth was dry. Rarely had he felt so wretched.

'Let's go Ted,' said the pilot and they began the short walk to the Lysander. Moments later they were strapped in and a small team of groundcrewmen got the big engine started with a roar that rent the night. Ted saw the now familiar jets of flame erupt from the exhaust and then the engine settled into a monotone roar. The entire craft vibrated. He could smell aviation fuel in the warm evening air. They waited for some moments while John checked his instruments. The chocks were dragged away, the revs increased, and they trundled forward.

'Just a normal take off, Ted. No fancy stuff till we get to the other side.' The words came through his headphones and Ted nodded his acknowledgement in the darkness. It was a pointless gesture but he didn't care. He was no longer certain that he could even speak. He felt as if his senses were shutting down one by one to protect him from the gruesome reality of what lay ahead.

He felt the bulk of the pistol in his jacket pocket and recalled the brief conversation he'd had with the armourer, a rotund soldier of the type the British public didn't suspect still existed in their slimline, modern army.

'I'm now handing over the British Government's entire stock of Walther PPs and magazines,' he'd said. With a flourish he passed Ted a single pistol and two magazines. Then he passed him a box of ammunition. Twenty rounds; Ted hoped he would need only one. 'That's it,' he said. 'Good, little pistol that,' he added approvingly. He looked very pleased, as if he had designed the gun himself, and Ted decided not to ruin the moment by asking if there was a silencer for it. He would have to make do.

Ted could see virtually nothing inside the aeroplane. He wondered why they hadn't plied him with their new night vision wonder pills. Just because they plainly didn't work wouldn't be sufficient reason to prevent these people from pressing them into immediate use. *These people*, he mused. Who were *these people*? They existed, no doubt about that. In backrooms, peering through one-way glass at weird experiments, organising trials with men's lives at stake and only hearing about – never seeing – the results. He was no more than a lab rat being sent on a field experiment. It didn't really matter if he killed this German or not. Not unless he was Hitler's son. *Did Hitler have a son?*

'Okay, in the back?'

'Fine. Just thinking.'

'Don't think too hard.'

The glow from the instrument panel gave John a rather muted aura as if he was divine but only slightly so. The aircraft was cold. They'd given him a fleece-lined Irvin jacket with unambiguous instructions about its removal before leaving the plane. His disguise as a French office worker would not stand scrutiny if he had an RAF aircrew jacket over his garb. They had even debated about the pistol – not standard French office worker issue – and had reluctantly let him take it simply because he needed a means to kill the German officer.

He tried not to think of him as a person, to separate Leutnant Feldhus from the things that made him human. Ted had killed before and for a while he had become inured to the horror of taking life, but it had *never* seemed easy and he had *never* been complacent about that repugnant act. Now, of course, he'd taken a break from it. He'd *trained* to kill but hadn't actually done so for weeks. The officer's face – really just a fuzzy black and white image – haunted the corners of his consciousness. How much worse would it be when he'd snuffed him out?

The blackness outside was complete. The moon was out there hiding behind clouds, seeming to peek out and then hide once more. The stars were briefly on view as they rode up above the clouds, but already they were descending again, cutting a path through those same white mists. Ted looked up. There was nothing. To the left and the right, there was nothing. Below was maybe a sliver of coastline painted with surf, and soon that too was gone, as if it had never been there.

He sighed and tried to think of the return journey, having sent the murderous German to hell. It seemed impossibly far away and there was so much to do in the meantime. He hadn't even started yet, and until he had, he couldn't bring events to a close. Even then he would be stuck as he waited for John to get him. Perhaps three nights was too much time. Perhaps it was too little.

The plane dropped suddenly, losing what felt like twenty feet in a second. Ted's intestines danced, tying another maypole knot and he felt warm, liquid fingers of stomach acid reach up into his throat. He groaned and tried to think about anything other than vomiting. He thought of Christmas, but an image of his brother staggering home from the pub, collapsing in the kitchen and throwing up supplanted anything else. He thought about summer days in the city, days out to Bangor… but all his mental diversions returned to throwing up. It was as if there was nothing else in the world.

'I think I'm going to puke,' he said to John.

'Well, you can bloody clean it up on Thursday when I come to get you.'

'Oh God,' he groaned. 'You're all heart.'

'That's me. Look we're nearly there.'

'How long?'

'Two minutes-ish?'

'Is that supposed to make me feel better?'

'It should take your mind off it. Here we go.'

The Lysander tilted over on one wing and plunged to earth sideways. Ted's stomach just did its own thing, gurgling, knotting, unknotting, tangling, untangling, lurching, heaving… and then they flattened out.

'Nearly there.'

The engine note changed and the plane tilted backwards a little as if shying away from an obstacle ahead. They dropped suddenly, then again and then again, as if they were going down gigantic stairs. Ted felt the wheels touch and the engine note change, and he braced himself as they slowed like a bicycle ridden through sand. They came to a stop, but the engine continued to roar, sending a blast of night air over the fuselage.

'Okay. Good luck, Ted,' said John without preamble.

Ted had already undone his straps and was crouching as he shrugged the Irvin jacket off. He dropped it onto the warm seat like a discarded skin and pushed the canopy open with the smooth noise of a well-oiled filing cabinet drawer. He stood. His head was pulled painfully to one side as he did so and he remembered to disconnect his mic and remove his flying helmet. He checked his pocket for the Walther and then without a word jumped to the spongy French soil. It had taken just a few slick seconds. The blast from the huge propeller tugged at his jacket.

Ninety degrees. He could see nothing and he stumbled, got to his feet and kept running. He heard the plane taxi away and turn, ready for take-off. He turned to watch, could see almost nothing and then tripped over a low wall, falling back into a ditch.

'Oh shit,' he said to the blackness. The Lysander roared away into the night and in its place a profound silence settled. 'Oh shit,' he said again.

Chapter Twelve

Ted felt like a criminal on capture's cusp. He waited for his eyes to grow accustomed to the dark. They didn't. It wasn't just quite dark or a bit gloomy, the darkness was complete: championship, record-breaking darkness. The air was still warm but the ground was becoming damp under his feet, seeping through the leather soles of his shoes and into his French office worker-style socks. If he was captured now, he'd have a job explaining what aspect of his profession had brought him to an isolated field at night, with a German pistol, a wad of banknotes and a small wash kit in his pocket. He was not lavishly equipped. *He was espionaging on the cheap*, for want of a better phrase.

He forced his thoughts to remain roughly in line with those required to complete his task, but even when he did so he simply had no idea where to go. He wasn't sure if he was in the actual field he'd studied on the map or from which direction they had landed. If he took the bull by its metaphorical horns and struck out manfully and with determination in any particular direction, he was more likely to be heading away from his target than towards it. In addition, he was bound to look like someone who'd spent a good part of the night tramping through muddy fields, rather than a semi-sophisticated town dweller. Suit trousers caked in mud to the knees was not, as far as he was aware, this season's look from the Paris fashion houses. (*They'd probably be looking at something in feldgrau with jackboot accessories*, he told himself, ruefully).

Ted found that he was effectively paralysed. Not with fear, as he might have expected, and not as a result of a parachuting accident, which until recently had been a real possibility, but rather he was paralysed by a lack of options. There seemed to be no viable course of action to take. Had he eaten nothing but carrots for three weeks, had the stupid night vision tablets been of any use at all, he still couldn't have seen anything. It was simple physics: no light – no see.

He crouched down in case he was being observed by someone who *could* see in the dark. He wanted to find somewhere dry and safe to gather his thoughts and fill in the gaps in his plan, the gaps that could only be dealt with *in situ.* Already he was thinking of what he was going to say in his debriefing, and it wasn't good. Others would learn from his experiences, benefit from his hard-earned wisdom.

But only if he got home.

The ground was stony and ridged underfoot. He could feel a hedge or a bush nearby and he knew there was a low wall, simply because he'd fallen over it. He was slowly building a mental picture, hoping that some extra sense would develop which would help him to move on. As mental pictures went, however, it was a poor effort, lacking detail and perspective like a four-year-old's drawing of… anything, really. A map produced by a lunatic would have been as much use. It would probably have been better, in fact.

He stood again and slowly turned through three hundred and sixty degrees. Or he thought that was the number of degrees through which he turned but he had no reference points against which to judge the extent of his rotation. As he did this, he looked hard, trying to strain his eyes and deciding, not for the first time, that such a thing was not really possible. If you couldn't see, then you couldn't see. You could strain all you liked, but it made no difference. He could have either been standing in the middle of a field or at the edge of it, but surely the hedge indicated the latter? If that was the case then how had John landed the plane? How indeed had he managed any of it? And what sort of field had a wall in it?

Ted tried to gather information by other means. What could he hear? He strained his ears, or rather he didn't, because that too was not possible. Could he hear a river, or a road, or cattle, or sheep, or voices or the hum of electric pylons? So many questions, one answer.

He sighed, took a step into the black night that lay around him and stumbled immediately. He swore but it did no good. He couldn't even sit down. He looked at his watch but could see nothing; he couldn't even see his wrist. Very sensibly he hadn't been provided with a torch. Nothing would have looked as suspicious as a lone man in occupied France, wandering through a field at night dressed as a… *et cetera et cetera.* But if he had a torch he would have used it now. Perhaps that was one for future missions. Give the agent a torch with instructions to avoid its use if at all possible. *Future missions?*

'Fuck that,' he said aloud. He wondered if someone would hear him. He hoped that they would, except if they were German, and even that was becoming an attractive proposition. Until he reminded himself what would happen to him if the Germans got him. There would be no POW camp. Desperation born of sensory numbness made him take another step. He didn't fall over. Encouraged he took another and did. His knees made contact with something damp but unyielding. He swore again as he picked himself up. He'd be a wreck before he got much further.

Suddenly, he heard a noise. He stopped, swaying as if drunk, for his footing was insecure. A light breeze shuddered past his ears but over that he heard dull footsteps. Slow, plodding, methodical and worst of all, coming towards him. He crouched again, seeking a better angle to observe this new threat, hoping to silhouette them against the weak and haphazard moonlight. He gave his eyesight time to adjust and then squinted. It felt as if his eyes were on the end of stalks, trying to catch a glimmer of light from the all-encompassing gloom. He listened for the footsteps but could hear only his own ragged, fugitive breaths.

Ted forced himself to calm down a little. He was armed and they couldn't see him any better than he could see them. On the other hand, they obviously knew he was there but probably not the exact spot he crouched. They must have heard the plane land and take off again.

Of course, he reasoned, they could be Frenchmen coming to investigate, but he knew that that was not the case. He pictured the German patrol, approaching in a stealthy crouch, machine guns cocked and ready to fire. They might have flares and torches. He listened again, not wanting to breathe or swallow. He felt a tickly cough form in the back of his throat.

Still the footsteps came closer. It was definitely more than one man but their approach was leisurely, measured. There was no rush for them, caution and surprise were their greatest asset. Ted reached for the Walther, slipping it from his pocket with infinite care. He used two hands to remove the safety catch, trying to avoid any click that might seal his fate. He needed to cock the weapon to make it ready to fire but that would be far too noisy, and no noise in nature sounded like a pistol being cocked. Ted felt the gossamer layer of oil against his skin. He was reassured but firing in the dark was generally a futile exercise.

Footsteps. How on earth could they see him? But there was little doubt in his mind that they could. Perhaps they had some other sense guiding them. But he knew that that wasn't really possible. *What other sense?* He turned his head and squinted, trying to get a fix on his adversaries, but was greeted with only impenetrable blackness. They were close now. He could hear the ridged soil being compressed by their feet, the occasional brush against the long grass. It was at once eerie and terrifying. Ted was transfixed by that unseen spot in front of him, trying to guess the distance between himself and his opponent. Should he call out, or fire, or run? None of these seemed to offer him much hope. *What would he even do if they called out?* In French? In German? In English? Was it a trap, or the hand of friendship on offer?

The tickle in throat became more pronounced and he felt the need to urinate too. Was his body going to betray him?

Was it a trap? The question remained, nagging, just as the answer continued to elude him. He tried to *smell* an answer, or at least a clue. Cologne? Or sweat? Anything? They were no more than ten yards away and still they approached, calm yet dogged, unstoppable, unwavering… Ted moved his left hand to the slide on his pistol. He'd have to be quick. He might only get one shot, and he'd lose his night vision – such as it was – then he'd run. It was the best, worst and only plan he had. Clump, clump, clump…

***

The landing was easier this time, for he was bringing the Lysander down on a proper airfield, with adequate illumination. Predictably, Murray was waiting for him, anxious about his agent but relieved to see his pilot again.

'He's there?'

'Yes, sir. That part went smoothly enough.'

'Good. Let's hope his luck holds so that we can get him back out of France. Well done, Flight. We can have a proper debriefing tomorrow. 0900 hours.'

Chapter Thirteen

The horse was about a foot away when it finally stopped. He could smell it now: stale, oaty, like an old musty blanket. He reached out a hand and stroked its nose.

'Fer fuck's sake,' he muttered. He laughed and then spoke to the horse. 'Do you know the way to Lille?' The horse didn't speak; it was a horse.

'No, didn't think so,' he said. He was reassured by the sound of his own voice as if he were hearing a friend offering guidance. Perhaps, he mused, he *was* hearing a friend speak, that for the time being companionship would come from within. The horse sniffed Ted's face with a jerky lunge and made a strange spluttering noise as if offended by the smell. Ted could only just make out the outline of the great beast. It could have been a pantomime horse for all he could tell. They both stood there in what might have been a companionable silence, although Ted wasn't convinced that horses thought that deeply about such matters.

'Well, what now, Trigger?' he asked. 'Trigger' responded with a seemingly inexorable deluge of urine that splashed onto the ground like rainwater from a broken downspout.

'Thanks,' he said, backing away hastily. 'So, you're not called Trigger, then. Is that it?' The horse shuffled sideways and then turned slowly. Ted peered into the gloom to follow the animal's movements. The horse slowly walked away, apparently satisfied with the result of his investigations. Ted applied the safety catch gratefully and returned the pistol to his pocket. He followed in the horse's wake, feeling very much like an unwanted but persistent visitor. He stumbled over the little wall again and swore again. The horse kept walking, undeterred.

At this point Ted knew only one thing for sure; the horse was going *somewhere.* If that somewhere happened to be better than the somewhere he'd been before, then so much the better, and if it wasn't then he was no worse off. To find himself relying upon a dumb beast for guidance wasn't ideal but his only other option was to stand in the field until daylight. This way he was doing something, taking the initiative. He might only find himself in another part of the field, and perhaps further from his destination, but at least he was no longer passive. He thought that he remembered one of his instructors saying to him, 'whatever you do, do something.' It hadn't made much sense at the time.

He stumbled again but the horse kept walking towards some unseen destination. Ted regained his feet and brushed himself down. It was like a slap-stick comedy act played out in a darkened theatre.

For the next few minutes, they both padded resolutely through the field, Trigger unbothered about the peculiar man who seemed to be following him.

'Does this sort of thing happen to you a lot?' Ted asked the horse. 'A strange man following you home?'

Clump, clump, clump. Now and again he could make out some aspect of the animal's shape: a black curved flank, a swishing tail, but other than that he followed nothing more than a sound. Ted's shoes got heavier and heavier as he gathered layer upon layer of mud and dung. He imagined his feet resembling big mud pies. Or *dung* pies.

Then the horse stopped. He didn't turn or lie down or make a noise, he just stopped. There was some indefinable quality to the way in which he ended his journey that told Ted they had arrived at a definite place and not just another featureless part of the field. He took a few more steps until he was next to the beast and peered into the gloom once again. He heard an owl and then something, probably a bat, fluttered violently past his face. Was that a hedge? And next to it a gate? And beyond that a road? He took a pace forwards, gingerly feeling his way. More confident now, he strode towards the gate.

The thin crust of mud in the ditch wasn't enough to support Ted's weight and his left foot plunged through into the stinking watery sludge beneath. The smell was what his Auntie Ellis would have called a *good country smell,* which was a euphemism for something less than good.

'Christ,' he said, hauling himself out. He still had one leg that didn't smell of animal waste, but the other leg more than compensated. He turned to look at the horse, accusingly. 'You could have warned me,' he said. The horse stubbornly refused to comment. 'Well, thank you for showing me the gate,' he said, grudgingly. 'I haven't got a carrot for you but then you can already see in the dark, can't you?' He took a couple of paces then turned again. 'Lucky I didn't bump into an enemy horse, eh?'

He was astride the gate when it swung open, dipping alarmingly at the same time. Despite the tension, or possibly because of it, he laughed. Feeling immensely silly, he jumped down onto the road, glad to have something firm under his feet. The road was lined by hedges and trees, a sanctuary for animals of the night, which now protested at this intruder's presence in their demesne.

He walked tentatively, barely able to pick out the dramatically sloping verges from the road; everything was night grey. He paused occasionally, hoping to hear a sound or smell an odour that would somehow indicate he was proceeding in the right direction. After a few minutes he came to a junction and paused to find a road sign. He shuffled blindly to the road's apex, his arms outstretched like a Hollywood mummy. Nocturnal animals noted his progress and scuttled warily in the undergrowth. The signpost was a hollow tubular affair, the metal cold to the touch. He let his hands reach up to find three flat, elongated plates. The outer two were at ninety degrees to the one which pointed back in the direction he had come from. He could see nothing. He ran his fingertips along the plates and detected the embossed words that gave each one a destination. Had he been blind he could probably have read the place names, although he might not have known where each of them was in relation to Lille, his destination.

'Oh, fer God's sakes,' he said through a weary sigh. He looked round for signs of daybreak but there were none. He looked at his watch. He might as well have been blindfolded. If he could even find an outbuilding to take shelter in…

The noise of the vehicle came to him slowly, hints dropped, signals detected, discounted, picked up and considered. A car? A truck? French or German? Probably the latter, he decided and time to get off the road. Keeping the signpost to his left he stumbled forwards, making contact with a wall, beyond which was a thick thorny hedge. He groped for a gateway but realised that there was unlikely to be such a thing situated on a junction. He cursed and retraced his steps back to the road he'd been on. It too was bordered by thick jungles of thorny hedge.

He carried on looking for a tree against which to mould himself but there wasn't one. The engine was louder now and he heard a none-too-smooth gearchange as the vehicle surmounted an incline. Ted began to panic and tried to force himself through the hedge. Thorns tore at his exposed flesh and plucked at his woollen clothes. The elastic branches where intertwined and seemed to push him away. With each thrust he was thrown back onto the road as if he were charging into a huge piece of sponge rubber.

Now he could see the headlights peeking dimly through blackout slits which gave the driver just enough light to drive. The vehicle was coming his way and he was caught in the road like a startled animal. Ted threw himself in the ditch, his hip connecting painfully with a rock. Perversely, the ditch was much shallower at this point than any of the ditches he had previously fallen in. Now that he needed a hole to swallow him up there wasn't one.

'Bastard!' he cursed with the sort of vehemence he could only summon for inanimate objects which refused to bend to his will. He stretched out, flattening himself into the ditch. The truck drew level with him moments later and halted at the junction. He could hear German voices from the rear – drunken soldiers heading back to camp in the passion wagon, was his guess. He'd been one of their number often enough. He heard a rough gear change and the engine note pick up. The truck began to move off laboriously, then with a resounding bump it stalled. Ted sighed inwardly. He shuddered. 'Fer fuck's sake,' he muttered.

From the back of the truck there came jeers and from the front good-natured abuse. The engine turned over like a sick old man with a hacking cough, but didn't catch. Ted's frustration grew like an ache. He clenched his fists. One of the soldiers used the unintended halt to relieve himself over the tail gate. Little drops of warm urine splashed onto Ted's sleeve. Still the engine refused to catch. *So much for German engineering*, he thought bitterly. This was the one time when he actually wanted something in the German armoury to function properly.

There was another exchange between those in the back and those in the front. It sounded like the driver was telling the men to get out and push. Ted tensed, ready to run, his mouth dry and eyes wide. He didn't know where he was going to run to. He wondered if the soldiers were armed. Could he shoot his way out of trouble? His thoughts flew like banknotes caught in a cyclone, each one an idea, a scrap of information, a plan, or an obituary. And then the engine coughed back to life. There was an ironic cheer from the soldiers. Ted felt no urge to kill them. He didn't even begrudge them their night out.

He carefully released his breath. The driver revved the engine and pulled away into the blackness. Two minutes later all trace of the vehicle had gone but Ted still lay in the ditch. Only now did he feel the pain in his hip.

Chapter Fourteen

Ted crawled along the ditch until he found a softer patch of earth and then curled up. Pulling his jacket tightly round his slender frame, he decided to wait until dawn broke before continuing. Once he could read the road sign he would be able to establish his whereabouts and then head for Lille. It shouldn't be far.

He knew now that future missions – and he didn't intend that they should involve him – would require the provision of a map. A torch and a map; not much to ask... but then again, a map was quite incriminating should it be found in the possession of a supposed French local. *Not as incriminating as a pistol, of course*, he reminded himself.

His hip throbbed but he assumed it wasn't broken because his movement wasn't affected. In recognising that, he had more or less exhausted his medical knowledge. To pass the time, he tried to list his mission's good points. It didn't take long. For a start, he hadn't been captured, he hadn't broken his leg in a parachute drop and he *was* armed. Against that he was cold, hungry, lost, covered in mud and had the whole of the mission ahead of him. He had achieved nothing thus far.

Despite the cold, he slept, curled up like a stray, and awoke some time later with a globulous patina of dew on his clothes. It looked as if he had been sprinkled with tiny pearls during the night. He stood and shook himself like a dog. He rubbed his tongue over his teeth, winced, yawned and stretched. Lurid lights flickered before his eyes and perspiration sprung from his brow. Ted sat heavily and let his head drop between his knees, waiting for the moment to pass. He needed food and some more sleep. His brief, uncomfortable slumber had exacerbated his weary depression rather than alleviated it.

As the sun slowly drew itself into the sky, he was able to pick out details from his surroundings: dew-sprinkled spikes of grass, the undulating form of the ditch, a tree with drooping branches that reached into the road like gnarled hands. Bile rose in his throat and he shivered. He tried to draw from some mobile cache of determination that he hoped he'd brought with him.

Chocolate. The third thing on his 'future missions list.' Chocolate provided energy and boosted morale. It was easy to carry. He wondered briefly, and without enthusiasm, if he had a knack for this type of work and at the same time realised how ill-equipped he really was. *Torch, map, chocolate…*

If he felt so weak and fatigued on his first day, how would he feel by Thursday when John returned? He glanced at the signpost and stood gingerly. This might be the moment of truth, the point that he took charge of his situation and actually began the job he'd been sent to do.

'Right Ted. Get on with it,' he told himself. He made his way over to the sign and looked at his three choices: Belloire, Coutilles and Paetenaire. The first of the three was on the way to Lille. He looked down at his muddy trousers, shook his head and began his journey. His breath floated before his eyes in little clouds and he yawned repeatedly. He vowed that this was his last foray into France or anywhere else as an agent. Murray would be disappointed but not necessarily surprised. Churchill? Well, he wasn't likely to meet him again. Jean? If she loved him then she should be glad that he wouldn't be risking his life in future.

Would it make him less the man? He scoffed inwardly at the very idea; only he knew that he was already less the man than they all seemed to think. All this – this half-baked 'mission' – was the result of his escape from France. More fool them if they couldn't see that he had merely been doing what any man would do in the circumstances. It had been a question of survival and nothing else.

He could abandon his mission right now. All he had to say was that he couldn't locate this Feldhus and who could argue? He still had the problem of finding somewhere to hide out until Thursday, but if he didn't kill the officer then no one would be looking for him. His morale was at a low ebb, but it certainly wasn't the first time, and he understood the reasons: fatigue, cold, hunger, danger, discomfort. He'd experienced them all before and felt exactly the same way. These things were parts of a soldier's life and had been since anyone had ever called themselves a soldier.

***

'We know he got there but, overall, how was it?' asked Murray. A cigarette lay in a heavy brass ashtray which looked like a relic of the Great War. A thin spiral of smoke rose in the still air.

'Fine really. It was a bit too dark perhaps – I would say we needed more moonlight to be on the safe side. It clouded over heavily after I landed so I doubt if Ted could see much.'

Murray nodded.

'And you'll be able to find the same spot for next time?'

'I hope so, sir. I'll have more moonlight, hopefully. We need people on the ground though.'

'It just wasn't possible. Perhaps we'll have a network of helpers in future but we don't have anything terribly organised at the minute.'

'If the landing zone is marked out...'

'That'll make it easy for the Germans to capture our man if they infiltrate.' Brigadier Murray poured two cups of tea from a pot and offered one to the pilot. John nodded his thanks. He added a sugar lump with a little pair of silver tongs, feeling faintly ridiculous as he did so. *Where did the brigadier get this stuff*, he wondered? 'There are no easy answers at present. He is a guinea pig to some extent. You too, really.'

John laughed. 'That's not very reassuring, sir,' he said.

'Not really,' admitted the officer. 'It's honest though. How did he seem to you? Corporal Dexter, I mean.'

'Fine. Nervous, as you'd expect. Do you have doubts about him, sir?'

'Should I?'

John shrugged an answer.

'I would have doubts about anybody in the circumstances. It's a risky business. To be honest he doesn't seem terribly enthusiastic,' said Murray.

John laughed gently, thinking of his friend. 'Perhaps it's nerves, sir. He might not be enthusiastic but he's tough and that's more important.'

'I think you're right Flight Sergeant Guy. Nevertheless, I don't send people on this type of trip lightly.' A silence followed in which John began to wonder if he was expected to take his leave of the officer. 'Did he ever mention Captain Pomeroy to you?'

'Captain Pomeroy? I don't think so.'

'He was the officer who sent Dexter off on what turned out to be several wild goose chases.'

'He mentioned that that had happened but I don't remember the name.'

'Okay. Well, I'll see you on Thursday, no doubt.' John drank the last of his tea, then stood and saluted.

Murray watched the pilot leave and then retrieved a note book from his desk. He wrote *'Captain Pomeroy?'* and put the pen lid to his lips. With a sigh he replaced the notebook and sat back in his chair. For the moment he could only wait. There would be no news, no indication of any sort that Ted had succeeded or failed. Indeed, when he returned, he would just have to accept his word of success, at least until his source came through with his report gleaned from the radio traffic.

He thought about Churchill, the man who had selected him for this job. The PM expected so much, not only of him, but of men like Ted. Winston thought that everyone ought to be like Winston: displaying the same strengths, the same determination, the same imagination, the same fire, and compensating for the same failings. *Was the PM even aware of his own foibles?*

The PM simply wasn't ordinary, thought Murray and *thank God too.* The time for ordinary men would be when the war was finished perhaps. He felt suddenly weary, just as he had in the Great War. The prelude to each battle seemed to draw energy from his body like a blotter on an ink spill, and so it was now. He was no more enamoured with risking the lives of others than he had been with risking his own. He had a desk job now and yet he didn't feel safe, other men's peril feeling like his own.

He picked up the paper and quickly scoured it for good news. It was the usual mixed bag of war stories, generally weighted in the Germans' favour as usual. Seventeen Luftwaffe aircraft reported shot down versus nine RAF, Italian sabre rattling, British ships sunk by merchant raiders and submarines, the establishment of a collaborationist government in France under Petain. He yearned for news of victory but would have made do with something that didn't sound like defeat. The great air battle was a numbers game. No one knew exactly how many aeroplanes Hitler would throw at Britain in order to achieve his aims. Would a ratio of seventeen losses to nine ensure Britain's eventual victory? He didn't know.

***

The Lysander was refuelled and ready to go. John looked above him at the contrails of another great air battle. Perhaps he should volunteer for fighters. He'd flown an old Gloster biplane a few times in the late thirties but he guessed they'd be desperate for pilots pretty soon, pilots with any experience at all.

The idea had no real appeal for him. He still felt as if he had fought his war and that no more could rightly be expected of him, and yet here he was still risking his life. The risks were less perhaps than those faced by a

Hurricane or Spitfire pilot, but nevertheless his was a dangerous profession.

He kept low on his return, skimming the underside of the aerial conflict high above. There was no guarantee that the battle wouldn't come to him of course and this time he had no rear gunner, just the two forward firing guns in the wheel spats. He'd be no match for a Messerschmitt.

Increasingly, he doubted his ability to survive the war, either physically or mentally. There was only so much strain a man could take. He knew that Ted must feel the same way and wondered about Murray's questioning of him. Had he seen some weakness in Ted's make up that might lead to him unravelling when tested? He sighed. Ted had had his war too. He'd done more than most men would ever do, even if the war lasted five, ten or twenty years. He shuddered at the thought.

John searched the skies around his head, craning his neck this way and that, looking for enemy aircraft, knowing that losing himself in thought, even a moment's inattention, might lead to a loss of life – his. The air, even that above his own country, was hostile. He flew at one hundred and sixty knots, making fine adjustments to the controls, feeling the vibration of the engine through the plane's metal, wood and fabric sinews. The skies were clear and blue. It was easy to forget the war for a moment and think about a time when peace had been re-established. *Would he still want to be a pilot*, he wondered? He glanced at his control panel and looked up again just as the Dornier Do17 plunged through the air ahead of him. The Lysander bucked in the turbulent air left in its wake. The elegant, twin-engine bomber screamed like a dying beast as it plummeted. Flames burst from its port engine like a comet. John could see the rear gunner trying to open his canopy. His face contorted in panic, he thumped and thumped... For a second John could picture the pilot trying to wrest control of the aircraft from the force of gravity that it had once arrogantly defied. But no more.

Below, but well ahead of his position, the slender fuselage of the bomber struck the earth with a resounding bang. The fuselage snapped, then concertinaed. A spray of dry clay erupted and then an explosion tore the aeroplane's mortal remains asunder, casting them skywards. A chunk of metal wheeled in the air in front of the Lysander but John flew on and missed it by feet. He swallowed hard, shaken but glad that it was not him at the Dornier's controls. *How much longer?* he wondered.

***

Jean rather enjoyed her new job. The car was a Wolseley, originally black but now painted matt olive green. She was in the MT section, run by Sergeant Harris, and was dispatched to various airfields to collect and deliver officers who, for one reason or another, chose not to fly between bases. Some were groundcrew officers, some too old to fly and some simply didn't want to fly when the air above them was crawling with Luftwaffe predators looking for easy prey. Mostly they were polite – dismissive of her, but rarely rude. Some of the younger ones took the opportunity to chat her up, despite the fact that she was merely an NCO. She smiled, made small talk, held the doors open for them, saluted, helped them with their bags and pined for Ted. All of which went largely unnoticed, especially pining for Ted.

The other drivers, mainly older men, called up, or from the reserves, were friendly enough and the girls were... girls. She liked them, of course and they her, but her relationship with Ted set her apart somehow. Few of them had boyfriends actually fighting the Germans. The army sat at home licking its wounds and recovering, ready for the next phase of the war, but Ted was back there. He was fighting and she couldn't even talk about him. No wonder they thought she was odd. War, of course, threw people together from all walks of life. It was a great leveller, a unifying force. Things wouldn't be the same after the war. It would have to be a better world… if they won of course.

Chapter Fifteen

The spare figure of Hugh Dalton was shown in to the PM's office. Dalton was the Minister for Economic Warfare, a Labour politician in Churchill's coalition cabinet. Churchill respected his subordinate's intellect and his application. He was an economist by training and, like most of his generation, a veteran of the Great War. His task was an unexpected one: to oversee the development of what would become the Special Operations Executive. Their task in turn was, using Churchill's own phrase, 'to set Europe ablaze.' The PM was eager to see his rhetoric transformed into action. Dalton wondered if his instructions were almost meant literally. Perhaps nothing short of a burning continent would do.

The basic structure of the organisation had been defined years before through various studies, but Dalton had to turn theory into reality. He appreciated the PM's enthusiasm and determination but this appreciation was tempered by wariness of his unrealistic ambitions. Churchill's imagination was one of his great strengths, but also one of his greatest weaknesses. He was a polymath and a man of extraordinary energy. He was passionate, obstinate, obdurate; he had an artist's vision, the drive of an industrialist, and yet despite his great personal gifts he rarely seemed to take account of the abundant complexities in his wild schemes. He skilfully used simple words to convey huge ideas and expected them to become reality almost as they tripped blithely from his lips.

'Sabotage?' he asked. He'd never imagined himself to be the head of such an organisation.

'Sabotage. We must keep Britain in the war. The free world must see us fighting the Germans. We can't sit back and let them bring the war to us.'

'There is the question of how the Germans will react.'

'React?'

'Will they exact retribution upon the French themselves? I don't foresee them putting up with acts of sabotage in their new empire. It is now that they will be stamping their authority on the new provinces of the Reich.'

'True, but that danger always exists. This is total war, is it not?' His argument might have sounded specious – *they started it* – had it not been unalterably true. Churchill patted his stomach as if to emphasize the physical difference between him and the lean Dalton. 'I would expect them to recruit patriots to fight the Germans too. We could supply weapons and explosives.'

Privately Dalton doubted this; they were struggling to equip the new army let alone giving weapons away to irregular forces of dubious value. 'Are the French interested in fighting? Their best chance to defeat Germany was prior to their surrender when they had the most powerful army in Europe. They squandered their chance,' he said, sardonically. Churchill smiled. He understood the numbers game – the French had had more of everything than the Germans, therefore they ought to have won the war. He also understood that nothing was ever so simple. The Germans had outfought the French. They might have outfought the British too had they been given greater opportunity.

'Don't let General de Gaulle hear you say that,' he said.

Dalton chuckled.

'So, what do you want me to do?'

'Find the men to establish the organisation. Recruit agents. Ask Giles Murray for help. This new organisation will need specialised weapons and new tactics; you will need men working on that. We need ways to get these agents into Europe and, just as importantly, out again. You are recruiting fighters, not spies, but they will need the same virtues as their MI6 brethren.'

Dalton glanced at the decanter on the table between them. He was not offered a drink and wondered if this was a slight or an oversight. The PM touched his chin. 'You will need training facilities and a suitable syllabus. Unarmed combat, languages, demolitions, that sort of thing. Parachuting as well probably.'

Dalton wondered if he didn't have enough on his plate. Where did he start?

***

Later in the day he visited General Brooke, the newly appointed Commander-in-Chief, Home Forces.

'Forgive the mess,' said the General, guiding his visitor out of the removal men's path. 'General Ironside left me a Rolls Royce and very little else. I don't even know where his papers are!' He led the minister to one of the few chairs already installed. 'Please sit. I'll try and rustle up some tea.' The General, one of the PM's most trusted officers who had recently distinguished himself in France, was gone for a few minutes. Upon his return he said, 'I hope the Wehrmacht doesn't invade today. I'm in total disarray. Not my normal state, I hasten to add.'

'I know it isn't, General. You wouldn't have been given this post if that were the case. The PM has asked me to establish some sort of force for sabotaging Europe.' He paused to let the information sink in and to study Brooke's face. There was something about the general's manner which led him to believe that he would not be in favour of such an organisation. He was a soldier of the old school, unlikely to be a proponent of private armies.

'I see,' said Brooke, guardedly. An orderly brought in a silver tray with tea and biscuits. 'I brought these with me from France,' he said nodding at the delicate biscuits arranged artfully on a plate. 'I think we shall be doing without such luxuries soon.' Dalton smiled. Most of the population did without such luxuries all their lives. 'He's already recruited one young man. He's under the care of Giles Murray. He might be your first recruit,' suggested the general.

'What do you think of the idea, General?'

'Me? Oh, well I...'

'Off the record.'

'Rather like you, I was a conventional soldier in the Great War. Off the record, I think it's potty. Whilst I think we are fortunate to have Winston at the helm I also think we need to be careful with him. That he is inspirational is not in question. He is ruthless, forceful and determined. He will never see this country bow to the likes of Hitler.'

'But?'

'But some of his ideas are impracticable and some of them are deleterious to our common goals. He needs advisors to keep his imagination operating within the bounds of what is possible. I fear that if the prosecution of the war was left to him alone, he would spread our armed forces so thinly, attacking so many different targets, that we couldn't mount a serious defence of any one part of the British Empire.' Brooke sat back and then poured the tea, as if to prevent his hands from shaking.

'So, you wouldn't be in favour of this sabotaging force?' asked Dalton.

'Well, where do the men come from? And the weapons and the training? Right now, we need soldiers in organised formations: brigades, divisions, corps and so on. We need conventional troops with tanks and artillery support to repel an invasion.'

Dalton said nothing. He presented an impassive exterior but his mind was racing, trying to find a way to bring the General's views more into line with those of the PM. Brooke would be a formidable ally. Equally he could perhaps be an obstructive foe.

Brooke looked at the minister and then spoke. 'But I appreciate also that Winston's view of things is necessarily different to mine. From his perspective the world is looking on, expecting us to crumble. He wants the world to know – the United States in particular – that the fight goes on.'

'So, can you help me? This organisation is going to... em, happen. Regardless of the practicalities of the situation I have to see it through. And who knows, it might pay dividends one day.' The two men studied each other, both doubting that this would be the case.

'Yes, of course. If we are not overrun in the coming weeks then we will have the nucleus of this force ready for action.' Brooke smiled at the politician, his scepticism undiminished.

Chapter Sixteen

Nonchalance, Ted decided, was the key. The problem was he didn't feel nonchalant. He felt tired. He felt filthy. He felt frightened. These were not the building blocks needed for a display of nonchalance. In the distance he could see the spires and roofs of Lille, his ultimate destination, but before him lay the town of Belloire.

Belloire wasn't ruined but nor was it pristine. An abandoned French tank stood like a gate guardian beneath the eaves of a barn, and cattle peered curiously at him over hedges as he strode along the road. Two men stood next to a tractor and trailer, the latter piled high with hay, artlessly arranged and seemingly ready to slip off onto the road. Each watched him suspiciously from beneath the brims of their caps. One of them had a pungent cigarette clamped between his jaws, a little white chimney poking out from beneath a grand moustache. Ted's newly acquired knowledge of French seemed to desert him, leaving him only with the vestiges of his available vocabulary. He wondered if he could even get the single word out if it proved necessary to converse.

'Bonjour,' he said, airily. His seeming levity was quite at odds with the prevailing mood in these parts.

'Bonjour, monsieur,' said one man, suspiciously. His voice was gruff, laced with distrust and barely concealed malice. The other man declined to speak but took time to look at Ted's mud-spattered clothing. He spat on the ground like a naughty cinematic cowboy. Ted forced a smile and kept walking. The street consisted of tall town houses with wrought iron balconies, shuttered windows and peeling paint. There were shops, some of which remained in business. There was an air of tension. The

locals, thin on the ground as they were, tried to keep going amidst the uncertainty of the times.

Lille, their sprawling neighbour, had become like some sort of evil empire, growing malignantly on their doorstep; the German garrison was established there. The war had gone through Belloire in a flash but Ted could see bullet holes and at least one house ahead of him that had begun to collapse into the pavement following heavy shelling. Bricks and rubble made an ugly slope, like a sort of domestic landslide. Two grimy boys in shorts stood at its pinnacle like conquering mountaineers. As he passed, Ted glanced into the house, noting the plaster walls, a fireplace, curtains, wooden furniture... no one had attempted to tidy up.

At the boulangerie, a small, bedraggled queue formed. Housewives, uniformly disconsolate, pondering the fate of their husbands, old people wrapped up despite the heat of the sun. Ted's thought s turned to his own family as they always did at times like these.

A young woman stepped into the street in his path, causing him to stop abruptly. He smiled and gestured to her to proceed.

'Pardon, monsieur,' she muttered. She strode off, turning her head once to look at him and his muddy attire. Ted, who rarely felt insouciant under any circumstances, began to feel even less so with each step he took. He simply couldn't carry this off. He couldn't appear in Lille dressed like a peasant who'd been pelted with mud.

'Pardonnez moi, mademoiselle,' he began. The woman turned and frowned. Ted closed the gap between them. These were strange times, she thought, pulling her

cardigan closer to her chest. *'Ceci semblera étrange mais peut je lave mes vêtements.'* He was asking if he could wash his clothes. Ted pulled what he hoped looked like an honest, open face but the woman turned to walk away. *'Je peux payer,'* he added, hurriedly. The woman paused again and tucked a strand of hair behind her ear. He thought he had made a minor breakthrough in Anglo-French relations. She wasn't being friendly but nor was she terribly hostile.

'Je ne pense pas alors, monsieur,' she replied. She was extremely wary and he didn't blame her. Who in their right mind wanted to take a chance on a stranger, especially one who looked as dishevelled as he did?

'Please!' he blurted out.

She glanced around lest anyone else heard. This was not the time to strike up a friendship with an 'Englishman'.

'Et alors serai sur ma journée,' he added, wondering if that hastily tacked on phrase made any sense at all. He felt exhausted with the effort. The woman closed her eyes briefly and then indicated that he should follow her. Ted did so, feeling very conspicuous, like a disreputable fishing boat receiving a tow from a plush motor yacht.

A van rumbled up the street, sounding as if it only just had the power to move at all. A shopkeeper languidly swept the pavement in front of his business as if doing so was basically a waste of time. Life went on. What else could these people do but those things they always did? Ted kept a few paces behind the woman, looking uncomfortable and conspicuous. She acted as if he wasn't there and he wished it were true. Her pace was fast, her cardigan still clutched protectively around her. She nodded to another woman and paused briefly to speak to a shopkeeper without much apparent friendliness.

Ted stood close to her like an inept detective on the trail of a suspect. She glanced at him and then moved off again, finally taking a right turn into a street, so narrow and flanked with such tall houses that daylight seemed like nothing more than a rumour. A gendarme stood guard outside one house, looking puzzled and dejected, perhaps wondering if there had been any point in turning up for work. Ted stopped for a minute thinking that she was going to turn him in but she breezed past the policeman and kept walking apace.

In another few moments she crossed the street and turned left without bothering to look for traffic; it had obviously never been a busy thoroughfare. There was no let-up in her pace as if she hoped he would flag, fall behind and lose sight of her. She glanced round but he was still there, and she stopped. There was a key in her hand and this she placed into a lock in a door with peeling blue paint. The lock opened slickly, belying the general condition of the building they were about to enter. The door looked as if it would creak but didn't.

Without glancing in either direction she stepped inside and waited impassively as he did the same. The hall smelt damp despite the cloying warmth of summer. She checked a mail box but it was empty, as it had been for days. In a downstairs room, a dog barked and was sharply reprimanded by its owner. She moved a black bicycle from her path and ascended the stairs. Wordlessly, he followed. She was slim and walked nicely, but was rather plain, he had decided. Her clothes were old but well cut.

From the first landing he heard a baby cry and then a toilet flush with a noise like a ship's fog horn. It looked as if each floor had two rooms or flats. They ascended the next flight, their footsteps leaving dusty traces on the wooden stairs. The stairs themselves were warped and old, solid enough but treacherous. The woman sighed and began her ascent of the last flight of stairs. She glanced behind her and he ventured a smile. It was not reciprocated. Finally, they reached a door. She held a key in her hand like a surgical instrument ready for an incision. The door was bare wood, cheap-looking, but he could see traces of paint on its edges as if someone had once tried to cheer the place up. It had obviously not been a recent attempt.

She entered the hall and kept walking. He followed, closing the door softly behind him. The hall was confined and dark. Ted felt a surge of weariness wash over him as if a previously undetected sleeping potion was starting to take effect. He brushed past a woollen coat hanging from a peg, past doors on either side of the hall and into the room at the end; the kitchen as it turned out. He peered in warily, feeling essentially uninvited. He was nothing other than a tolerated intruder. The woman had put a kettle on the gas ring and was in the process of taking two cups from a cupboard. The kitchen was spartan and cramped, precisely as he would have expected from a garret like this. It was the sort of place in which a struggling artist lived. *Was she a struggling artist*, he wondered? She was a struggling *something*; struggling to whip up any enthusiasm for his presence in her home. He didn't blame her for that either.

A small table was pushed against one wall and two chairs were wedged into the narrow space at either end.

He pulled one out, lifting a newspaper from the cracked seat. The front page had a photograph of an elderly French officer shaking hands with a German counterpart. Old news, he set it aside.

Ted sat, uninvited. He glanced out of the tiny window at a similar one across the road. A man leaned out, smoking as if worried that the cigarette smoke might infest his tiny hovel with an unpleasant smell. The woman kept her back to him the whole time, concentrating on the task of producing two hot drinks which smelled like coffee. He assumed that one was for him and was encouraged. Presumably, this was some sort of acknowledgement that he actually existed. He adjusted his position, the Walther digging into his thigh. He thought about setting it on the table but decided against taking such a liberty. *Probably bad manners*, he thought. He had never visited someone before whilst carrying a small arm but there was bound to be some sort of associated etiquette.

The chair creaked as he leaned back. It was glued together and felt as if it had fallen apart many times and been reglued. Ted sighed, puffed out his cheeks, slowly releasing his breath. The woman turned, a plain white China cup and saucer in each hand. Steam lifted from each, mingling with the air and seeming to disappear.

'Thank you,' he said. 'I mean, *merci*.' The woman retrieved a pair of glasses from a box on the table and put them on as if to get a proper look at her guest. She suited them, he realised, revising his opinion of her.

'You're taking a big risk being here,' she said, plainly.

'You speak English?,' he replied, astonished. He set his drink on the table.

'I *am* English. You can wash those clothes here but then you'd better be on your way. I don't even want to know what you're doing here. It is not safe for you... or me.'

'My God. But what are *you* doing here?'

'No questions.'

'Aye but...'

'Unless you can get me back to Britain, then there's no point in giving away any information to you.'

'Well, okay then. Supposing I can.' Ted held his hands out, palms uppermost. The woman scoffed. 'Supposing I can get you back. Back home.'

'You'll be lucky to get yourself back.'

'Oh, I'm getting back alright,' said Ted with the touch of defiance that normally eluded him in these situations.

'You look shocked,' she said. Was she thawing a little, he wondered?

'I am. I had no idea. All the time I was following you here and you didn't speak or anything. I can't help wondering what you're doing here.'

'I should probably be wondering what you're doing here also,' she said. There was no hint of coyness in the way she spoke. 'But I'm not,' she added abruptly. 'Now get those clothes off.'

He removed his shoes and then his trousers. If he was captured now... He held the muddy trousers out to the woman. She looked at them as if she was being offered a baby's nappy.

'I'm not bloody washing them,' she said. 'The sink's there.' She pointed at a small sink with a few dirty dishes poking above its rim. 'You can clean those too if you'd like to earn your keep.'

'Oh, right,' said Ted, sheepishly. 'I was hoping I could have a sleep,' he said. She grabbed the trousers off him as if saving him from disaster.

'Bed's through there,' she said. Her tone was curt, exasperated but not entirely hostile, maybe just disapproving.

***

The trousers drip-dried into the sink with an insistent noise: plip, plip, plip. Veronica knew that it was going to drive her mad. She couldn't lie on her bed because *he* was there, and the only other room she had – the bathroom – was even more uncomfortable than the kitchen. She sighed heavily and looked at her cigarettes as if they were dear friends. She was husbanding her last few packets of Players, suspecting that they were not to be imported again for some time. The alternative was to smoke the abominable French things but she had never acquired a taste for them. Even *they* might soon be in short supply.

She rose and walked to the window. For several minutes she stood, looking *through* the view and thinking of nothing. Her eyes were unfocussed as if such absent-minded reverie could keep her troubles at bay. She wondered idly if anyone's life ever went according to plan. Hers certainly hadn't. *Not that she had a plan to follow*, she thought. She glanced at her cigarettes once more. Life went on. *Why not have a cigarette?*

If she had planned her life, what would it have been like, she wondered? Most lives were just a series of inescapable events, one running into the next in some sort of random continuum. Hers was no different. It would be easier to list those things that she'd rather have avoided: being trapped in a foreign country that had just been overrun by another foreign country, renting a grotesque little flat using a rapidly dwindling stock of savings, giving refuge to a strange man whose newly washed trousers were dripping into her kitchen sink with a noise that was going to drive her insane.

She picked up the waistband on the trousers and examined it as if looking for a name left by a protective mother. The thought made her smile. She was just a little bit curious about him. She turned, walked past her cigarettes and into the hall. The bedroom door was ajar – only she had the knack of closing it properly. There was a sound of gentle snoring. She opened the door slowly.

Ted was curled up, on top of the sheets with his back to her. His shoes were on the floor and his jacket was hung up. She wasn't too surprised to see a pistol on the bedside cabinet next to the alarm clock. She smiled like a mother gazing upon her favourite child. He was quite nice really; unthreatening. He wasn't tall but he looked to be in good shape. Despite her misgivings it was reassuring to have him here but she quickly reminded herself that she didn't need a man, and certainly not one whose very presence would lead to her arrest. Harbouring a spy? She was likely to be shot.

From the kitchen she heard plip, plip, plip. He would have to stay – at least until his trousers had dried.

***

It was after three when he awoke. He lay still, letting consciousness take him by stages and trying to assess his situation. He wasn't sure if the sleep had made him feel worse or better. He didn't stir. Instead, he listened and thought. Somewhere, outside the flat, a door slammed. He heard footsteps on the stairs and then another door, further away this time, slammed. He thought the windows shook in reply. The street below was silent but he imagined that he could hear the woman in her kitchen.

Ted yawned and turned over on the bed so that he was lying flat and looking at the light bulb suspended there like a hanged football. A glance at the bedside table told him that his pistol hadn't been touched, which he supposed was reassuring.

'Time to go, Ted,' he said, rubbing his eyes and yawning again. The bedsprings shook lightly as he stood. He caught his trouserless reflection in the mirror. Ridiculous. Precisely what sort of assassin was he? Having no name added a sense of mystery. Having no trousers just added a sense of idiocy. He padded into the gloomy hall and knocked gently on the kitchen door, pushing it open.

She reached for her glasses as he entered as if they were a disguise or protection from strange men.

'The trouserless man returns,' she said, gently mocking. A slight smile played on her lips, taking the edge off a rather stern look. Ted felt that she had begun in some small way to accept his presence. 'You're going to look very conspicuous you know. Wherever you go you'll stand out from the crowd.'

'You mean the other men will have trousers on?' he quipped.

She laughed, indulgently and raised an eyebrow.

'I was thinking of putting them on again and getting out of your way,' he said by way of reassurance.

'They aren't dry. I couldn't send you away damp,' she said. She pictured him walking down the main street in Belloire with steam rising from his trousers. 'What I meant was there won't be many young men in civilian clothes walking about. They're all in uniform, fighting, or in prisoner of war camps now.'

'I know. Look, I appreciate what you've done. I know it's a risk. I might be able to get you home.' She looked at him askance. 'Seriously,' he added.

'What's your name?' she said suddenly. She walked over to the window and looked out. A German open-topped armoured car rolled through the street below. The rumble of tyres on cobbles, the muted roar of a petrol engine and the whine of its four-wheel drive transmission gave it a distinctive sound. 'Germans,' she said without drama.

Ted looked at her, studied her face for emotion, but there was none. 'They're gone. Be seeing a lot more of them, I'm sure.'

'Ted.'

'Hmm?'

'Ted. You asked my name. It's Ted. I thought you didn't want to know anything about me?'

'That was before you said you could… can you get me out of here? Can you really?'

'I can but maybe I'll have some questions for you,' said Ted, cagily. She seemed to ignore this as if she recognised him for the inexpert inquisitor that he was.

'So how can you get me out?' she asked. It sounded like a challenge.

'Ah, so you want to know all about me but you won't even tell me your...'

'Veronica,' she said hastily. She spat the word out.

'What?'

'My name's Veronica,' she said. Ted thought it was a horrible name, redolent of verruca.

'That's a nice name,' he said.

'No, it isn't. It's bloody awful.' She looked at him directly, goading him into disagreement. Ted looked over her shoulder as if spotting something outside. 'Isn't it?'

'Well, it's not my favourite but it suits you,' he said with a smile.

'Don't try that bloody Irish charm on me,' she warned with mock severity. She made it sound like an affliction. Ted was confused. No one had ever accused him of having charm, Irish or otherwise, but he let it go for the meantime.

'It's the sort of name a glamorous actress would have,' he said innocently. She gave him a curious look in return.

‘Mmmm. Maybe,’ she said dubiously. ‘I’m no glamorous actress, I can assure you.’

‘What are you doing here?’ he asked. She turned her back and began making some tea, as if he hadn’t spoken.

‘There’s not much to eat but you might as well be fed before you move on. You can stay here until the morning if you like.’ Ted nodded.

Chapter Seventeen

Veronica pulled the curtains open with a flourish, admitting pale sunshine into her bedroom. Ted had slept on the floor like a faithful dog, and she had crept out to start breakfast and to make coffee. She'd had her first cigarette of the day leaning out onto her little pretend balcony. Henri across the street had waved as he did every morning, no more than the casual flap of his hand like a bored seal. She waved back and looked at the sky then down at the street, expecting to see some Germans queuing at the café. There were none. She had intended to bring Ted his coffee in bed in an act of tenderness, the origin of which she could not explain. Her simple plan was thwarted by two factors: firstly, he wasn't actually in a bed, and secondly, he woke up and came into the kitchen before the kettle had boiled. He was wearing his long underpants, a vest and socks which had slipped down his feet.

'Very fetching,' she said. 'You look like the Incredible Melting Man.'

He looked down and then pulled his socks up one at a time hopping from foot to foot as he did so. He said, 'is that a film?'

'It should be. I've made you coffee. There's some bread and butter, then you can go.' Ted nodded, smiled and then yawned in that order.

'Ta,' he said, sitting.

'Your trousers are dry, by the way. I no longer have any hold over you,' she joked. She watched him as he sipped at his coffee. 'Cigarette?'

'No thanks. I don't smoke much. I know I've said this but I do appreciate you looking after me.'

'It's okay. For some reason I took pity on you. You're not a bad sort, are you?'

Ted shrugged. He wanted to ask her how he could get to Lille without drawing attention to himself. He also wanted to know if he could stay again after the deed was done. It was a lot to ask. These were dangerous times but he was sure that she could help him. And in return? A flight to Britain, surely good payment in the circumstances.

She watched him as he ate. 'So where are you off to?' she asked casually.

'Lille.'

'Why there?'

'Oh, well… I've got something to do there and then back home,' he said vaguely. She nodded and smiled, as if everything was perfectly clear now. There was a silence, which both of them wanted to break. Eventually Ted said, 'So how did you end up here?' Veronica briefly wondered how she could avoid answering and then if it was actually worth doing so. He'd be shocked, but did it matter?

'I came to France with a friend. She worked as a typist at the British Embassy in Paris. I got work nearby with an export company. I was a bilingual secretary. Well, that's what I told them. I could barely speak French. Somehow, I managed to keep my job; I don't think they ever quite realised how useless I was at it. The boss fancied me a bit too, which must have helped. When the war came, she – my friend – was evacuated back to Britain, but I was left behind. She gave me some money before she left and I had some more of my own. I went to the coast but I couldn't get away. Eventually I went to Lille, but ended up in Belloire, rented this lovely flat and tried to find work. I got a bit of work in the café across the road but the owner hasn't opened for a few days. I don't know where he's gone actually.' She smiled, suddenly craving another cigarette. 'So now you know.'

'Now I know,' he added. 'I got left behind too.'

'I thought maybe you were some type of secret agent – the gun and everything. I'm not trying to pry.'

Ted took a deep intake of breath, reminding himself that part of his job might be to recruit people who would take on the Germans. Was this woman a suitable candidate? Either way, he needed her help now, not at some point in the future. Perhaps she needed to know a little bit about him in return. 'Okay Veronica. I *am* an agent.' Somehow his job didn't sound very impressive when he said it. He felt embarrassed, unworthy of the title. 'I've been back to Britain after the evacuation, trained up and then sent back here. I can get you home but I need your help in return.' She nodded but looked worried.

'Carry on,' she said.

'Will you help?'

'I might. It depends what you need me to do, doesn't it?'

'I need you to get me into Lille and I need you to put me up.'

'I don't have a car.'

'Get me on the right bus. In fact, if you came with me, that would make the whole thing a lot easier.'

'Lille is crawling with German soldiers,' she warned.

'That's why I'm going there...' She looked at him blankly. 'I'm going to assassinate an officer. I need to find him first, then kill him and then get out. That's it really. Quite simple, except that I don't know *exactly* where he is, or where he will be. He'll be based in the old barracks but I can't exactly stroll in there, so I need to get him when he comes out. I have to shoot him and hopefully not get caught.'

'I would have thought that the hard bit was getting back home. I don't see how...'

'Aeroplane,' he said simply.

'An aeroplane?'

'It's a special plane that can land and take off in short distances. Fields and that sort of thing.'

'And there'd be room in it for me?'

'I think so.'

'You think so!' She was about to berate him for trying to drag her into his sordid little 'mission' with only the faint chance of being repaid in the manner he had suggested. Ted hastily intervened.

'Yes,' he corrected. 'Yes, there would be room. Easily enough room.' He looked at her levelly, trying to gauge whether or not he was winning her support. 'If there wasn't room for both of us, I'd let you go and I'd stay.' He hoped it wouldn't come to that, but three of them had fitted in the little German plane in which they had escaped France just weeks before. He made the promise to get her support, but Murray wanted his trained agent back, not some unknown civilian woman instead.

'That's very gallant,' she said, smiling sadly. 'I'm a lesbian you know.' She didn't want him to think that acts of chivalry could win her over.

'That's okay,' he said, quickly. 'You can still come with me.' She smiled again and a brief silence descended. In the street below, they heard a lorry pass and some men shout greetings to each other. A dog barked and then yelped as if having been kicked. 'What *is* a lesbian?' asked Ted, eventually.

Chapter Eighteen

The bus was half-empty. They took their seats like an ordinary couple. Ostensibly, they were two people who had become companions through long standing familiarity, rather than young lovers. Love hadn't died exactly but nor was it in its first youthful flush. They looked content… with each other at least. No one looked at them and they looked at no one. *Trust no one.*

Trust had been the first casualty of the occupation. In the months and years ahead, there would be some otherwise decent, upstanding people forced to collaborate with the enemy just to survive. In doing so they sold their souls. Furthermore, there would have to come a time when the enemy – the Germans – ceased to be such. Invasions and the eventual integration of the invader were facts of history, oft repeated, fought against, frowned upon and then accepted. With each generation came a diminution of hatred and then grudging acceptance.

Ted glanced at her now and again, still a little bit shocked at her revelation. *A woman who slept with another woman,* she'd said before adding, *in a biblical sense.* That had really floored him; what had the bible to do with it? Realisation came slowly like a faltering dawn and she had smiled archly as snippets of understanding had formed themselves into a whole picture in his brain.

He'd heard the word before but hadn't given it any thought. Sammy McClelland had told him that a lesbian was a person from Lisburn, a small country town near Lough Neagh. It didn't really fit as an explanation when he thought about it. Back then he'd readily accepted this definition of the word. Now that he knew its true meaning he was fairly sure that no lesbians existed in Ulster. It really wasn't the done thing, at all.

So, she had a horrible name, *slept* with other women and didn't look quite so attractive without her glasses on. Nevertheless, he liked her, despite this modest catalogue of failings, and she had quickly become a resolute ally, having at first been unwilling to even speak to him.

They had cobbled together a hasty plan. Neither she nor Ted gave it much chance of success, although they didn't say as much. But it was a good plan in one respect: it carried few risks. So what if it came to nothing? Ted didn't care and he was fairly sure Veronica didn't either.

Veronica glanced over at Ted and smiled. His earlier discomfiture, when she had explained the basic tenets of lesbianism had pleased her; not in an unpleasant way. She was touched by his naiveté and by the fact that he had quickly got over his surprise. He didn't seem to judge her or think her strange. Men like that were few and far between. In addition, she felt oddly comforted by his proximity as if he could protect her come what may. Maybe that was what men were for – reassurance. Perhaps that was why she was putting herself at risk for him. That and her passage home, of course.

'Vous tout à fait êtes toujours étonné?'

'Un peu,' he admitted, with a rueful smile. He *was* astonished, but it was fine…

A moment later the bus slowed and then stopped. The driver shouted something over his shoulder at his passengers. Veronica tilted her chin defiantly but Ted sat impassively.

'La Boche,' she said through gritted teeth. Ted patted his jacket pocket, feeling the unmistakable shape of the pistol. A lady with an improbable hat craned her neck, trying to get a better look at the road ahead. Ted feigned disinterest but his mouth was suddenly dry and he felt tired and vulnerable like a man facing personal defeat.

The Germans soldiers *looked* like victors. There was no need for manners and certainly not compassion. Their commanders might be thinking of winning over the local populace with acts of fairness, apparent decency and magnanimity but they – the captains, majors and colonels – weren't here. *They* weren't standing on this road checking traffic for undesirables, French deserters, British stragglers. *To the victors the spoils.* The German soldiers were free to behave however they saw fit.

Ted cleared his throat nervously and looked over at Veronica. She was impassive, her face betraying no emotion of any sort. *She was certainly a cool customer*, mused Ted. He pictured her being introduced to Brigadier Murray…

A period of time passed during which they sat immobile while the German soldiers took it easy, standing nearby in a huddle. They were in high spirits, each of them shying away from the dubious honour of searching the bus. None of these men thought that there was any threat in their vicinity. The French were defeated, cowed. A beaten dog offered more of a threat. Finally, a boyish young soldier was pushed forward with a slap on his shoulder. His submachine gun was slung across his chest, his helmet pushed slightly back from his brow. He smiled dolefully but accepted his place in the pecking order; firmly at the bottom.

Leaden of foot, he approached the bus. The driver stood and opened the door. He was resigned to this new aspect of his life. He had already decided how he would play it – polite disinterest. He would co-operate but he would look neither happy nor upset.

The driver stood to one side as the soldier climbed the steps, not making eye contact. His passengers remained in their seats trying to look innocent but for the most part they only managed to look guilty.

Veronica gripped Ted's arm, although whether to give support, receive support, or simply to give credence to their loving couple act, he could not say. He looked over at her and smiled, hoping that he looked unconcerned. He would soon find out of his fake papers were up to the job. *Maurice Grima.* It still didn't sound like him.

The young soldier looked more ill-at-ease than the passengers who surreptitiously watched his progress down the aisle. He stopped to let a rotund housewife move her shopping basket from the floor but didn't smile or acknowledge her in any way. He was maybe eighteen years of age. Ted wondered if he actually knew what he was looking for… hopefully he did not. The other soldiers nudged each other and made disparaging comments about the young soldier. They were veterans, poking fun at the new boy. Ted recognised the signs; he'd once been the new boy, just as he had become the veteran.

The soldier was about a third of the way down the bus, moving slowly but deliberately when another vehicle, a small Opel truck came into view and then stopped. At once the other soldiers looked alarmed, exchanging worried glances, standing a bit straighter. Two military police descended from the cab and another two with attack dogs jumped down from the back. Ted had seen these MPs – *Kettenhund* – before and recognised the chest plates; shrunken armour slung around their necks. The *Kettenhund* looked over at the infantrymen with contempt. They saw themselves as the real professionals and revelled in the fact that other soldiers feared them and the power they wielded. The dogs, both German Shepherds, strained on their leashes, snapping and snarling. They would never be pets. There would be no retirement for these animals. When their usefulness ended, so would their lives.

Ted breathed deeply to steady his nerves, watching the MPs and willing them to remain where they were. He hoped that this was just a show of strength from France's new masters, aimed at keeping the populace in their place; subservient and afraid. The young soldier on the bus drew near and Ted took a moment to examine his uniform, remembering the time when he had removed the grenade from the sleeping soldier and then thrown it into the road. He'd been in a tight spot then and had quickly improvised a solution. This time, however, he felt as if he had only one option – to sit tight. Veronica's gaze remained fixed at some point ahead. Her face gave no clue as to what she might be thinking. She looked like a defiant young Frenchwoman; proud and not yet ready to kowtow to the invaders. It was a part she played well and, of course Ted knew it was just an act – she wasn't French for starters.

The soldier paused when he came to Ted. He looked at him, swallowed almost imperceptibly. Here was a man who should be in uniform. He clearly wanted to ask Ted for his papers but his confidence slipped and he immediately felt like a boy sent to do a man's job. A flurry of doubts whirled in his head: what if the French civilian didn't understand, what if he just refused to co-operate, what if he didn't have the correct papers, then what did he do? Ted tensed himself in anticipation but the soldier coloured slightly and moved on, wiping a hand across his cheek self-consciously and hoping that no-one noticed his weakness. He didn't know what genuine French documents looked like and he didn't know how to speak the language. He resented the others for putting him on the bus.

When he reached the back row of seats, he turned on his heel and began to re-trace his steps. He walked a little bit more quickly this time, then saw the *Kettenhund* outside and blanched. He hoped that they wouldn't ask him too many questions. *No* questions would be best. He didn't want to appear an idiot.

He paused again and pretended to examine the parcel shelf above the passenger's heads. *What was he looking for?* he asked himself. He had no idea but it created a delay and made it look like he was being thorough. He glanced at the driver but he looked away guiltily.

In fact, everyone on the bus looked guilty of something. One of the passengers, an elderly man, coughed but no-one spoke. The German soldier felt as if he was communing with the undead. The only sound was the dull rumble of the bus's engine and the occasional yelp from one or other of the attack dogs.

The soldier peered out through the windscreen, then looked at his watch, absently. He really didn't want to leave the security of the vehicle now. His section corporal – a veteran of Poland, Belgium and France, no soft touch by any means – looked distinctly uneasy, not quite afraid, but unnerved by the presence of the MPs. One of the passengers began to sob quietly, evidently giving in to the strain that they all – even him – felt. He almost wanted to tell her that he was just as fed up as she was, that he too feared the military police.

Reluctantly, when he could no longer extend the parameters of his search, he made his way down to the front and dismounted the bus. He headed over to the corporal so that he could deliver his report, sketchy as it was. The dogs snarled at his approach, not bothering to make any distinction between friend and foe. Ted watched him speak to the corporal, the latter nodding.

The NCO in charge cast an apprehensive glance over at the MPs and then waved the bus on. They lurched away from the road side and carried on until they reached Lille.

It was clear that the city had been fought over. Patches of rubble lay like huge cairns built to commemorate destruction. A few French army vehicles sat at the side of the road, apparently unwanted. There were civilians at large but not as many as Ted would have expected in a bustling city. Cafés had begun to open again and a few shops dared to trade. Those who had remained behind to test the water of the new regime thought about normality and what it might entail. That there would be normality was not in question; anything can become normal.

The bus stopped in the square and the passengers stood. Ted found himself irritated by their slow disembarkation just as he always did. The woman with the bag held everyone else up, the bag catching on every seat back as she lumbered forwards idiotically. Behind him he heard the old man curse her as if he was in a tearing hurry. The driver sat with his elbows resting on the steering wheel, his mind blank. For him, life went on. Ted felt the sun on his face as he stepped down.

He offered Veronica a hand and they walked confidently across the square watched by a small group of officers, smoking and drinking coffee at a pavement café. They felt safe and relaxed. Ted wondered if they were waiting for their de-mob, or did they expect to invade Britain next?

'I wonder if that's him?' she whispered to Ted. This, he supposed was the moment where the practicality of their plan was put to the test. Pre-war pigeons strutted around their feet undefeated, bravado aplenty. They never won, just as they never lost.

They stopped to look in a shop window and Ted casually turned to assess the huddle of officers. They were relaxed, complacent, the arrogance of victory written across their noble Teutonic brows. Each one had a side-arm, something compact in a neat little holster but Ted reckoned he could shoot them all before they had a chance to react. One of the officers, now perhaps twenty yards distant cracked a joke and the others laughed. Another kicked at a bothersome pigeon. Three of them smoked cheroots and two of them cigarettes. They were languid in the sun like siesta-time lizards.

Ted studied the faces.

'Well,' urged Veronica.

'No. He's not there.'

'Probably just as well,' she said.

'How's that?'

'They've seen us together. He probably wouldn't be too encouraged if he thought I was married already.'

'He might not care,' said Ted. 'A good-looking woman giving him the right signs…'

'I'm good-looking?' she said, scathingly.

'Course you are!' said Ted. 'That's why you're here.'

'No. I'm here because you said you'd get me home,' she corrected in a hoarse whisper. She clutched his arm tightly for emphasis.

'Yes, but if you were ugly there wouldn't be much point using you, would there? He's not likely to go for an ugly bird is he?' Ted realised with a jolt that he had never used the expression, 'ugly bird' before. Veronica was staring at him incredulously.

'So, you're just using me?'

Ted presumed she was joking but he wasn't too sure. 'Aye. And you're using me. Now let's go for a wander. We might bump into him.' Ted said this without conviction and his companion looked at him, doubtfully. 'Well, we might,' he said, with hushed emphasis. 'We'll head towards the barracks,' he added, nodding in the direction of a side street.

'You know your way about?' she asked, surprised. Ted was the newcomer after all.

'I know which direction the barracks is in, that's all.' A waiter at a nearby bistro watched them suspiciously. 'C'mon,' said Ted and they began walking. They passed a dejected looking Gendarme and in turn were passed by an army truck filled with weary soldiers; so weary that they couldn't even be bothered to leer at Veronica.

'Shits,' she whispered under her breath. She grabbed his arm protectively, as if she wasn't a lesbian. He might have quite enjoyed walking through this small, grand city with a stylish woman on his arm had it not been for the minor problem of his ultimate mission to assassinate a German soldier. It was hard to get in the holiday mood with the prospect of blood on your hands.

'We'll keep our eyes peeled,' said Ted, *sotto voce*. 'Or rather I'll keep my eyes peeled – you don't know what he looks like.' She nodded, grimly. The reality of what she was being asked to do was shocking to her when she was reminded of it. She was a honey trap, according to Ted, or part of a honey trap… the honey, she supposed. Veronica couldn't decide if being a lesbian made it easier or not. She didn't hate men – Ted was a case in point – she just didn't find them attractive… but not so unattractive that she wanted to lie in bed with one while someone else blew their brains out. But, she reasoned, she had to earn her passage home somehow. Ted had warned her that Murray might try to recruit her when she returned. She'd cross that bridge when she came to it, or rather, if she came to it.

The street was narrow and dark, despite the bright sun. It led them to a wider street, a boulevard in fact, lined with trees on either side and with another row of trees planted centrally. A few cars were parked and a bus lumbered towards them having surmounted a low bridge in the distance. Ted sighed. This mission required too big a helping of luck for him to be optimistic, which was something else for his debrief.

If the officer – Ted's target – for some reason, did not step out of the barracks, then there was no chance of getting to him. Even if he did leave camp, then Ted would need him to be in just the right place and at precisely the right time if he were to intercept him. If all that occurred, then, of course, he had to believe that he was going to bed Veronica and be able to get out at the appropriate time for their liaison.

None of these even touched upon the other imponderables, such as the fact that Feldhus might have been posted, or be on leave. Not for the first time Ted wondered how his bosses were able to avail themselves of so much information on this man… and then he wondered why they didn't use the person from whom this intelligence came to eliminate the target.

Obviously, they weren't an assassin. Like him. Ridiculous.

***

'This is like finding a needle in a haystack,' he whispered to Veronica. She nodded. He added, 'in fact it's worse because we don't actually know if he is in the haystack to begin with.' They were now a third of the way down the boulevard. The bus had passed them and a small convoy of German vehicles was just rolling over the bridge now. A little boxy field car first, followed by two small trucks with canvas covers and a ponderous looking eight-wheeled armoured car, which towered above everything else on the road. They moved slowly, maybe twenty miles per hour. Ted and Veronica kept walking.

'There's an officer sitting up front in that car. I'll try to get a look at him as they go past,' hissed Ted. He turned to watch a French civilian lorry come from the other direction. It was a flatbed Citroen carrying maybe two dozen large sacks. Ted looked ahead once more but heard the truck slow, then stop at the junction of the boulevard and another street across the road from where they walked. The German convoy seemed to slow too and Ted fixed his gaze on the figure seated in the field car next to the driver. Unmistakably an officer, his cap was low on his brow and when he turned his head, Ted could just see his blond hair.

'That might be him.'

Veronica spoke, 'let's go to that *tabac* and wait.' She pointed at the little shop across the road. So narrow was its frontage that it looked as if it had been squeezed in painfully after all the other buildings had been finished. A lurid canopy picked out in green, red and yellow added an incongruous splash of colour to a city that was haemorrhaging high spirits and good fortune. The name Ankoplar, written in cracked white lettering, was somehow familiar to Ted. Veronica headed for one of two tiny tables, each of which had a white table cloth, two folding chairs, a vase with a single dying flower and a menu. They paused to let the German convoy trundle past. Each of the vehicles took it in turns to pass through a gap in the central line of trees to reach the other side of the road where they seemed to meet up with the French lorry. The armoured car had to see-saw back and forth to get through, its turret and antennae array snapping off low hanging branches as it did so. Ted and Veronica winced involuntarily at the loose barrage of cracks that ensued. Leaves flew in all directions and one end of a great looping antennae broke free, swinging around like a fishing rod wielded by a lunatic.

'What if we don't find him?' she asked. Picking up the menu but not looking at it, she sat and invited Ted to do the same. He was still watching the vehicle as it tried to untangle itself. By now the officer had dismounted and was haranguing the driver, embarrassed at this unseemly display of German incompetence. He shouted something about Italians and removed his cap as if he was going to screw it up and throw it to the ground. With a great effort of will he stopped himself from doing so, put the cap under his arm and rubbed his forehead. His blond hair was wispy and thinning like a baby's. His face was broad and his nose long and pointed. Five feet, ten inches tall, reckoned Ted.

The owner of the *tabac* had appeared at Veronica's elbow. He was a neat man with just a hint of a gut beneath his apron.

'Madame, Monsieur?' he said, but his attention too was drawn to the vehicular chaos just up the road. The French truck driver had dismounted and looked on at the debacle with dead eyes. He was determinedly non-judgemental – it seemed the best policy in the current circumstances.

'Deux cafe, s'il vous plait,' said Veronica, folding the menu. The tabac owner scuttled off.

'That's not him,' said Ted. 'That's not Feldhus.' He sighed and rubbed his chin.

'You're sure?'

'Pretty sure.'

'We'll have our coffees and go, then.' Ted nodded. Ted felt as if his plan was coming apart at the seams. He might be going back without having achieved very much.

He didn't know if he dreaded that more than actually having to see it through. The coffee was bitter and black. He looked for milk in a jug but there was none. Veronica noticed his predicament.

'They drink it black,' she explained.

'No point asking for a cup of tea, I suppose?' he asked, humourlessly.

'Yes, you could and order some toasted crumpets while you're at it. Might as well be hanged for a sheep as a lamb,' she said.

'You're very sarcastic,' he pointed out.

'Lesbians are.'

Ted nodded. He didn't know if lesbians were really sarcastic but this was all new to him so it might just be true.

'Now what?'

'Will I still get home if we don't get him?'

'No.'

'No? Are you joking, Ted?'

'Yes. To be honest I'm not sure if we will get him but there's no reason to stay here, is there?' Ted pulled a face as he took another sip of his coffee. From inside he heard the owner re-arranging tables and setting chairs on the floor. The words of a mournful French song drifted out from behind the counter.

'Edith Piaf,' said Veronica.

'What is?'

'That singer.'

'She sounds ill,' said Ted. Veronica smiled. She glanced at the Germans. The armoured car was now free and parked at the side of the road. German soldiers were unloading the French truck, dropping the heavy sacks into neat piles. They had removed their tunics and wore shirt sleeves and braces. The officer and an NCO looked on as if doing so somehow helped. Two soldiers were passing tools from the back of the other truck and these were being stacked neatly.

Another French truck hove into view moments later and this, it transpired, carried a load of bricks.

'Wonder what they're building?' mused Ted. Veronica shrugged. She pulled two Gauloises from a packet and handed one to Ted. He lit them both and slumped in his chair slightly as if succumbing to the startling effects of nicotine. Suddenly, Ted leaned forwards and spoke again. 'Another car coming,' he said.

The field car pulled up just short of the other vehicles and an officer stepped out. Ted thought that his luck might just have changed.

Chapter Nineteen

Ted stood at once, the little folding chair almost toppling behind him.

'Where are you going?' asked Veronica.

'That's him. I think it is. I'm just going to wander off so that he thinks you're alone. I'll keep an eye on you, don't worry. Good luck.'

Veronica sat there nonplussed. *Now what,* she wondered, drawing heavily on her cigarette? She took a deep breath and then blew air out as if she was whistling noiselessly. As casually as she could, she turned to look at the newly arrived officer. He certainly fitted Ted's haphazard description but then virtually all of them did. He was engaged in earnest discussion with the other officer and the NCO, gesticulating, pointing and occasionally shaking his head. The men listened intently to him. Clearly this new arrival was in charge.

Veronica realised that she now cut a very unlikely figure. Perhaps Ted simply hadn't known that a woman would virtually never sit in or outside a *tabac* by herself. She felt conspicuous and wished that the owner would pop outside so that she could pay him. Obligingly he did so about thirty seconds later, giving her a strange look, which confirmed her fears.

'Madame?'

'Je voudrais payer, s'il vous plait.'

'Oui,' he replied and at once returned to his counter to fetch the bill. Veronica paid in haste and left a small tip before standing and smoothing her skirt. The officer

looked over at her momentarily, then snapped his head round again in silent reprimand for allowing himself to be distracted from his work. *But at least he has noticed me*, she thought. Ted was nowhere to be seen. She moved off down the street, glancing in shop windows. Most of the shops were shut and their window displays had gone, or been left frozen in time with the shopkeepers' departure. She was almost alone on the street, blending in with her surroundings about as well as a polar bear in a jungle. Her mouth ran dry and her heart thumped in her chest. The sheer idiocy of this plan was suddenly shocking. Her part in this stupid 'mission' was too much to bear. She wanted to run away. She wanted to hide or cry or get into bed and pull the covers over her head… instead of which she slowly turned on her heel and retraced her steps.

The NCO was marking the ground out with chalk and the two officers were still in discussions about their task. The junior officer was smoking now, nodding as the other man, Feldhus, spoke. As she passed the café, the owner gave her a wan, puzzled smile. He hoped that the Germans might be his next customers – business was business. Veronica's slow, deliberate footsteps seemed to resonate on the pavement and she forced herself to look in the empty shop windows. She still had no idea how she was going to play this without making it look like a deliberate trap. She felt unsuited to her new role; what was she a vamp, a flirt? Truth was she was a lesbian, horribly miscast in the circumstances.

Eventually, she drew level with the work party and paused, her back to them, her eyes fixed on the haberdasher's none too exciting window display. The window acted like a mirror and in it she could see the officers appraising her. She understood only a little

German but one of them seemed to dismiss her more or less instantly; she was glad it wasn't Feldhus. *Or was she disappointed? How badly did she want to lure this man to his death?* She took another deep breath, tried to calm herself and then turned. Feldhus smiled and she smiled back.

'Bonjour, monsieur,' she ventured.

Gallantly, he bowed but did not snap his heels together like an archetypal Prussian officer. Nevertheless, she was reasonably pleased by his response. Evidently, he wanted to make an impression; wanted her, in fact, to take an interest in him. He smiled at her, bemusedly, flattered and astonished at the ease with which he seemed able to initiate relations with the local women, or one of them at least. *This might be a good posting,* he thought.

A sudden image of him lying in a pool of blood presented itself to her. She felt sorry for him. Not only had he fallen for a woman who was only interested in other women but he'd fallen for one whose intent was to leave him dead. She was the worst possible female companion really. It would be hard to imagine him picking someone worse.

'Bonjour mademoiselle,' he replied. He hadn't quite expended his knowledge of French but he was coming close. She returned his greeting with a slight bow of her head and a coy smile. *Now what,* she thought desperately and not for the first time? Immediately, the officer had dismissed the soldiers from his thoughts. This woman was attractive but not beautiful, well dressed, sort of classy in a way which he couldn't quite define. She reminded him of his sister and he tried to quell those evil thoughts at once… sometimes they just sprung out on him from some

dark corner of his mind. He was often ambushed by incestuous lust.

He shook his head – just slightly – trying to dislodge the unwanted images from his mind. She smiled again then raised her cigarette to her lips. *How could it be so easy*, she thought?

He smiled back. *How could it be so easy,* he thought?

She hoped Ted was nearby. It would be helpful if he could shoot this poor man now, she thought. She'd never wished anyone dead before and really bore this man no malice but pragmatism won out. Over his shoulder she saw some of the troops leering at her like animals. They looked rough, muscular in a gone-to-seed sort of way. They were dangerous, no doubt, but not the cream of the German Army by the look of them. The officer intercepted her gaze and turned to find the men hard at work with shovels and bare hands. They were, he knew, cunning like wild beasts forced to live in towns and cities. He trusted them as far as he could throw them. They were rough men from rough places. One of them had been a docker in Hamburg – that said it all.

***

Their conversation was strained. He spoke a German-French patois mixed with pure German and she spoke good French, though she was glad that he was unable to detect her less than authentic accent. They returned to the little *tabac* – to the same table that she had vacated minutes before. The German seemed shy all of a sudden. *An introverted Nazi? What next?*

Veronica tried to decide if he was good-looking or not but she was no expert. He wasn't ugly but he certainly had the unmistakable characteristics of a good, thoroughbred Aryan. If you liked that sort of thing then he was perfectly acceptable. His uniform seemed tight and restricting and she almost urged him to undo a couple of tunic buttons, as if sharing his discomfort. It was too warm to be constrained by a heavy jacket. She refrained. She didn't know how to say it for one thing.

It was clear after a few moments that only Veronica really understood why they were there; the officer was clearly bemused. *If only you knew the truth*, she thought. She smiled pleasantly, hiding her fear of the shop owner's reaction when he saw her again but this time in the company of a different man.

When he peered out, he was startled but very briefly and regained his composure with considerable aplomb as if acts of treachery and deceit were carried out in his establishment every day. Perhaps they were. He'd seen a few illicit liaisons in his time, no doubt. This was just another one, perhaps a variation on a long-running theme. He smiled blandly and waited for them to order, determined to make the abnormal, normal. The officer muttered something under his breath as if he was looking at a menu displayed in his head and then ordered two coffees in German.

'Zwei cafe,' he said. His attempts at charm clearly didn't extend towards French shopkeepers. Veronica was glad in a way – glad the veil of artifice had been blown away in that one act. She really didn't want to like him and now she saw the cracks in his performance. He was charming her into bed, or so he hoped. As for the owner of the *tabac* he was worthy only of contempt in the German's eyes.

'Deux cafe, s'il vous plait,' she said, clarifying the order.

Perplexed now, the owner disappeared into the back once again. The woman was a collaborator, he supposed. *Was he anything better?* He would take these German's money the same as before, as if they were tourists. *It was too soon to judge people who co-operated with their new masters; perhaps they would all be collaborators eventually and once that happened, well, they wouldn't be seen as such any longer. Was there any point in antagonising these people? They were going to be around for a long time.* He felt a little happier having rationalised his position with regard to his new customers.

The officer turned occasionally to observe his soldiers at work. Never once did he catch their sneers or knowing looks. They clearly didn't think highly of him. Mutual antipathy. Feldhus hadn't been posted to a prestigious regiment following his officer training at the *Kriegsschule* in Hannover but he supposed this woman would not understand that or care. She obviously went for the uniform or perhaps was just eager to establish good relations with the new masters. It was hardly commendable and certainly not patriotic but pragmatic rather. French patriotism, he supposed, was dead in the water now anyway. Whatever the reason for her interest in him, he would capitalise upon it. *To the victors, the spoils.*

'*Was ist Ihr Name?*' he asked suddenly.

'Veronique.'

He smiled as if pleased by the sound of her name.

'*Tres belle,*' he said looking truly pleased with his grasp of the French language. Veronica smiled sweetly rather than rolling her eyes.

'*Quel est votre nom?*' she asked, although she already knew he was called Karl Feldhus.

'Frank,' he replied. *Frank?* She let it pass. She could hardly argue with him about his own name. If he said he was called Frank, then Frank it was. He smiled ruefully as if he was embarrassed about his name.

She decided to change the subject. This was harder than she had expected; the language barrier made it supremely difficult to strike up a rapport with this man. She pointed at the soldiers, one of whom now stood idle, his chin resting on the handle end of a shovel.

'Que vos soldats construiesent?' she asked. She didn't give a damn what they were building. As he turned yet another of his men lapsed into idleness, then bent over to examine the two rows of bricks they had laid. He tutted and then answered dismissively.

'Oh, rien!' Nothing. For the present he was not interested in his modest military mission. *'Kann ich Sie heute Abend sehen?'* he asked.

'Oui,' replied Veronica. The sooner she brought this ordeal to a close the better…

***

Ted watched the two 'young lovers' from afar and with a cynic's eye. If Feldhus's body language was anything to go by he had just fallen into the trap. He looked relaxed, a conqueror finding it all too easy. He leaned back in his chair and drew heavily on a cheroot as if he had already bedded the woman. Ted shook his head slightly. He thought of the few brief moments he had managed to snatch with Jean and wondered if things would be as intense and passionate when he returned home? How many men could he kill before he became an unfeeling monster? His eyes started to burn with what he supposed must be fatigue and his hip ached from the fall in the ditch. He had removed his jacket and enjoyed the warmth of the sun on his back but he missed the reassuring feel of the pistol in his pocket. He'd grown used to feeling it close to his body.

A tiny grocer's van struggled over the hump of the bridge behind him. The driver gave him a curious look for a young man at large in Lille was an uncommon sight, unless he was a German, of course. Ted tried to play it cool. Any one of these people could become his enemy if they were forced to provide information on agents, spies and resistors in order to prolong their own existence.

A little column of pigeons crossed the bridge under his feet, quite unperturbed about his presence. For a moment he envied them their simple life.

The streets lay almost empty save for a few determined French going about their normal business. It was as if a plague had wiped out the population and only now did the survivors dare to stray outside.

He glanced at his watch, unsure how his plan was going to work out and then he hefted his jacket just slightly, feeling the weight of the concealed pistol. Above him was an endless sky, pale blue, marbled with streaks of cloud. With shocking clarity, he realised that there was no war here. This was now a country at peace, defeated admittedly, but at peace. For these people there seemed to be no hope. They had new rulers and new rules. They had to rebuild their lives and make a new future. They had to drag opportunity from the suffocating burden of domination by a foreign power. They could accept this form of peace or be pacified; either way the result would be the same. They were subjugated and saw no hope of that situation changing. Britain wasn't their saviour. Britain was, in all likelihood, just the next country to fall, deluding itself that it could resist the might of the Nazis.

Peace. They had peace. Ted had no place here because he brought war into their midst once again when all need for violence had been taken away. These people had nothing to fight for and so they didn't.

He felt as if he was being crushed by the responsibility put onto his shoulders. More than that, he felt foolish at having fallen for the Prime Minister's flattery. Periodically he was felled by his own gullibility. He was risking his life for men who cared not for him. He imagined himself with all the things he never had, a cottage with a rose garden, the sun set to shine forever and Jean by his side. He'd be lucky to get any of those things. Avoiding capture, torture and the firing squad was as much as he could realistically hope for.

Chapter Twenty

Ted tried to make sense of this latest version of the plan as the bus took them back to Belloire. Feldhus was to drive over to Belloire that evening and she would meet him at the western edge of the town. Then they would drive to her flat. Simple, really. At some point Ted would come in and kill the German. Then they would vacate the flat and…

'But the plane doesn't come until tomorrow night,' said Ted in a whisper. In truth it was a loud whisper because the old bus was so noisy that he struggled to make himself heard. His fellow passengers were the usual mix. The driver was a thin man, careworn body cloaked in a careworn uniform. Despite the heat he wore a grey cardigan with so many holes that it was more like a string vest. He grappled with the huge unyielding steering wheel like a man wrestling with a playful but determined crocodile. The bus seemed to resent his physical inputs, frequently veering off the road and into the verge as if drawn there by a huge electro-magnet. Had it been muddy, they might have been sucked right into the ditch. He had always wondered about the sanity of bus drivers in general.

Behind him sat a middle-aged couple. He was as thin as she was large. They were almost caricatures of the hen-pecked man and domineering wife. Beneath her skirt her glutinous thighs spread like dripping ooze off the side of the seat. The man looked ahead as if ashamed. The next few rows were empty but then there was a young woman with a baby. She was plain but well-dressed and Ted decided that she was an officer's wife. The baby was her remaining connection to the life she'd led before the

Germans came. Immediately behind her was a man in early middle-age and unremarkable in appearance until he turned his head to look out of the window. His right cheek had, many years ago, been sliced open by shrapnel in three places and left to heal without even the most primitive medical intervention. Ted knew of other men – men in Belfast with similar injuries, all of them veterans of the Great War. The scars left were deep clefts, which reddened horrifically on cold days. This particular man looked as if he had been lucky to keep his sight.

Belatedly, Veronica responded to Ted's observation. It had almost sounded like an accusation. 'That's as maybe, but what was I supposed to do? I can't say to him, *look we can't kill you until tomorrow night so could you come round then instead*, could I?'

'No. No, you couldn't and I'm not complaining. You did a great job. I'm just wondering what we do with him afterwards.'

'Put him in his car and then dump it somewhere?'

'He'll be missed.'

Veronica shrugged. As far as she was concerned Ted would just have to kill the man, preferably before he stuck his 'thing' in her. She shuddered inwardly. The bus lurched to one side as the driver swerved round a cyclist. Ted was thrown against Veronica and she pushed him away. He wondered if she was annoyed with him. The bus seemed to take an age to overtake, running up the centre of the road long after the cyclist had fallen off and landed in the ditch. Ted turned but could only see the front wheel of the bike and a small cloud of dust to indicate that anyone had ever ventured out on two wheels.

‘This driver is fucking insane,’ he said.

Perhaps two minutes later they pulled over at the side of the main road through Belloire and a selection of passengers along with Ted and Veronica stood, preparatory to disembarkation. It was hard to comprehend that such a degree of calamity could be shoe-horned into a journey so brief. Ted glanced at the driver as he stepped down. The driver looked straight ahead, displaying the humanity of a hat stand.

‘Thank God, that’s over,’ said Ted, too loudly. A rotund man, an erstwhile fellow passenger, turned to glare at him then hurried off like someone putting distance between himself and a potential assailant. Being British had gone out of fashion since Dunkirk.

‘Sssh,’ said Veronica, grabbing him by the arm and pulling away from the flank of the bus. ‘You’re bloody French, remember,’ she added through gritted teeth. Ted flushed. He wasn’t generally prone to careless moments and now was not the time to develop that habit. One mistake and they could both end up dead.

‘C’mon. Let’s get home,’ she said. Belloire seemed to be closing up for the day, insofar as it had ever *opened* up. A gendarme, unshaven and demoralised stood at a street corner ahead. He knew his orders were to change soon; no longer would he be a protector of the French people and nor would he be viewed as one.

In the side street, a middle-aged woman, with her hair in a ragged bun, grappled with an awning trying to push it back into place indicating that the boulangerie was shut for the day. Next to her a man stood, holding his black bicycle by the handle bars and offering her no assistance of any kind. Ted guessed he was her husband. He sneezed suddenly, sending a spray of sticky droplets into the air. Ted made a mental note not to buy bread from his establishment. As they hurried along Veronica spoke briefly to another woman, roughly her age, but pushing a pram.

They reached the security of the door to the block and were inside moments later. Veronica stopped, letting the tension drain from her. It would build again soon when she met the officer for the second and final time. She looked at Ted but didn't speak. He looked back, wanting to say something encouraging but no words came and eventually she turned, trudging up the stairs laden with anxiety.

Veronica reached for the kettle automatically and filled it with water. She lit the ring and then took one of her Players from its packet, offering one to Ted. This time he accepted.

'I hope it's worth it,' she said. He sat heavily but she continued to stand. There was silence, the exact nature of which Ted couldn't quite fathom. Was she worried, angry, or just exhausted? He drew on his cigarette and watched her furtively. Veronica turned to look out of the window and didn't make a move when the kettle began to boil.

Ted placed his cigarette on the edge of the table, then stood to turn the gas ring off. He splashed boiling water into the two cups and began looking for a tea spoon.

'Are you scared?,' he ventured, pulling open a drawer next to the sink. It squealed as it came out and then got stuck. He pulled at it and wiggled it until Veronica turned.

'A sharp tug,' she said. He pulled again and this time the drawer flew out. Ted staggered back against the table, as cutlery rained down on the floor in a storm of metal.

'Bugger,' he said. She spoke again as he retrieved her paltry collection of mismatched spoons, knives and forks. He held a strange, long-handled fork in front of his face. 'Is this for eating food at long range?' She didn't seem to find it funny.

'I'm really scared, Ted,' she began. 'This isn't really my type of thing at all.'

'I'll let you get out of the room before I do it,' he assured her. She had taken over coffee making duties from him, doubting if he could do it without injuring himself.

'It's not just that. I know his name for God's sake.'

'I know but he's a German. He's the enemy.'

'Yes, but I'm not a soldier. It's not my job to kill people. He probably has a wife and kids.'

'Well then! He's being unfaithful.'

'You don't usually kill someone just for that, do you?'

'Okay. That's true but it's not actually you doing it. It's me.'

'I'll have to help you move the body.'

'We can leave the body in here.'

'What and we sleep next door to a rotting corpse?'

'He won't be rotting…'

'Ted, that's hardly the point. I can't spend a day in a flat with a dead body. And don't say that I won't have to live here anymore. I know that but it's just not right.'

'Suppose I do it outside.' He let the thought take shape in his own mind; the dynamics of murder. 'He pulls up outside. You get out and walk towards your door. I step out of the shadows – sounds a bit melodramatic that – *'steps out of the shadows'* – but you know what I mean. Then I shoot him.'

'And leave a dead German officer outside in the street beneath my flat?'

'No. I drive him away. Dump the car somewhere. Walk back.'

She looked at him doubtfully.

'What if someone sees you?'

'They're not likely to say anything. These people must hate the Germans.'

'They do but once our friend Frank has disappeared the German Army is going to want to know what happened to him. They'll come looking for answers. They'll want to find a murderer. Someone here may just point the finger before they get accused of it themselves.'

'Frank?'

'The German officer.'

'He's called Karl.'

'No, he's bloody well called Frank. I know more about him than you do now.'

'Okay, okay. Frank then. But we're back to square one. We kill him inside.'

Veronica nodded unhappily.

'Where are you going to wait?' she asked at last. She sidled over to the window and looked down into the street as if he might be there, waiting. She flicked ash into the breeze.

'The bathroom?'

'What if he wants to pee?'

'I won't look.'

Veronica rolled her eyes.

'Okay, have you got a cupboard. Preferably one I can stand up in?'

'Just the wardrobe.'

'Talk about a dramatic entrance. He's just getting started, his bare arse flapping about like a…'

'Stop! I thought you said he you were going to do it straightaway more or less.'

Ted continued in the same vein as if he hadn't been interrupted, 'and I step out of the wardrobe like someone from the gas board.'

'Why would someone from the gas board…' she cut herself short, shaking her head in frustration. 'Look! You'll have to wait outside. I won't close the door tight.'

'How will I know when you're ready?'

'Just give it a few minutes.'

'You might be sharing a romantic bottle of wine and gazing at each other over that dead flower on the table.'

'I haven't got any wine.'

'He might bring some to impress you. He's not expecting to come round and just get started on… er you know… He'll want to impress you. He's not just going to drop his trousers.'

'How do you know that wouldn't impress me?'

Ted sighed. 'I'll wait down the street. When I see you go in, I'll follow.'

'The outside door shuts tight.'

'Well, just close it gently. It only needs to stay open for a few moments.'

'How can you be so cool about this?' she asked suddenly. Ted shrugged. He could have said truthfully that he was a trained assassin. But it still sounded ridiculous to his ears…

***

Veronica picked out a dress to wear and her best shoes.

'How do I look?'

'Stunning,' said Ted.

'Really?'

'Well, you look okay.'

'Hmmph. Glasses or no glasses?'

'Glasses. They make you look…'

‘Attractive?’

‘Intelligent.’

‘My God Ted, you know how to make a girl feel special.’

‘Look you’re one of those lesbians, aren’t you? Why do you care what I think?’

‘I’d still like a compliment.’

‘Fine. You look very attractive.’

‘Really.’

‘Yes.’

‘Such a liar.’

‘I can’t win, can I?

‘Not really. Anyway, it’s time to go. It’ll take me a few minutes to walk down there. I expect he’ll be bang on time or early so you’d better make a move as well.’

‘Right,’ said Ted with a sigh. ‘Good luck.’ Veronica nodded, apprehensively. ‘Try not to worry,’ he added, uselessly.

‘Oh, I’m always like this on a first date,’ she joked.

Despite his nerves, Ted chuckled.

Ted stood on the doorstep and watched her go. He felt a sudden and inexplicable warmth towards this strange woman. He had no doubt that she could look after herself but felt protective of her nevertheless. It wasn’t, he realised, love but friendship.

She turned the corner and he moved off with a leisurely pace. He was a man at ease with the world… or so it would seem to anyone who was watching him. No-one was. He had nowhere to go and nobody was expecting him. It might have been relaxing had it not been for the finale that was required of him. He could easily lose himself in these back streets, escaping the war he had brought with him. He could abandon his cause and just melt into the local population, become one of them. He had nothing to prove and, after all, he didn't exist. *Does that mean I can't be court-martialled*, he mused?

Of course, if he had to disappear then this probably wasn't the ideal place. He'd have to spend the remainder of his time as a fugitive, or risk being shot as a spy. That was no life. A French police car passed him, its engine sounding laboured. He looked straight ahead and kept his pace even. He was growing used to disguising his guilt. He could probably be some sort of criminal after the war. But when he thought of Jean, as he did often, the idea vanished. He wasn't sure what sort of life they would have after the war or even if there would ever be a time called, 'after the war' but he planned to make it a good life if he could.

From a doorway he smelt food being prepared. Some sort of pungent seasoning attacked his eyes but the smell was good. He heard a pan sizzling and a muted radio in the background. A few doors down a dog sat next to a bowl of water. It looked like a terrier but without the streak of madness that afflicted those breeds. The dog watched him with interest as if he was a student of the human form. Everything was apparently so normal and yet in truth it was extraordinary.

The weather helped lift his spirits. Whereas the sun seemed like an infrequent visitor to his home city it felt like part of the fabric of France. Belfast people got used to being damp and cold – rain was a permanent threat; it made them tough but not necessarily optimistic. In many ways the men and women of Ulster generally were a breed apart but Ted wondered if that definition extended to him. Was he part of that breed still? Or was he a one-off who would never fit in anywhere? Maybe, by increments, he was becoming either a citizen of the world, or an outcast from it. Time would tell.

He saw few people but those who were out and about wore short sleeves, the women in light flowery dresses, children in shorts, all dressed appropriately for the weather. Their summer attire made his jacket – worn only to disguise the bulk of his pistol – even more incongruous.

He was overheating now, familiar oppressive weariness dragging him down like spiritual gravity.

An elderly man with a well-fed dog spoke to him and Ted smiled. The adage about dogs and their owners certainly held true in this case; both of them waddled along as if they had become synchronised over the years of companionship. He thought of his own dog, the inexplicably named Seamus and how no-one could ever explain to him why a family of Ulster Protestants had settled upon such an archetypal Roman Catholic name for their pet.

He came to a church at the corner of the street and paused to look at the notices imprisoned behind a discoloured glass case. Unsurprisingly, they were in French but pretending to read them provided him with a good a waste of time. *As good as any.* The door was open, like an invitation to be saved or simply to rest. The Virgin Mary watched him from afar as he shuffled uneasily in the doorway. He couldn't tell if she was judging him or not. Was he just a murderer in her eyes? What would her son have thought?

Ted scratched his head, then smoothed his hair down. He was creating a delay to give Veronica a chance to lead Feldhus into his… his what? Final resting place, death bed, tomb? Ted wondered if he was no longer the killer he had been. Where had these unwelcome doubts come from? Was it Jean's influence, or the mere fact that he had someone to live for? She gave him a reason to avoid taking risks and to get back to Britain in one piece.

Or was there something else at work here?

Clarity came suddenly like the answer to a puzzle leaping from the page. The difference between this time and the other times – the times when he had killed – was that this was not a case of kill or be killed. He had a choice now and he had chosen to take a life. It just didn't seem right.

He could talk himself out of it, if he chose to let that happen. To complete his mission, he would have to block out such thoughts.

Instead of talking himself out of it, he turned and began the slow walk back to Veronica's flat. The cast of locals had altered in the interim, only the curious terrier still *in situ*. He passed a teenaged boy leaning his bike against the wall of a house and a young woman sitting on a step smoking a cigarette. Her blonde hair was cut fashionably and she wore baggy trousers, very Katherine Hepburn. She smiled at him and he smiled back. She was very pretty. His stomach churned. The juxtaposition of such beauty and the ugliness of the task he would have to perform, was almost too much to bear.

In the distance he could see the little boxy car parked on the street. Feldhus was inside with Veronica. He pictured them greeting one another, with a hug and a kiss on the cheek. Or something more discreet? Either way, her number was up as far as her neighbours would be concerned. Fraternisation with the enemy… she couldn't stay in Belloire even if she wanted to and he had made no effort to be discreet for her sake, which seemed naïve. Leaving the car parked outside her block…

Ted swallowed. He had stopped walking and stood on the street. He felt out of place and awkward, like a worker forced to mingle with the bosses at a function designed to instil good industrial relations. His confidence had almost gone. Images of faces flashed before him; Churchill, General Brooke, Murray, Mig, John, Jean, Mrs Torrance even. They were like a jury. Then, in his mind, he saw Veronica. Veronica alone with the German he'd been sent to kill. Feldhus might be trying to undress her already. Was she resisting or just going along with it? Either way, Ted couldn't prevaricate.

He saw that the door was closed over but not shut tight, just as she'd said it would be. *Right*, he decided. He began to cross the road, resolute once more, but paused as a large truck trundled past, creating a turbulent wake in the confines of the narrow street. The wake was just enough to create a pressure differential which sucked the door inwards slightly. It returned on its closer and snapped shut with uncharacteristic Gallic precision.

With the truck now gone, Ted saw what had happened and his heart began to beat out of control, for their simple plan hinged on being able to get into the block. Ted rarely panicked but he did so now.

He was a drowning man with one last chance, grasping for the rope thrown to him and missing. Ted gasped. He was locked out.

Chapter Twenty-one

Feldhus said something as he followed her up the stairs but she didn't understand. It could have been a compliment or some kind of smutty remark. She didn't know him well enough to judge. He had two packages with him, one of which was clearly a bottle of wine. Whether he'd had to buy it, or was in a position to just help himself, she couldn't say. *What was the word for it? Appropriate? Was that it? Could he appropriate goods if he chose to?*

Procure. Another good word. Maybe she was doing him a disservice. Again, it depended on what sort of man he was. Was he altruistic, trying to make the best of a bad situation, trying to win the locals over? Or was he, as seemed more likely, simply consumed with the conqueror's arrogance? Whichever it was, she hoped that this ordeal would be over soon.

She glanced over her shoulder as she led him upstairs. He smiled at her. It wasn't even a leer. Was he all bad, she wondered? Did he really deserve to die? She had no idea why this fate had been chosen for him by people who had almost certainly never met him. Why had Ted been dispatched from England to kill him? She smiled at Feldhus as she unlocked her door and then stood to one side to let him enter. He returned her smile, removed his hat and stepped in.

She noticed the pistol belt for the first time and wondered what the etiquette was for dealing with a visitor's side-arm. Did she offer to take it? Was it good form to put it in a cupboard or a drawer until they left? Twice in as many days she was faced with the same conundrum. An image of him naked apart from his leather pistol belt and holster flashed through her mind and she grimaced.

'Was los?'

Veronica smiled and shrugged. The officer handed over the wine and the package with a suggestion that she should open it. The mauve tissue paper came apart in her hands easily to reveal a small box of hand-made Belgian chocolates. They would have cost her a day's wages and again she wondered had he bothered to pay or just taken them as booty.

'Merci, monsieur,' she said.

He smiled at her hopefully. She marvelled at how straight and white his teeth were.

They found themselves in her kitchen. It was the only room in which she could entertain visitors. So far, he had been a perfect gentleman but she knew that he hadn't really come here simply to extend the hand of friendship. It wasn't the thought of his hands that alarmed her most. He was categorically not an informal ambassador trying to improve relations between the vanquished and the vanquishers. The question was, at what point he wanted to… er, get down to it? She would put it off for as long as possible… or should she try to get him into bed so that Ted could dispatch him without being detected?

She squeezed past him to get wine glasses and set these apologetically on her tiny table. From a drawer she lifted a corkscrew and passed it to him with a hopeful smile, acknowledging his manly credentials in the process. He took the bottle and began removing the cork and Veronica made her excuses to check the bedroom – the room in which this man was scheduled to lose his life.

The quilt was pulled invitingly to one side, leaving a white triangle of sheet exposed. She wondered if this was being too forward, too obvious perhaps. Was this the time to be discreet? *How the hell do I know?* She paused for a moment and wondered how she had got into this situation. How had Veronica Hamill, former deputy head girl of St Clements Girls Grammar School, found herself trapped in a foreign land with her only escape to be facilitated through being an accessory to murder?

Her life had been so simple at one time, especially once she and Sue had made their move to France, away from the judgemental, disapproving eyes of provincial England. They had been free to be a couple, not because their relationship would be viewed any more favourably by their new French neighbours. It was simply the case that no-one really knew them or understood the nature of their… friendship. There may have been a few who thought they were a couple, in *that* sense, but no-one said as much, or at least not to their faces.

She felt oppressed by her situation, wishing that it could all be over without any further involvement from her. She found it difficult to maintain the deceit required. She was no Mata Hari. She wasn't an expert seducer of men, a calculating deceiver. She swallowed hard and took a last look around the room. Maybe if she had a drink it would make it easier; after all who really wanted a clear head when they were luring an innocent man to his death? And he might as well have been innocent, for she had no knowledge whatsoever of his crimes or even if they were real. What had he done that he couldn't be taken away and tried for?

She removed her glasses and cleaned them on a corner of the sheet, shaking her head and pulling a dismayed face as she did so. *Come on, Ted*, she thought.

When she returned to the kitchen, Frank was sitting at the table exactly where Ted had sat so recently. He stood fractionally as she entered and then passed her a glass of wine. She noticed the gun belt slung on the upright of the chair. *Make yourself at home.*

The colour drained from her face when he next spoke.

'Bottoms up,' he said and she at once feared a trap. Had he known all along that she was a Britisher? But he smiled and then laughed. Evidently, she had inadvertently stumbled across that near mythical creature; he was the German with a sense of humour. She smiled weakly and raised her glass.

For a moment or two they savoured the wine. It was good. Even with her inexpert pallet she recognised its quality. She sat and glanced at the box of chocolates, wondering whether to offer these little brown delicacies or to keep them, for later? She imagined that luxuries of this nature would be disappearing from the shops very soon. This was a time to horde. The hard times weren't around the corner – they had arrived and there was no conceivable end in sight.

The sound of light traffic came to them through the open window and she stood again, crossing the room to close it. She glanced outside as she reached for the frame and almost recoiled in horror. Below her Ted grappled with the door, clearly unable to gain entry. Somehow, in the time it had taken him to get here, the door had slipped shut. He looked upwards but she quickly pulled the window closed, her mind a maelstrom of terrifying thoughts and bleak outcomes. She was close to panic but managed a deep breath before she turned to face the German again.

The difference in language was proving to be a saviour and a curse. In respect of the former it meant that she couldn't really form much of an attachment to the man whose death was shortly going to occur in her home. In respect of the latter, however, it meant that there was a distinct lack of conversation available to them with which to pass the time until his demise. She wondered again how she could even be thinking like this. How could she be so dispassionate about taking a life or more accurately assisting the process in which a life was taken?

'Trés bon,' she said, holding up her glass. He smiled appreciatively. It was a nice smile, damn him.

She still couldn't decide if he was handsome or not – not that it mattered – but she concluded that in years to come he would run to fat. He had that look of incipient chubbiness. She was shocked all over again with the realisation that he didn't have 'years to come.'

Veronica remained outwardly calm and demure, but she thought about Ted, stranded outside. She thought about their options. He could wait until someone else entered or left and slip in before the door shut once again. That might create a rumpus as the tenant in question sought to remonstrate with the intruder. Alternatively, she could take the initiative, make her excuses, go downstairs and let him in. But Frank might demand to know where she was going. Once again, the language barrier would be useful if that was the case. She stood with her back to him as these possibilities cascaded through her mind.

He took her reticence as being a sign of shyness and stood, looping his arms around her waist. She stiffened momentarily and then relaxed, after all what had she expected to happen? It had to begin somehow. She felt him push his face into her hair and then he kissed her neck delicately. She knew how to respond although she felt not the slightest inclination to do so.

With surprising tenderness, he turned her round to face him and they kissed on the lips. He wanted more. She held him tight, smelling his cologne and his hair oil. Veronica needed time to think. At this rate they were going to finish up in bed together with no prospect of Ted coming to her rescue.

'Frank,' she breathed. She ran her fingers through his hair and massaged his neck.

He responded breathlessly, 'Veronique' and pulled her tighter to him. Throughout, she was looking over his shoulder, willing Ted to appear and knowing that he was unlikely to do so. Her luck was going to have to change dramatically and soon.

They separated for a moment and he took both of her hands in his. Her heart began to pound; he was going to lead her to the bedroom. *It might help if you knew where it was*, she thought. He kept his eyes fixed on hers. She noticed that they were blue but flecked with grey, almost a flaw, as if he wasn't quite the perfect Aryan specimen he should be. He smiled, delighted at the manner in which his evening was panning out. This was too easy. Veronica felt her stomach rumble. She was hungry without feeling hungry and she certainly wasn't hungry in any other sense, although she was obviously putting on a good show of being seduced.

He backed out of the doorway as if he had rearward vision. He began to lead her down the short hall, brushing past her dark winter coat as he did so. He wheeled round in a slow backwards arc and deftly kicked the door open with a back heel. She wanted to warn him but the words wouldn't come. His eyes were still fixed on hers, his gaze intent, his passion manifest. He only diverted his eyes away from her face when the backs of calves made contact with the edge of the toilet bowl. Despite, or possibly because of, her tension she laughed. Frank reddened. *Shoot him now Ted to spare his blushes*, she thought but Ted was nowhere to be seen.

Disguising her reluctance, she now began to lead him back out of the little toilet room and towards her bedroom. He shuffled forwards, his sleeve catching on the pointed door handle. He winced his annoyance, his good mood disappearing in large chunks.

This time *Veronica* back-heeled the door and led him into the correct room. Had she ever felt inclined to swing a cat in her bedroom it would not have been possible. As he began to undress her, he appreciated that the bed offered the only feasible living space available to them. He pushed her down gently. She sat pliantly and he sat next to her. They kissed again, with more passion this time, his genuine, hers affected. Frank reached for the strap of her dress and stroked it from her shoulder, repeating the gesture on the other side. He looked at the fold of fabric just above her breasts as she reached for his shirt buttons. They kissed again, a long lingering kiss as she snapped each button open in sequence, starting from the top and working her way down towards his waist. His tongue darted around her mouth and she began to make those little noises she thought he expected to hear.

His hands reached down and he began to pull at the hem of her dress. At first, she didn't move to assist him but then, bowing to the inevitable, she raised herself slightly so that the light fabric slipped past her thighs. She pulled the dress off over her head and he gazed at her breasts, cupping one with his hand. He bent to kiss the erect nipple and she closed her eyes in apparent ecstasy but actual disgust. She wore only her knickers and shoes now. He pulled his shirt off and flung it on the floor like a matador sweeping a bull away with his red cape. It was a flamboyant gesture. Veronica noticed that his skin was white and hairless. His torso was flabby, his shape ill-defined and vaguely feminine.

He stood swiftly, fumbling with his fly buttons and then pushing his trousers down with a flourish where they became stuck on the top of his boots. His off-white underwear bulged. She felt nauseated. *Where the hell was Ted?*

'Ach,' he said in disgust and sat down again awkwardly, pulling at the tight boots. He couldn't get proper purchase on them and was forced to stand again to pull up his trousers. Veronica crossed her arms across her breasts as if feeling the cold.

His ardour was frustrated but not undone. He worried that the moment had passed for her, not realising that it had never even been close. His right boot came free suddenly and he threw it on the floor. His sock hung off his foot ridiculously like a partially shed snake skin. He grunted as he pulled at the other boot. It came off suddenly and he accidently rapped his knuckles on the opposite wall. He swore under his breath, using words she didn't recognise.

Veronica gulped nervously as he stood again, having triumphed over his footwear. His teeth were gritted now, his concentration complete as he pulled his trousers down again. He stepped out of them, leaving them crumpled on the floor like a discarded towel. He smiled at her, hoping she shared his excitement. He had two thumbs hooked into the elastic waistband of his underpants. She was about to come face to… er, face with his 'thing.'

'That's quite enough of that, pal,' said Ted sticking the muzzle of his Walther into the German's temple. 'I'll do the shootin' round here.'

Veronica thought she was going to pass out with relief.

Chapter Twenty-two

Veronica watched in horror as Frank's underpants filled with urine. The damp stain spread from the epicentre of his now flaccid 'thing' like a pale yellow explosion. At the same time a smell of faeces assailed her nostrils.

'Eugh,' she said, standing urgently. She bent to collect her dress, Ted catching sight of her breasts for a moment, and then she left the room with the dress held protectively in front of her.

Ted spoke to her as she dressed in the hall. 'I had to wait until some ol' boy came along and let me in. He didn't look too pleased about it.'

'Just in the nick of time, as they say. Frank here was just about to get his willy out for me.' Ted laughed. The word 'willy' sounded very odd coming from a woman. It wasn't the sort of thing said by any of the girls he had ever met.

'Well, we couldn't have that now, could we?' He jabbed the muzzle of the pistol painfully into Frank's temple. The German flinched as if the bullet was on its way and pulled his head back. 'Come on now Leutnant. I'm about to carry out a long-held ambition – shooting an officer.' It wasn't quite true. He'd given it no thought at all, certainly not to the point where it became an ambition. He didn't even want to shoot Pomeroy although he'd raise no objection if somebody else did.

Despite his eagerness to bring the whole distasteful matter to a close Ted wanted the officer to know why he was being killed. He wanted to tell him that he knew all about the soldiers in Mig's platoon who should have been taken prisoner but who had been shot out of hand instead. To kill Feldhus without him realising that this was simply a liaison with destiny seemed futile. The man had to go taking a message to the afterlife so that those who preceded him *and* those that followed him would understand.

Ted found it odd to be in the position of judge; odder still that he was also jury and executioner. For one thing, killing a man such as Feldhus sounded like a job for an officer, not a corporal.

To kill him, to remove his brains from his skull on the end of a piece of lead was to leave his mission incomplete. Ted wasn't a murderer; he was an agent of retribution. He was an arbiter of right and wrong. The problem lay with making his point effectively. But one way or another, despite the difference in language, Feldhus had to know why he was going to die.

Feldhus made his way into the kitchen on the end of Ted's gun.

'Turn round,' said Ted and the German complied. 'Oh shit,' said Ted.

Veronica looked over at him, quizzically. He was constantly amazed at her calmness, her adaptability. She spoke.

'What is it?'

'This isn't him.'

'But you said…'

'I was wrong. It's not him.' He jabbed the gun at the soiled German in front of him.' 'Your name?,' he demanded. Then he tried it in German. *'Die Name?*

'Frank Ebbinghaus,' said the German. His bewilderment was complete, and undiluted by the will to fight. However, he had regained some of his composure.

'Fuck it,' said Ted. 'Now what? We've got the wrong bloody German.'

The mystified German looked from one tormentor to the other, hoping to find salvation in some unlikely form. He was in the position of the man who wasn't qualified for Hell but not quite right for Heaven either. His future hung in the balance. His jury consisted of two people who really didn't care what happened to him.

'This is a bit of a disaster,' said Veronica.

'A *bit* of a disaster? You make it sound as if some of this is working out quite well.' Silence descended upon the three of them. The German began to speak, his tone hopeful, compliant and agreeable. He was the very soul of reason… but they didn't understand what he was saying and so his efforts were wasted. Veronica looked at him with something like contempt. She had never been fond of men who lost control of their bowels and bladders.

Ted sighed. 'I don't suppose you have any handcuffs?' he ventured.

'Yeah, I'll just go and get them,' she answered, sarcastically.

'We need to tie this bugger up. And gag him.'

'Then what?'

'Oh. I don't know. Hide him away.'

'Hide him away?'

'Put him somewhere.'

'Such as? For God's sake, Ted. We need to get rid of him.'

'Get rid of him? You were the one who didn't want a dead body in her flat.'

'Yes, I'm an old-fashioned girl alright. Some people like corpses in their homes but it's never really appealed to me.' She paused, exasperated. 'I'm not *actually* suggesting we kill him but we need to store him somewhere.'

'Clean him up first…'

'Yes, clean him up.' She was exasperated but not panicking.

'Don't forget his car's outside.'

'Oh God.'

'Let's gag him and tie him up first. He can clean himself up inside the bathroom. I'll stand guard. When we've done that we can come up with a plan. Can you drive?' asked Ted.

'Not really. Even if I could I think I might look a bit conspicuous driving along in a German Army car, wouldn't I?'

'True,' said Ted. He was shoving the officer in the direction of the bathroom. 'I don't suppose you have any men's underpants?'

'Next to the handcuffs.'

'Yes, okay…'

They heard the taps go on in the bathroom and looked at each other as if expecting the other to come up with a solution to their problem.

'This is a mess, Ted.' She wasn't referring to the state of the German's under garments.

'It is, but he's not dead so we don't have a corpse to deal with.'

'I don't know which is worse really…' Veronica absentmindedly picked up the officer's clothes and left them in a heap outside the bathroom. She returned to the kitchen. 'Do you still have to get the real Feldhus?,' she asked. It was a reasonable enough question. Perhaps he came across as being considerably more dedicated than was actually the case. *Did he seem like a merciless assassin?* It wasn't a description that his Mum and Dad would have recognised.

'No. That's it. I've blown it. I should have known something was wrong when you said he was called Frank. I just thought they had made a mistake with the name.' They heard the bathroom door open. 'I'd better keep an eye on Frankie boy. Don't want him running off.'

Ted returned thirty seconds later with the German on the business end of his gun. Veronica was in the process of removing a pot from her lowest cupboard and swung it upwards in an arc as Ebbinghaus plunged for the pistol belt hanging on the chair. The cast iron base of the pot caught him full on the chin, sending his head back. He fell heavily, his outstretched hand brushing the tip of the holster. The German lay for a second, then groaned before turning onto his back. Veronica smiled triumphantly but her mouth fell open as Ted unhooked the leather belt and holster and threw them onto the floor next to the German officer.

'Is that what you want?' he asked. There was a hint of contempt in his voice.

'Ted, what are you…' asked Veronica.

Warily, Ebbinghaus glanced up at Ted and then slowly reached for the holster. He looked at Ted again, then unclipped the holster's flap, already realising from the weight of the item that there was no pistol inside.

'I hid it,' said Ted, plainly.

'Oh,' said Veronica, her disappointment evident.

'But you did very well. Your reactions were excellent.' The German sat up rubbing his chin. His flabby stomach bulged whitely over the waistband of his trousers. 'But now we know we have to tie him up. Think you can do it if I keep this gun pressed to his head?'

'I can do it. I'll use the belt to tie his hands behind his back. I've got stockings and things to tie the rest of him up good and proper.' She smiled. The phrase 'good and proper' sounded completely alien to her as if she was learning lines from a play about working class people. 'Then we can have a nice cup of tea.'

Ted sniggered at the sheer, unadulterated Britishness of her response. Perhaps there was hope for a world in which people drank tea to settle their nerves.

The fight was knocked out of Ebbinghaus now. He stood, like the obedient soldier he was and allowed Veronica to bind him. Further resistance seemed utterly pointless to him now, his humiliation was complete… or rather it would be when he was found and returned to camp at some point in the future. At least, he supposed, they weren't intent on killing him, although their motives were a considerable puzzle to him.

Ted checked the bindings when she had finished and nodded his approval. He looked admiringly at Veronica. 'You're a natural,' he said.

'Don't get any ideas,' she warned him, half serious. 'I'm a secretary by trade.'

Ted pushed the German down so that he was seated. 'Let's have a drink while we think about what to do. *Ein cafe?*' Ebbinghaus nodded. *'Zucker, milch?'*

'Ohne milch,' he replied. It was all rather civilised. He wanted to ask them what their intentions were. If he lived, as seemed increasingly likely, then it was only to be subjected to a court-martial.

They might have been three friends had it not been for the rather stilted conversation. They were subdued, thoughtful, tense. The German had relaxed to a certain degree now that he knew he wasn't going to lose his life. His chin was bruising nicely, yellows and blues blended, dissolving into one another like coloured inks on a blotter. He sipped his coffee as it was offered up to him by Veronica. She was gentle now, like a nurse.

'You realise that you're going to have to take him to the toilet as well,' jibed Ted.

'No, that's your department, I think,' she replied, hastily.

'Do you think you can manage him while I get rid of the car?' She nodded and Ted pulled the German to his feet. 'We'll tie him to your bedframe. I'll leave the gun with you.'

Ebbinghaus was secured to the metal bedframe with a canvas belt Veronica retrieved from a drawer. He looked subdued like a beaten dog.

'I'm not sure about the gun,' she said. Ted pulled the Walther from his pocket, cocked it and passed it over.

'Safety catch,' he said pointing at the lever on the rear of the slide. 'Trigger. Any problems just ask Frank. He's got one almost the same.' The officer seemed to get the gist of Ted's briefing and gave a snort of self-mocking laughter.

'I'm borrowing your jacket,' he told the German. Ebbinghaus made a gesture which seemed to say, *be my guest.*

Veronica looked down at the pistol doubtfully. Ted held her shoulders in his hands and spoke to her like a proud parent.

'I couldn't have got through this without you. He's not going to give you any trouble. I'll take his gun and I'll be back soon.'

He was surprised when she gave him a hug. 'Don't read too much into that Ted. I still prefer women.'

'That's fine, Veronica,' he said and was gone. Veronica leaned against the wall in the cramped hallway and sighed heavily. The sooner she was on that plane the…

There was a knock on the door and she froze. Several scenarios crashed through her mind, none of them good. She looked at the gun and then at the door. Whoever it was would need a good reason to get into her flat.

'It's Ted,' came the voice.

She released the breath she'd been holding. 'Thank God,' she said as she released the door. Ted bounded in.

'I forgot the bloody keys,' he said.

Chapter Twenty-three

She watched him clamber into the car and grapple with the ignition. The engine burst into life with a clattery rumble. Ted glanced around him and then pulled the jacket on. He swiftly selected a gear then lurched away from the kerb. Seconds later he was gone from view and she closed the window.

She might have been attracted to a man like Ted, if things had been different for her, she thought. She reminded herself to warn him against talking about her sexual preferences when they got home. She didn't want to escape to her home country just to squander freedom rotting in jail.

She looked in on her prisoner. He was quite relaxed, his head resting against the mattress and his gaze directed at the ceiling as if it offered him hope. He glanced in her direction and gave her a tired smiled. He seemed utterly defenceless. She might have felt sorry for him but stopped herself even thinking that way.

The gun felt heavy and unnatural in her hand. She honestly couldn't imagine herself shooting someone, no matter how threatening or odious they might appear. She especially didn't fancy shooting Ebbinghaus. She found him inoffensive at worst; chinning him with a pan was the utmost act of violence she could picture herself inflicting upon him. She paced the hall, waiting for Ted's return. His presence somehow gave her the confidence to carry on whereas his absence made her feel isolated and vulnerable. It went against her nature to feel dependent on a man and she never had before, but then she hadn't ever been trapped in a hostile country before, either.

***

Ted took it easy through the back streets, driving courteously despite the lack of competing traffic. He was thankful for the fading light, the officer's tunic and the lack of witnesses. The car would be left somewhere out of sight but not too far from the flat – he had to walk back, after all. He tried to keep a note of the route he had taken but soon became disoriented as he sought the ideal dumping ground. The streets began to look identical, more so as the receding light drained the shops and houses of colour. It wasn't as if the car could be mistaken for anything other than what it was. It was camouflaged for one thing and more angular in outline than even the most utilitarian French vehicle. It was synonymous with the German Army; obviously the most common form of transport for junior officers.

On one street, Ted found a small lorry park and considered using it to drop the car off. He drove through the gates but then reversed out again at speed, alarmed at the noise the little air-cooled engine made as it reverberated from the high brick walls on either side of the depot. It was not a vehicle designed for stealth, its unsophisticated engine sounding like a dozen spanners being vigorously shaken in a chef's pot.

He drove on and then pulled into a shady spot, stepped out, enjoying the silence as the engine rattled to a halt.

With a heavy sigh he set off on foot to explore the truck depot. If he and Veronica even got away with it for twenty-four hours then they should be on their way home. It didn't seem like much to ask. He placed a hand on the butt of the little Walther PPK he had taken from the officer. It was a slightly smaller version of the weapon he'd left with Veronica and operated in exactly the same way. There was no equivalent in the British arsenal – the service issue revolver, the Webley, was enormous and impossible to conceal.

His shoes crunched on the gritty concrete beneath his feet. A series of lights shone down from a single wooden pole located centrally, bathing the area in a dull yellow glow that gave everything it touched a look of jaundice. One of the lights flickered on and off. A fleet of grey-painted trucks stood regimented in front of a long, enclosed garage area. The light infused them with the colour of urine. The ground was marked out with an archipelago of oil stain islands. Over to the far right stood an array of oil containers and boxes of spares, the latter looking as if it had been delivered in haste, stacked in haste and subsequently abandoned in haste. If this little operation had ever thrived then it certainly wasn't doing so now.

Ted steered a course to the left, keeping close to the high wall and then darting into the garage area. Almost at once he stumbled over the hose of an air compressor and cursed in English. He waited, listening to the sounds of the late evening. He wanted to park the car at the far end of the line of trucks, in the hope that it wouldn't be visible from the road. He was growing in confidence that there would be no workforce turning up when the morning came.

Some sounds belong irrevocably to their locations. Woodland has the sound of leaves and birdsong during the day and the ethereal banter of owls and the shuffling of night hunters when the sun has gone. Factories have the monotonous day-time drone of machinery and the secretive scuttling of rats at night. Garages and truck depots, by contrast, are almost silent at night once the clicking of cooling engines has stopped. It's as if the sound has been vacuumed out, leaving a temporary aural wasteland.

As he stood there, however, Ted did become aware of one sound, like the remnant of a noise, left behind, not quite extinguished when the day's work had been done. It became more pronounced as he moved cautiously towards it.

Ted knew that he should *not* be hearing the noise of crackling fires, knots of wood exploding, embers slipping down through the grate in a dozen fiery cascades. The *deserted* truck park was no such thing. He pressed himself into the shadows. Stray tendrils of acrid smoke reached out to him and he backed away from their ghostly attentions. He held his breath and then wafted the fumes away from his face.

That there was a night watchman was a considerable inconvenience but, he supposed, not a total surprise although it was hard to imagine someone daring to steal a truck in these dark, oppressive days. Ted shook his head. He grew concerned with the length of time he had been away from Veronica, briefly picturing their captive trying to escape and her pulling the trigger. He wasn't convinced that she could do so, or that she would necessarily hit him if she did. Ebbinghaus was a trained soldier, after all. He would use everything he could to his advantage.

Immobile, Ted tried to picture the confrontation that awaited him: the old man wrapped up against the cold of early evening, his sudden appearance, a gasp of surprise and then what? He cut his reverie short. This man, whoever he was, was not the enemy. Ted had already spared the life of a German – to then kill a Frenchman not only robbed his mission of any value but made a mockery of everything he stood for.

He was temporarily paralysed with indecision. Could he simply present himself to the man and ask that he hide the car? He could say 'no' and that would be the end of the matter. Would that work? The man might then have to explain where the car had come from… *Mmm, that won't work*. He glanced over at the trucks and wondered how long it would be before the local garrison pressed them into service.

Ted stepped out of the shadows, still taking care to be quiet. He picked his way through a low jungle of garage detritus, taking his time, using his senses, thinking through his options. He made for the far wall where he had spotted a grimy window with four panes of glass held in a metal frame. This gave him the means to carry out the next stage of his reconnaissance. As he approached, the glow of the brazier became more apparent and he could see the figure of a man picked out in orange as he moved to and fro. He heard wood being dropped into the powdery ash and saw a shower of sparks rising like tiny luminous insects disturbed. For a moment he thought he could see the ominous outline of a German helmet and he froze; his plan abandoned in an instant and no alternative springing to mind. But then he gave a near silent snort and shook his head; he was getting windy. Better to bring this little adventure to an end or find another place to abandon the car.

Ted speeded up, made it to the window and glanced outside. He saw the tall brazier, an elongated metal basket but no-one standing next to it. He nodded and made his way along the wall to the front of the garage. Ted kept the gun in his pocket and made his way round the corner, discarding stealth, replacing it with openness. He would close the distance to the man and simply say *'bonjour.'* Perhaps he would accidentally kick some tiny object on the way or scuff his foot on the ground to warn the man of his approach and then he could begin his negotiations.

***

The German soldier was scouring a bin for some newspaper like a huge alley cat as Ted made his approach. He wanted to have it on hand in case the fire started to go out for he still had another chilly forty-three minutes of sentry duty to go before his replacement arrived. He turned, alerted by some indistinct sound behind him and saw the Frenchman approaching him. He was sure he heard the man gasp in surprise. His job was to keep an eye out for looters. Was this a looter? He didn't look like one but he reached for his rifle nevertheless and in that instant the man drew a pistol out of his pocket.

In a panic he fumbled with the Mauser rifle's bolt, cursing the clumsy gloves he wore. He felt a round slip into the breech but his gloved fingers were too fat to operate the safety catch. He looked up and heard the report of the pistol, saw the flash and heard the bullet whistle off into space.

Ted had panicked and loosed off a round without taking proper aim. He knew better than that. Stupid mistakes cost men their lives. The German seemed to be struggling to bring his rifle to bear as if his hands had been anaesthetised. It gave him time to take another shot, an aimed shot this time. The element of surprise had gone, his stealth had been in vain. Now he needed to get rid of this German soldier. He could barely see him now and realised that the man was crouching, making himself a more difficult target. He could just make out the soldier pulling a pair of gloves from his hands. Ted fired into the gloom. The bullet hit the brazier and tore a tunnel of sparks through the fire.

He heard the German call out and then fall to the ground. He had to close the distance now, get that next and final shot in. Ted stumbled over a pile of logs, falling to the ground and striking the muzzle of the Walther on the concrete. Ahead of him, unseen, the German cried out but Ted had regained his feet and bounded over to where the injured man lay.

The soldier tried to sit up. His rifle lay beside him and he nursed a shoulder injury. He spoke, pleading for his life, gabbling away in Bavarian German. Ted could see the man's eyes, wide with terror, illuminated by the fire from the brazier. His own shadow fell across the scene and he lifted the gun, aligning the man's head with the foresight and then the rear sight.

'Nein!'

Ted pulled the trigger.

***

He ran to the road and jumped into the car. It started noisily and he crunched the gears. Without headlights he drove through the depot, past the trucks and then parked up at the space he had picked out earlier. He killed the engine and then bounded over to the dead soldier, bending to pick him up by his shoulders and then dragging him round to the back of the garage. Ted's breath came in ragged gasps now. He choked on smoke from the fire and felt warm sticky blood on his forearm. He turned awkwardly and wedged the body into a space between two oil drums. Then he returned, picked up the rifle and stood it against the wall but obscured by a wooden upright. He threw Ebbinghaus's tunic onto the fire and pushed the PPK into his trouser pocket.

Ted glanced around. He wanted to leave no obvious evidence of his presence. He took a deep breath, patted his pocket once more and then began to walk from the truck depot, trying to look casual. His legs felt weak and his gait was awkward as if was learning to walk by following instructions from a manual.

At the entrance, he paused, took another deep breath, wished he had a cigarette and then looked both ways. To his left, the street was empty and quiet, just a row of houses, each one the same as its neighbour. To the right, something similar but with the addition of a shop and a man walking a dog. The dog, some small thing on the end of a weedy-looking lead paused to anoint a telegraph pole. There was nothing to indicate that either man or beast had been alerted to recent events. Ted turned right and began to walk back to Veronica's flat. He was cold without a jacket but he was eager to get off the streets for other reasons than simply finding warmth.

He wondered when the German would be found. Once the alarm was raised things would become very complicated indeed. *If only I'd parked somewhere else.*

***

Veronica stood next to the window listening to night sounds. A car drove up the main road, a dog barked and music came across the street to her; some sort of old music hall refrain, belted out in breathless French. She lit a cigarette and stood with one arm across her chest, wishing Ted would return and thinking about tomorrow night's escape. What would she do once she was back in Britain? Would she try to find Sue or was that episode in her life finished? She wondered what steps Sue had taken to try and smuggle her back home when the Germans approached Paris. Had she taken any, at all?

She still couldn't picture the actual mechanics of their departure. *A plane that could land in a field in the dark?* It sounded fairly ridiculous when she thought about it. She scratched her cheek absent-mindedly, her gaze fixed on some infinite point above the rooftops of Belloire. Ebbinghaus called out, disturbing her reverie. He wanted the toilet.

'Oh hell,' she muttered. She hoped that he would take the hint if she ignored him but he called out again. She stubbed out the cigarette and left the butt perched on the window sill. The gun was on the sideboard looking out of place next to a loaf and a coffee cup. *How was she going to manage this?*

The answer came suddenly; she wasn't. He would have to wait until Ted returned. He called out again. Veronica tutted and shook her head. He was clearly a man used to getting his own way.

He was already looking in her direction as the door swung open.

'You'll have to wait until he gets back,' she said slowly and deliberately as if Ebbinghaus was hard of thought.

'Nein. Ich mochten das Toilet.'

'I'll give you a bowl and you can pee in that,' she said. She thought regretfully about the hand painted bowl in the top cupboard. She hadn't intended to take it on the plane with her but nor had she intended to fill it with German urine.

When she returned with it moments later he shook his head.

'Nein, nein. Ich… assis,' he said in fluent patois. He needed to sit on the toilet.

'Oh,' she said. 'You'll have to wait.'

Chapter Twenty-four

Ted tried to look casual, rather than lost.

But he was lost.

The streets looked like those he had followed on the way there but they didn't lead him back to Veronica's flat. Things appeared different on foot of course and each section of the return journey also took longer now. He tried to picture the maze of streets from above and having done so he pin-pointed himself on this mental map. Sadly, the map was wrong and Ted was actually about two hundred yards to the east of where he thought he was. The moon was almost a complete disc, lighting his route to safety.

He kept a steady pace, glancing at street names hoping that something would jog his memory. He was desperate to get back to check on Veronica and their prisoner but more than that he didn't want to be on the streets when the metaphorical 'balloon went up.' For now, everything was quiet but he was virtually alone on these strange, narrow streets. A few fellow pedestrians wouldn't have damaged his cause. If anyone did begin looking for the man who'd killed the soldier and stolen the car then he was the only apparent suspect. He had his ID but would avoid putting his *bona fides* to the test if he could. *Maurice Grima.* It still didn't feel like he was that man.

Maurice Grima was middle-aged with a pot belly, braces holding his trousers up. He chain-smoked and rarely spoke. That was how Ted pictured him, at least.

If he was stopped, he would also need to ditch the gun in a hurry. He could do it right now – its purpose was served – but he liked the reassurance of being armed. A shoot-out was slightly more appealing than trying to pass himself off as Monsieur Grima. He still had the other pistol in the flat – the one he'd brought with him.

A dark side street offered him concealment and he stepped into it, gladly allowing darkness to swallow him up, shadow and all. He took time to think, his mind clouded by frustration and weariness. In the distance he heard the distinctive rumble-whine of a four-wheel drive vehicle traversing a cobbled street and pictured the German patrol dropping off their sentry at the truck depot. It was a guess but if he had guessed correctly then his time was running out. He thought about the river that ran through Belloire. It was behind him somewhere and if he could find it then it should lead him close to the flat and Veronica.

He set off again with a fugitive's desperation, a soldier's optimism and an Ulsterman's realism tugging at each other for dominance in his mind. He ran, just a gentle trot that he knew he could maintain for mile after mile. Not that he should have to; Belloire didn't have mile after mile! Unless he ended up going round in circles.

He came to a junction with a well-lit street and stopped, gathering his wits, using his senses. To his right he saw a little bistro, nothing more than a few tables and chairs outside double doors and a brightly coloured awning. As he watched, the owner popped his head out to check for customers and then retreated once again, disappointed. Ted considered asking the man for directions but caution made him decide against it. He didn't know where he was trying to get to, or at least not in terms he could readily describe to a foreigner.

To his left he saw the row of shops he had walked past on his first morning in the town and smiled his relief. He was sure that he could find his way from this point. He began walking once more, trying not to think of the multiple hurdles that still awaited him before he returned to Britain. With shocking clarity, he realised that his mission was a total failure and that failure was just as hard to achieve as any success he might have hoped for. Maybe that would persuade Murray to think again; to find someone more suited to this type of work. Just the possibility of this being his last mission lifted his spirits. If this was the last time he would be required to perform such an impossible task, then his life could go back to normal. *Who knows I might even be allowed to 're-appear,' to re-join the human race.*

The thought of seeing his parents again spurred him on. So what if he had to go back into the infantry – it was hardly more risky than what he was doing. He'd enjoy seeing the look on Pomeroy's face when he returned from the unmarked grave.

He was walking briskly now, cheered, knowing that he was close to the flat and therefore closer to safety, closer to getting home. He just had to keep his nerve. He heard it again, the noise of a vehicle: four-wheel drive transmission, large petrol engine, tyres scrabbling for grip on night-damp cobbles. The German Army was at large in sleepy Belloire.

***

Murray jumped as the phone began to ring on his desk. He'd spent the day interviewing men who had volunteered for his new organisation. Dalton had only just left. They had both been shocked and dismayed at the mixed bag which had come forward. Phoney adventurers, disgruntled pay clerks, even an RAF cook.

They had opted for a new way of doing things, assuming that the necessary talent for their new force existed in all walks of life and not just amongst the alumni of country's public schools. But they were already rueing their optimism. Perhaps the old way of doing things, of making decisions based upon a candidate's influence, wealth, breeding, patronage, had some merit after all. Maybe that was the only way to find the 'character' required for this dangerous work.

Whatever, they needed another method of selection or a means of advertising their new 'job' without completely destroying any semblance of security they had established.

'Murray,' he said, tersely. He closed his eyes as a voice on the other end gave him the news. Murray rubbed his temples and sighed, heavily. 'How do you know?' he said at last. 'I see. Thank you,' and he put the receiver back in the cradle.

***

Embury was flying the next day, taking an unnamed VIP up to a bomber field in the Midlands. Routine stuff but he didn't drink when he knew he had to fly. The maroon wingback chair in which he normally sat was occupied by some new bod who'd been moping around for days without any obvious purpose. He could have been a spy. He shrugged. There was no sense having a favourite chair. With his drink – a ginger ale and his newspaper, The Daily Mail – he headed for his second-favourite chair. He didn't like the lighting in this corner as much, too harsh but good for reading.

The paper contained the latest news on the air battle being fought in the skies of Kent. He scanned it quickly with a mixture of fascination and guilt. Fighter command was undoubtedly putting on a great show but its pilots were also dying in droves. In comparison, his job was relatively safe, so much so that the comparison didn't really stand scrutiny at all. It wasn't that he was a coward but this was the job he'd been given. He'd see it through. The glamour and glory were for others, at least in the meantime.

He puffed out his cheeks and expelled a slow breath as he skipped the front page and began working his way through the news. There was little to cheer about. A quick glance at his drink and he felt the urge to have a nice whiskey added to it. The rule about not drinking was largely of his own making. Things were relatively lax in wartime. People who didn't expect to see out their three score and ten could hardly be denied a simple drink. He was sure the fighter boys had a drink in the evening. The door opened and an orderly walked in.

He approached and cleared his throat unnecessarily. 'Excuse me, sir. Telephone call.'

Embury looked at his drink again, then stood, his whiskey craving gone. The orderly led him to the phone in the entrance hall and pointed. Murray gave him the news. 'Don't be surprised if you two find yourselves doing a spell at Fighter Command.'

Embury re-took his seat. He was decidedly deflated now. His stomach fluttered with fear but he tried to convince himself that it was something else. Excitement perhaps. He thought about that whiskey. *All things considered where was the harm?* He would wait until the morning before he shared the news with Flight Sergeant Guy.

Chapter Twenty-five

Ted banged on the door; they didn't have a sophisticated plan for his return. Perhaps they should have decided upon a special knock or some other discreet, unique signal. He'd seen two trucks pull in to the square and soldiers spilling out from the tailgate. Everything was purposeful but directed, urgent but contained. Another truck had arrived shortly afterwards. Three dog handlers with German shepherds had piled out of that one. An officer stood talking to an MP warrant officer. The two men looked around them at the side streets that spread from the square like an orderly web. They were organising a search and Ted felt distinctly uncomfortable. He was the prize. In his favour was the fact that they didn't know who they were looking for yet. Against him was everything else.

As he watched, the warrant officer, a tall man in his late thirties, broke away from the officer and began directing operations. His manner brooked no arguments, his instructions were orders not suggestions. In groups of four the soldiers took off, each group heading for a designated street. They acted as if they had trained all of their lives for this moment. The apparent precision, involved was quite staggering as if the event had been choreographed and practiced relentlessly. Ted pressed himself into the door trying to become part of the grain, hoping desperately that Veronica would appear soon. He watched as one of the dog handlers was dispatched along the river bank. The other two looked on, their dogs barking and yelping, eager to join the pursuit like excitable huskies waiting to pull their sledge.

The door snapped open and he almost fell into the foyer.

'Oh Ted, what's happening out there? I was beginning to think they'd got you.'

'Long story. How's our friend?'

'He's fine. Do we have to get out of here?' There was a trace of subdued panic in her voice. They ran up the stairs.

'I don't think so. Not yet. They're scouring the streets so we're better off inside.' He paused as Veronica pushed open the door. They scrambled inside and she pushed the door firmly behind her. 'What they'll do after that is anybody's guess.'

'It's you they're looking for?'

'Pretty sure it is. I had to kill a soldier. I reckon they found his body a few minutes ago and phoned the camp to get a search going.'

'Will they search the houses?'

'I don't know. If they do, we'll have a job explaining why we have one of their officers tied to a bed.' Ted thought for a moment and then said, 'is there a back way out of here?'

'Downstairs just. I don't know if it's locked up or not. It leads to a yard with a wall at the end. I think there's a door out but again I don't know if it's locked. I never really looked out there.' She was calm but spoke with urgency, her mind clear and clinical. Ted let a feeling of relief temporarily suborn his other emotions. Veronica continued, 'the thing is, if they did come in here looking, we couldn't really get downstairs to get out that way anyway. The window from the bathroom leads onto a flat roof. We could hide there if someone comes. It's dark enough to not be seen.'

'Unless they have a torch? And so long as Frankie doesn't give us away.'

'Oh yes. I'd forgotten about him. We could take him with us,' suggested Veronica. She fully expected Ted to reject her idea but he paused and looked at her. He nodded thoughtfully and then said, 'let's just check on him. Then we can have a look at that window.'

Ebbinghaus was exactly where they had left him, no more and no less distressed than before. His expression was pained.

'Oh, he needs the toilet. Can you attend to that? I couldn't do it while you were gone.'

'I'd love to. Let's have a look at the window first.'

The bathroom had a white enamel bath and a plain porcelain sink, the latter just below the window. It was sparsely equipped for a lady's bathroom; utilitarian and bleak. Ted looked quizzically at Veronica.

'I wasn't planning on settling down here,' she explained. 'That sink makes things a bit awkward,' she pointed out.

'If we do hide out there, we need to make it look as if we haven't just climbed out the window. Footprints in the soap'll be a bit of a giveaway.' Despite the tension, Veronica giggled. Ted took a step closer to the window and moved a discoloured upright mirror out of the way. The window was almost seized shut but he pushed it open with difficulty. They heard a cat hiss and caught sight of its tail as it jumped out of the way. The window opened by jerky, protesting increments, admitting a stream of cool night air. Ted stood on tiptoes to get a look at the roof.

'Can't see much,' he said.

'It's got a flat bit but some of it is slopy if I remember rightly.'

'Is the flat bit big enough for three of us?'

'I've never actually climbed out the window, Ted. There was never any point before,' she said reasonably. Veronica followed this up with a shrug.

'I suppose not. If it comes to it, we'll send young Frank out first. If we hear him fall to his death, then we'll stay where we are. How's that for a plan?'

Veronica shrugged again.

Ted continued, as if trying to sell this variation on her escape idea back to her. 'If they do come, there's nothing here to connect either of us to the killing. Apart from him, of course.'

'They might be suspicious if they go outside again and find a dead German splattered on the pavement.'

Veronica reminded Ted of Ebbinghaus's toilet needs and with reluctance he untied the German's hands and led him to the little room. He stood guard outside, Ebbinghaus's own Walther in his hands and a round in the breech.

'Don't try escaping. We could have shot you already – remember that.'

'Ja, ja,' said the German from behind the door. It didn't sound like he was trying to escape, rather that something was escaping him. Ted recoiled at the sound of explosive bowel movements from within; Ebbinghaus and his intestines were clearly having a bad day.

The German, still wearing only his trousers and a vest, emerged, looking shaken and muttered something apologetic in his native tongue. It might have been something along the lines of *I wouldn't go in there for a few minutes, if I were you.*

Veronica prepared some sandwiches and coffee while Ted re-applied the officer's bindings. She was smoking her second to last Player when he re-entered the kitchen. The window was ajar but the curtains pulled to and it was quiet in the street below. Ted wasn't sure if that was a good sign or not. He wondered what the Germans would do next, supposing, as seemed likely, they didn't apprehend a suspect on the streets. If they did, it would be wrong man, of course. *God help anyone picked up now*, thought Ted.

Veronica held out the cigarette packet to Ted.

He looked inside and said, 'your last one. I can't take it.'

'Just have it. I'll buy some more when we get home,' she said, smiling bravely. Ted returned the smile, took the cigarette and lit it from the gas ring with scant regard for his eyebrows. He thought of his parents, both of whom often lit their own cigarettes with a red-hot poker taken from the fire. Only now did it seem odd to him. He smiled again, sadly this time.

'Are you okay?' She looked at him with something like affection. At times he seemed to her like a little lost soul, rarely a killer.

'I was thinking of home. Mum and dad.'

'Ireland?'

'Northern Ireland,' he corrected. Often, he didn't bother to make the distinction. 'Belfast.'

'Who are you, Ted?'

'Just Ted.' He drew on his cigarette, screwing his eyes up like a movie gangster. 'Gun for hire,' he added in his approximation of a Chicago accent.

She laughed. 'You don't seem the type. Apart from the fact that you have a gun, that is.'

'No, I don't think I am really. I got into this business by accident.' Veronica gave a scornful laugh. Ted continued, 'it's true. I don't even feel like I'm a proper… er… I don't really know what it is that I'm not a proper one of.'

'Killer?' suggested Veronica. 'Assassin?'

'I suppose. I was just a soldier before. Much simpler.'

'I'm glad you're here.'

Just then they heard the sound of more trucks pulling into the square. Tailgates dropped noisily, boots landed on the cobbles, more dogs joined the search, shouting, torches, orders. Doors were kicked in and soon they heard the protests of innocent civilians being dragged from their houses. There were screams and intermittent gunfire. The air was filled with fear like crackling electricity. The shouting continued. Ted and Veronica looked at one and other. The blood had drained from her face and her fear was manifest once more. Three storeys down, they heard the crack of splintering wood. There were more shouts, banging on doors. A woman screamed and a baby began to cry. A dog barked and then yelped in obvious pain. Heavy footfalls on the stairs, more banging, a door kicked in…

'Time to go,' said Ted.

Chapter Twenty-six

John was reluctantly in the habit of chatting to Embury at breakfast. Partly this was due to the lack of an alternative source of stimulating conversation but mainly it was plain courtesy. Flying was the only thing they had in common. The officer was polite enough he supposed and rather less condescending than some of his contemporaries. Their conversations were necessarily stilted and formulaic, however. There was no trace of bonhomie between the two men, simply because there was no room for it within the rigid rank structure of the RAF and John certainly knew his place. These were the times when he missed the company of the old guard of NCO pilots he'd known in the early days. Most of them were dead.

The RAF, the newest, least traditional and arguably most forward-looking of the three services was born from the army and therefore officers were officers, NCOs were NCOs and aircraftsmen were… there to do the dirty work. John understood that many of Embury's fellow officers and possibly Embury himself seemed to view NCO pilots like John as second-class citizens. Their unspoken, but commonly held belief was that they were only NCOs because they weren't good enough to be officers. Using that logic, it followed that any of them would accept a commission like a shot should the stringent requirements for commissioning be waived. It would require a drop in standards. The thought that they might actually be happy as NCOs was anathema.

'I have some news for you,' said the officer as John placed his tray on the table. He didn't sit but acknowledged the officer with a tilt of his head. Embury was looking neither happy nor glum, so for the meantime the exact nature of the news was unclear. His voice was clear of any inflection which might have imbued his statement with greater import.

'Tea, sir?' he offered. Priorities.

'Not just now, thanks.'

John returned moments later with a cup of tea. He said, 'what's the news, sir?'

'You're not going over tonight,' he said simply. John's blood ran cold.

'What's happened?'

'They think your man has been captured.'

'Captured? How can they possibly know something like that?'

'I don't know but we have to assume that it's true.'

John's appetite had gone. He shook his head. This wasn't some stranger he was being ordered to abandon, this was Ted. Ted, the man who had rescued him.

'I just don't see how they can know for sure, sir,' he repeated.

'It gets worse. We're both being seconded to Fighter Command until this flap is over. Our operations are being suspended until further notice.'

'When?'

'Today I suppose. You're going to Middle Wallop – Spitfires I think. I'm off to Biggin Hill. Fighter boys now,' said Embury. He didn't look thrilled. 'So, pack your stuff and get over there. Might as well fly. I'm sure they can tuck our Lysanders away in the corner of a hangar for the foreseeable…'

John pushed his fried bread around the plate with his fork. 'Right, sir,' he said, thoughtfully. He closed his mind to the babble of conversation around him. If his friend really had been captured then there was little hope for his survival. He didn't expect that they would even grant him a quick death; they needed to show no mercy towards a spy. Embury noticed his pilot's dismay and briefly considered some sort of pep talk, something along the lines of, *in wartime it is necessary for us to make sacrifices.* He decided against it.

'I can't eat this,' John said at last, pushing the plate away. He stood and strode from the room. Embury, concerned, watched him go and then stole his bacon and sausage.

Chapter Twenty-seven

'Out the window and wait for me,' ordered Ted. He pushed her roughly into the hall and into the bathroom. Her cigarette fell to the floor and smouldered unseen as she stumbled out of the room.

'What are you going to do?' she asked. Her tone was pleading.

'I need to get Frank. Just go – we'll join you in a minute.' Veronica was pushing at the window frame as Ted ran out. He heard shouts from the flat below owned by an elderly man. He hoped that his slow, infirm movements would gain them some time.

When he reached the bedroom, Frank was sitting up as best he could, his face impassive, his look inscrutable. 'We need to get out of here, Frank,' said Ted as he scrabbled with the knots he had tied in such haste. He pulled at the binding on the officer's left wrist – it was actually a stocking, thinking that it would come apart with relative ease. To his horror the knot actually constricted, becoming a tiny ball. Ted gasped and swore. The knot was an impenetrable weave of fibres, so tightly packed they threatened to reform into a solid mass of some new substance. Ted heard another shout from below and then heard what sounded like a body falling to the floor. Frank looked at the knot and shook his head. Frank and Ted exchanged glances.

'*Messer,*' said the German, urgently. Ted understood. As he sprinted to the kitchen he wondered if he had cut off the man's blood supply to his wrist. Why, otherwise, was he being so helpful? Ted slammed the drawer open with a violent tympani rattle and selected a stubby fruit knife. As he ran back to the bedroom he wondered if he heard the sound of heavy footfalls on the stairs over the noise of his own feet. The bindings came undone like springs in tension and Frank stood. *'Gehen!'* he ordered, pushing Ted ahead of him. Ted moved reluctantly at first. A glance at his erstwhile prisoner revealed nothing of his intentions.

He stumbled into the bathroom, Frank behind him. He reiterated his original command, *'gehen!'* There was urgency in his voice and he pushed Ted towards the window. Ted scowled, confused but the banging at the door encouraged him to move. He stood in the sink, heard its fixings groan as it took his weight and then propelled himself through the window. He slipped on the wet slates and landed heavily against Veronica. He turned to look at the window only to see it slam shut.

'What's going on, Ted?' she asked from the blackness. From beneath them came the sounds of terror and panic.

'I think he's helped us escape,' hissed Ted. 'We'll soon find out.'

***

Inside, Frank hastily wiped away Ted's boot print from the sink using the heel of his hand. He straightened as the flat's door crashed open and leapt from the bathroom. A corporal with an MP38 ran in, another soldier close behind. Normally the corporal would be shouting instructions in a facsimile of fury, keeping the terrified residents off guard and acquiescent. On this occasion he stopped dead, astonished, his mouth dropping open at the sight of a half-dressed officer in front of him. He normally ordered the residents out at gunpoint, pushing, shoving and giving no scope for alternative courses of action other than leaving. He knew how to intimidate. On this occasion, however, he was utterly stumped. *How to proceed?*

Ebbinghaus spoke first, breaking the deadlock.

'Guten abend,' he said casually. The corporal nodded, comprehension still an elusive commodity for him. He had entered a French flat to find a half-naked Wehrmacht officer standing guiltily before him. He would have to be careful.

'Abend,' he replied. He turned to look at the private behind him.

'Guten abend,' said the private.

Frank regained his dignity in small steps. He spoke to the corporal.

'Ich bin Kapitän Ebbinghaus.' Apart from his officer's trousers there was little to indicate his precise status.

'Was machen Sie hier, herr Kapitän?' asked the corporal, uncertainly. The officer gave a little dismissive snort. He would try to rescue some small fragment of his career and reputation from this bewildering situation.

'Es ist eine lange Geschichte,' he said truthfully. It *was* a long story and not one he was going to share with two soldiers.

'Sie haben mich Gefangerer genommen?'

He laughed at their description of the two people who'd held him; *fugitives*. They were now, he supposed. What they had been before, he could not say.

'Ich denke dass sie weggerannt sind. Vor fünfzehn Minuten.'

'Wir werden Sie zürück erhalten, zu lagern herr Kapitän.' The corporal looked at him hopefully. Ebbinghaus nodded his assent. He had to face the music sometime. He'd be lucky if that was all he faced.

He held up a hand to indicate that he wanted the two soldiers to wait in the hall and made his way to the kitchen to check for his belongings. He hoped he might find his pistol on the table but it was missing, presumably in the Englishman's pocket. He sighed. He wasn't looking forward to delivering his explanation. He spotted Veronica's cigarette still burning on the floor just as the corporal entered the kitchen, holding his peaked cap. The corporal held the cap out as he stepped into the room. Ebbinghaus stubbed out the cigarette with his bare right foot. The soldier looked at him oddly as he winced with the pain. He imitated a man with lower back problems and shooed the soldier back outside into the hall. The extinguished cigarette he dropped in the sink and then sat heavily to examine the blister on his foot. He winced again as he brushed away the ash. If he was passed on to the Gestapo that wouldn't be the last cigarette burn he'd be suffering.

When he was dressed in all the pieces of uniform he could salvage, he made his way into the hall. The soldiers turned and led him out of the flat. The stairs were littered with small belongings dropped by desperate people. Each landing had splintered wood, kicked-in doors, evidence of the clumsy German operation. There had been no finesse in their dealings with these startled civilians.

He followed the soldiers out onto the street, resisting the urge to glance at the roof where he knew his two captors were hiding. The square was a scene of bedlam as hordes of French civilians, many of them in their night clothes, were herded into hastily assembled corrals prior to some sort of crude processing. One half-naked woman lay dead on the pavement, her body slumped like that of a drunk. Her body was draped against the wall of her house. Blood stained the side of her head, matting her hair. From various directions parties of soldiers came with civilians in their none-too-gentle 'care'. Ebbinghaus made his way to a truck as the soldiers spoke to their sergeant. He feared for these French people but he feared for himself more.

***

Ted and Veronica cowered on the roof, pulling closely together for warmth and comfort. Ted put an arm around her protectively as if he could shield her from all the bad things in the world. She closed her eyes and listened to the drama below. The people seemed quieter now, perhaps resigned to their fate. The only noise that remained was that of orders barked out in German. She imagined people being loaded onto trucks perhaps for transportation to the barracks at Lille. Their subsequent fate? She shuddered to think. Every now and again, an engine started and a vehicle would pull out of the square. Eventually, some of those trucks returned, having completed their short transfer.

It began to rain and Ted pulled his jacket around Veronica. She sat curled up miserably, listening to the cacophony on the streets gradually die away. It felt as if they clung to each other for hours like shipwreck survivors on a slippery log. The rain stopped and the wind picked up, then died away. A pigeon came to investigate his new neighbours but waddled away again after a momentary inspection apparently satisfied that these two bizarre and rather enormous interlopers posed no threat. Veronica tried to alter her position, to stretch her legs, as her muscles deadened with the cold and inactivity. Her leg shot from beneath her and she slipped down the roof a few inches before her heel caught in the iron guttering with a dull bang.

'Shit!' she said under her breath. She felt Ted reach down from the darkness and pull her back next to him. She was surprised at his strength.

'You okay?' he asked. She nodded but then spoke, realising that her gesture couldn't be seen in the dark.

'I'm fine,' she said. 'Well, stiff and cold actually.'

'We'll give it a few minutes then we'll go back inside. Okay?'

'Okay. I hope he didn't lock the window.'

'We'll soon find out.'

As they waited a new noise gradually replaced the burgeoning silence. It was a long, low groan, that took on its own form as it intensified, changing from a monotone to a reverberating, pulsating mass of sound. It came to them from high above and to the east. It was an evil sound.

'Bombers,' said Ted. The noise drew level with them and passed overhead before dissipating and fading to nothing. Ted and Veronica used the bomber's drone to cover the noise of their scramble to the window. The slippery roof tiles gave them little purchase but cursing seemed to help. Veronica pushed the window open and then let Ted help her back through to the safety of the flat.

He heard her fall on the floor with a painful-sounding thump.

'Oh fuck,' she said. She spent a few seconds rubbing an injured shin and then stood. 'Try not to hit the sink on the way in,' she advised. Ted smiled and hefted himself through the window like a cut-price gymnast. The soldiers had left the light on and Veronica looked around her as if assessing the damage they might have caused, or the goods they might have taken. Everything was as she had left it. She walked through to the kitchen, taking care to keep away from the window. Again, everything was as he'd left it. The only thing gone was Frank.

She turned. Ted was in the doorway watching her. He smiled and gave a shrug. The smile, she decided, was one of relief.

'Why did he help us, Ted?' she asked at last. They sat at either side of the table like two old friends.

'I've been thinking about that. Firstly, maybe he realised that we could have shot him, but didn't. Secondly – and this might well be the main reason – with us out of the way he can come up with a story to explain what happened to him. By that I mean a story that casts him in a better light.'

'You mean, not captured by a British lesbian?'

'Er… yeah. Something like that. He can say it was a gang of… I don't know exactly… deserters, or criminals, or something.'

'So, it wasn't just altruism, then?'

‘No definitely not,’ replied Ted, assuredly. Veronica gave him a look and then smirked.

‘What’s altruism?’ he asked.

Chapter Twenty-eight

They squeezed together into Veronica's bed. Space was tight; a move by one generally required a move by the other. When they finally slept their twists and turns became synchronised; choreographed slumber.

'Don't get any funny ideas, either Ted,' she warned.

'But you're a lesbian,' he countered. His brow was furrowed.

'Yes, but you're not,' she said. The ensuing silence lasted perhaps thirty seconds but was laden with thoughtful energy. Eventually Ted spoke again.

'That doesn't make sense,' he said.

'No. Do you have a girlfriend? Or a wife?'

'Are you offering?'

'No,' she said defiantly and poked him in the ribs.

'She's called Jean. She's in the RAF.'

'Wife or girlfriend?'

'Oh, I see. Girlfriend.'

'Pretty?'

'Very. Don't *you* get any ideas,' he said and she poked him in the ribs again.

'Are we safe here?'

'Safer than anywhere else. I can't imagine them coming back.'

'Unless Frank tells them about us,' she said, softly.

She felt Ted's whole body stiffen next to hers and then relax. 'He won't. We'd only make things awkward for him.'

Veronica nodded in the darkness.

'So, we just have to keep our heads down until tomorrow night?,' she asked.

'Yes. And get to the field.'

'Can you find the field again?'

'I think so.'

'You *think* so?'

'Yes.' He decided to clarify his meaning. 'Yes, I can find it.'

The town was more silent than it had ever been in its history and they slept soundly as if the world was at peace with itself. It was just after eight when they woke up. Ted had a bath and got dressed as Veronica made a final breakfast with her dwindling supply of food. The bread was dry but not mouldy. She smiled as she watched Ted chewing determinedly.

They had decided to leave at one o'clock, taking the back roads and cutting across fields. Their morning was filled with tension, fear and boredom. Now and again Veronica took a discreet peek out of the window to reassure herself that they were living in a ghost town. Nothing stirred apart from a gentle late-summer breeze, its effect heightened by a lack of competition from other sources. There was no traffic, there were no footsteps, no voices to be heard; just the breeze filtering through the roofs; a twisting ethereal snake that joined and parted invisibly and on a whim.

'And he'll definitely turn up?' She found herself talking very quietly, not quite a whisper. She felt as if the Germans knew that they'd left someone behind and even now were trying to detect them.

'John? He'll turn up. No doubt about it. There aren't many people I trust the way I trust him.'

***

At the same time John was standing quite forlorn, leaning against the little briefing hut used by the pilots near dispersal. His aircraft was there, fuelled up, armed and ready to go. All he lacked was someone to pick up – Ted. He'd known so many men lost in one way or another but this was different. He owed this one man so much, although Ted modestly insisted that it was the other way around, of course. John couldn't bear the thought of leaving Ted to his fate. If there was just one chance…

He imagined Ted undergoing torture and closed his eyes hoping to dispel that dreadful image. *How could they possibly know for sure that he had been captured?* The idea tormented him, gnawed at his sensibilities. A picture of Ted standing in the cold, dark field waiting in vain for his salvation, haunted him. He thought that it would probably haunt him forever. He wondered just how callous Ted's controllers were.

Behind him, he heard an engine cough into life and turned to see Embury in the cockpit of his Lysander. He hadn't expected him to be quite so keen to join the fight, especially since they weren't expected at any particular time.

John wondered if these fighter squadrons really wanted someone like him. From their perspective he might be seen as a liability, likely to waste a perfectly good aeroplane through his lack of experience in fighters. Embury had some hours in a Gladiator admittedly but John was a bomber pilot by training. He was no less skilled than a fighter pilot but those skills were different in nature. He had little experience of aerial gunnery for instance. He didn't doubt that he could master the controls of a Spitfire but it wasn't just a question of flying the aeroplane from A to B.

Seemingly from nowhere, the seed of an idea had dropped into the soil of his fertile imagination. It germinated and grew with astonishing speed. What if he landed at Middle Wallop with an unexpected passenger?

They *could* subject him to a court martial. *Would they do that to a holder of the VC? Did he even care?*

He watched Embury strap himself in. Two groundcrewmen scuttled about busily and then backed off. He heard the engine note change, take on a deeper timbre but had decided not to watch the take-off. His mind was already elsewhere working out the practicalities of his flight to that field in France.

It would be fraught with difficulty and he knew that both sides were trying to get effective night fighters into the battle. He was almost as likely to be shot down by his own side as by the Luftwaffe. The worst part of his flight would be finding the field and then landing but that had never promised to be easy under any circumstances. Pulling that feat off was no more difficult now that it was illicit.

He straightened up and began to walk back to the control tower. The map room was situated on the ground floor. On the way he passed Aircraftsman Brown.

'I got that Jerry you know, Flight.'

'I heard. Well done. Just be careful they don't try to get you into bombers as a gunner,' joked John. It wasn't much of a joke insofar as he meant every word.

'Well, I've already volunteered. I start my training next month.'

The boy looked so happy but John felt the urge to warn him about his life expectancy once he climbed into that turret for raids over Germany. Instead he said, 'well done. You'll do a great job.' It sounded like the preface to an obituary.

***

He scanned the shelves in the map room looking for charts of Northern France, then selected the appropriate roll and slid it out. He felt like some sort of amateurish spy who was bound to be caught. A corporal with two white mugs held before him looked in briefly and smiled before continuing his journey up the tower. *Perhaps a pilot looking at a map was not so suspicious after all…*

He unrolled the map on the table and placed a sheet of Perspex over the top to keep it flat. In his mind he could translate the lines and symbols into landmarks and features, stretching two dimensions into three. It was a genuine gift and particularly useful to a pilot charged with this type of work. Where another man might methodically work his way through the seemingly jumbled mass of information on the map, John could see valleys, hills, rivers, forests, roads, towns, villages as an entire, flowing entity. He could take his mind's eye in any direction, stimulated solely by the map and *see* the land, its colours and shapes. He picked out the area he needed almost at once and remembered his approach from his last foray across the channel.

John decided he would set off in late evening. He wanted some daylight to assess the actual situation he was flying into. His mood had lifted and his appetite had returned. He could live with failure knowing that he had tried. Conversely, he couldn't stomach the idea of not trying at all.

He wondered if the little cookhouse still had some grub…

Chapter Twenty-nine

'Ready?' Veronica smiled weakly but nodded. Her actions were dictated both by resolve and by a lack of alternatives; they had to flee. 'Right, let's go.'

Ted opened the door a crack and looked out into the street. They had decided that a brazen approach, nonchalant and confident, would not work for them on this occasion. By rights they should be in German custody so there was no way they could simply stroll out with an air of disregard. They couldn't act as if they were catching the bus or going to work or for a walk… they simply shouldn't be at large and therefore had to keep hidden.

The street was deserted. An already depleted population had been finished off completely the previous night. Veronica felt as if she was walking through the final act of some silent apocalypse. Their footsteps resonated unchallenged off the walls that lined their escape route. Everything about them was out of place in this new eerie world. The smells of the town were noticeable by their dramatic absence but the birds sang cautiously. Perhaps they sang in German now, or at least included a few German bird hits in their repertoire. From the small park they heard a cuckoo, an incongruously cheery noise.

The streets were strewn with personal belongings discarded by terrified residents. Ted shook his head, sadly. Dolls dropped by little girls, wooden toys dropped by boys. He wondered if they were separated from their parents. The Germans had little apparent compassion in their dealings with the residents of Belloire. Each was guilty by association with a man they had actually never met.

This would make up the main thrust of his debriefing, if this was how the Germans reacted to the death of one soldier, then missions of this sort were simply not worth the bother. It wasn't fair to leave innocent French civilians at the mercy of vengeful Nazis. All that was before you even took into the account the fact that the mission had been a spectacular failure. Furthermore, they were unlikely to be able to create the so-called 'safehouses' they would need in future or to recruit fighters from within the population. British agents would be unwelcome in France, where they would probably be viewed as harbingers of German retribution. If it was an occupied Britain being infiltrated by French men coming to 'help,' they wouldn't be tolerated for long.

Across the road, a little dog of some indeterminate type sat and watched them skulking through the streets. Veronica thought him quite appealing, sad and lonely as he was. In a sense he summed up everything that was wrong with the world in general and with Belloire in particular. He was vulnerable and innocent. The dog was a victim of war or it would be if it didn't get fed.

'C'mon,' said Ted, quietly. Their footsteps were as light as they could make them. It wasn't long before Veronica had assumed the lead and took them through dark side streets and silent back alleys. The only real obstacles were cats *in* bins or cats waiting *next to* bins. The cobbles were dry now after the night's rain and the sun was beating down on them, its heat oppressive. Ted felt a film of perspiration form on his brow.

When they reached the edge of the town, Veronica paused as if she wanted to say goodbye to her old life. She looked at Ted, frowned and said, 'let's get out of here.'

Ahead of them lay the road Ted had come in on but it offered them no concealment and they at once made their way into a little copse that edged the first two hundred yards of tarmac. A path mined with tangled roots led straight down its centre and they were able to increase their speed to reach the open field beyond.

'Not much cover. We could easily be seen if anyone comes,' remarked Ted.

'Well, you're a soldier. How would you normally get across?' asked Veronica.

'Crawl.'

'I'm not bloody crawling through that.'

'I wasn't saying you should. You asked me how…'

'Okay, Ted. You're right but it's a long way to crawl.'

'Precisely. We'll walk. If we hear anyone we'll duck down in the grass. When they've gone, we'll walk some more.'

'Is the grass long enough?'

'It'll have to be. There's no other way of doing it. Don't forget no-one's *actually* looking for us. That makes a difference.'

Myriad unseen animals scattered, running for safety as they made their clumsy human passage through the ankle-deep grass. To their far right Ted saw a hare, immobile but alert, watching them with curiosity and wariness. He wondered if his field craft training all those years ago had been designed following a study of woodland animals. Animals were unwitting masters of camouflage and concealment, applying all the rules superbly without even knowing that they were doing so. Rabbit and hares were experts at evasion and camouflage. Hedgehogs and badgers wisely used the cover of night for their activities. It was survival of the fittest. *Where had he learned that phrase?*

In front there was another field, this one populated by cows. The grass was much shorter as a result of their monotonous attentions.

'These'll need to be milked,' said Veronica, casting a glance in the cows' direction before crawling through the fence.

'I don't think we'll have time,' quipped Ted. Veronica shook her head in mock exasperation.

'Come on,' she said, striking out across the field. The cows backed off at their approach, taking short, hollow steps that thudded percussively on the ground. This field had a slight rise and at its crest another fence. Either side of the fence was an elongated mire, a coagulated broth of mud and cow shit. 'I'm not crawling through that,' commented Veronica with disgust.

'It'll hardly be the first time you've been in the shit.'

'I don't care. I'm not doing it.' She seemed not to appreciate the joke.

'Well, what are you going to do? Pole vault?'

'I'll go round it.'

'There's miles of it. It's like a lagoon of…'

‘Okay. I’ll do it.’ Veronica set off and immediately sank to her mid shin. ‘Oh Christ!’ she exclaimed but kept going, reaching the fence seconds later. ‘I hope I’m allowed on this plane of yours smelling like this,’ she said over her shoulder as she scrambled under. Ted laughed and followed her. From their new vantage point they could see an isolated hill upon which had been built a castle or monastery that sat like an untidy crown.

‘Who lives there?’ he asked but her reply was shrug. ‘That looks like our field,’ he said pointing.

‘Don’t you remember that building then?’

‘Too dark. I couldn’t see a thing. That’s the field though. I can see the junction on the road and the signpost.’ He paused. ‘In fact, I remember that horse.’ A black horse stood in the far left corner of the field, its back turned as if it was counting to ten whilst another horse hid.

‘You remember the horse?’

‘It led me out of the field.’ She looked at him sceptically. ‘It’s a long story. Shall we go?’

They stood in unison and made their way in a diagonal to the hedge and stubby wall.

He examined it carefully, exploiting the daylight.

‘I see,’ he said as if great wisdom had been foisted upon him.

‘See what?’

‘This flamin’ wall. I fell over it in the dark. It’s the remains of an old hut or barn or something.’

'This is definitely the right field then?'

'Definitely. We just need to make ourselves comfy and wait.'

'And hope that this pilot can find the field as easily as you did.'

'Have faith,' said Ted. He sat on the slight bank in front of the hedge.

'And what time is he coming?'

'When it's getting dark. He needs a bit of light but not too much. Probably nine o'clock or so.'

'So, we wait?'

'We wait. We should have brought a picnic.'

'Is that what soldiers do when they're on manoeuvres – bring a picnic?' Her tone was mocking. He supposed that she felt a little bit more relaxed now, closer to safety.

'Yeah. Little sandwiches, lemonade, strawberries, that sort of thing. I remember someone once forgot to bring the picnic rug. Disaster.'

Chapter Thirty

John did all his pre-flight checks and then did them again.

'Old pilots and bold pilots, eh?' John turned to see the smiling face of Sergeant Donaldson at his shoulder. Donaldson was from Belfast and spoke just like Ted, with the same lilting humour and dead pan delivery of sarcastic put downs, of which he appeared to have an inexhaustible supply. He was also a good mechanic and an old-fashioned NCO of the regular RAF. John imagined that he'd be a Station Warrant Officer before too long.

'Yeah. Sam – just so that you know – I want to be one of the old pilots.'

'An increasingly rare breed mate.'

'Don't say that!' exclaimed John, only half joking. Donaldson shook his head in dismay.

'Sorry. It's a bit too close to home for you.'

'Off to Wallop later. What about you?'

'Wallop. That's why I came over, actually. Wondered if I could cadge a lift?'

John was taken aback. He tried to think of a lie but nothing came to him.

'Er, em I can't, Sam.'

'Regulations?'

'No, not that.'

'Okay. Just thought I'd ask.' The sergeant looked slightly put out as he climbed down from the undercarriage. John felt the need to explain.

'I'm not going there directly. I have to pick someone else up on the way.'

'Fair enough, John. I'll see you there.' Donaldson turned on his heel, walked a few paces, then stopped. He turned again. John smiled.

'On the way? There is nowhere 'on the way' between here and Middle Wallop.'

'When I said on the way I meant…'

'You meant?'

'France,' said John, plainly. He tried to sound matter-of-fact. He looked around guiltily lest anyone should overhear their conversation. Donaldson's mouth fell open and then shut again with an almost audible snap.

'France? Fer God's sake, man. You can't go there. What are you talking about?'

'I was supposed to be picking someone up tonight but the sortie was cancelled.'

'Well, there you go. Why was it cancelled, did they tell you?'

'Yeah.'

'And…'

'He's been captured.'

'Captured?'

'That's what they say. He might not be.'

'If he's captured, he's captured John. There's no point.'

'Well, I'm going anyway. I'd appreciate it if you said nothing about it.'

'John, they'll hang you out to dry. That's if you even come back.'

'I don't care. Besides they won't even know.'

'How can they not know?'

'I'll just land at Wallop as planned after I've got him. If I don't get him, I'll still land at Wallop. Who's going to know I've been to France?'

'They're going to know if you bring him back, aren't they?'

'Obviously if I bring him back but they can't exactly say much, can they? If I rescue their top agent, they'll look a bit stupid court-martialling me.'

Donaldson raised his eyebrows. 'Well, I think you're mad but I won't say anything.'

'Good man. I'll see you tomorrow. I'll tell you about it over breakfast.'

'Yeah okay. I'll come to your cell.' With that Donaldson walked off. John looked at his watch. He had hours to go before he set off. He hated waiting. Everything between now and then was just dead time. He could try to read or sign for a car from MT and go for a drive in the sunshine. Neither idea appealed. He looked again at the aircraft. There was nothing more to be done.

High above him vapour trails like ethereal fireworks criss-crossed the sky. He would soon be part of that battle.

He tried to imagine himself up there at the controls of a Spitfire. He felt doomed. Survival seemed like an abstract idea at times like these. He was deep in the emotional abyss that preceded a sortie. His dread prior to take off was of much greater duration than the elation he felt upon landing – an unfair trade-off. If it was battle of attrition, with his nerves acting as casualties, then he was losing. Only a swift end to hostilities, or at least his active participation in them, seemed to offer him the chance of surviving intact.

He slept, fully clothed, for half an hour, woke briefly, decided to get up and then went back to sleep. When next he woke, he felt as if someone had poured stale coffee into his mouth. He felt the beginnings of a headache and his eyes were raw and sore. He swallowed hard. After a few seconds, during which his brain adjusted itself to the possibility of protracted movement, he began to stretch, starting with his arms and working his way down until he finally waggled his feet. He yawned again, realising that he could easily go back to sleep. Instead, he rose and padded to the bathroom which he shared with some of the other NCO's. He splashed cold water in his face and examined his reflection. John decided that he looked… unremarkable.

The sergeant cook smiled at him as he joined the short queue for tea. From behind a steaming pot of boiled potatoes he said, 'thought you'd gone already, John.'

'Nah, not yet. Didn't want to miss your cooking, Ed.'

'Well, that's understandable. Venison tonight.'

'Venison?'

'No. Pork. But if you close your eyes...'

'You could have got away with that. I don't know what venison tastes like.'

'Not like pork,' assured the cook.

He shuffled forwards in the queue as if he was attached to the man in front with shackles. Only once their meal was completely assembled did the men seem to break free of each other. Another cook, who looked as if he cooked but never ate, slapped a lank piece of pork onto his plate. It was the worst cut of meat either of them had ever seen; mainly gristle and fat, with thin streaks of pale meat running through it like a token effort at nutrition.

'Did the autopsy give you any clues as to what this pig died of?' he asked the cook.

'Hunnh?' said the cook in reply.

'That's *hunnh Flight*, to you,' corrected John. The warrant officer behind him in the queue tittered.

'It was bred in Germany to sabotage the British war effort,' he suggested. The emaciated cook looked on, seemingly without comprehension.

'Are you Polish or something?' asked John. The warrant officer laughed again.

'Hunnh?'

'For fuck's sake,' said John moving on and having lumpy gravy splashed onto his plate. The next cook offered him carrots. 'No, you're spoiling me. I couldn't.'

He took his seat on a bench and the warrant officer sat next to him.

'Remember when you were a young airman and didn't dare criticize the food?'

'Yeah. Just making trouble for yourself really,' said John. The memory was not a fond one.

'Are you off to Biggin then?

'No. Middle Wallop.'

'They're taking a hell of a pasting,' said the warrant officer. He was hacking at his meat with a blunt knife. He accidentally catapulted a piece of carrot off his plate like a tiny discus.

'You'll have someone's eye out,' said John. 'What about you? Are you being sent somewhere?'

'Dunno. Stores bods like me are ten-a-penny. I'll get sent somewhere eventually, I expect. Rumour is that this little operation is being shut down.'

'Who told you that?'

'Just what I heard. We get gossip as well as supplies.'

'Permanently shut down?'

'So I heard. Too dangerous. You were supposed to be dropping agents into Europe but they're not bothering with that sort of thing now. Winding it all up… that's what I heard.' The WO continued with his meal as if it tasted nice.

John tried to make this new information fit with what he knew and yet it did not make complete sense. As far as he was aware they had only sent one man across – Ted – and even if he had been captured was that really any reason to abandon the whole operation? Abandon it all after the first set-back? Perhaps it was reason enough in someone's view.

In any case there was one last task to perform before the metaphorical plug was pulled. He finished his meal with the disconcerting thought that somehow Ted had been betrayed by the very people in whom he needed to trust. But if Ted was there, waiting for him in that field, then he would get him home.

Chapter Thirty-one

'I'm starving,' said Ted. His stomach rumbled as if to prove the veracity of his claim. Veronica said nothing. She looked ahead of her, across the expanse of field. Cows wandered aimlessly, feeding according to their relentless routine, suiting themselves and expecting in their own vague bovine way to be milked. Their discomfort was not yet apparent.

Ted tried to gauge Veronica's feelings but her face betrayed no emotion, hinted at nothing. If she was depressed or scared or generally disappointed by life he could not say.

'You okay?' he asked finally.

'Bored,' she said.

'Ah.' Ted took up the mantle of silence she had laid down. The air was still and warm. The birds sang languidly but without any determination to produce great music or to bring cheer.

'Are you hungry?'

'I suppose so.'

'You'll have your next meal in England,' he said. He hoped that it might lift her spirits but she seemed unmoved as if his words were deceit. Ted scanned the skies without any realistic expectation of seeing John's aircraft. 'Steak and potatoes.'

'What?'

'That's what I'd like to eat – steak and potatoes. And gravy.'

‘Sounds good,’ she said without any enthusiasm. He wasn’t managing to engender a sense of detachment from their predicament.

Ted puffed out his cheeks and exhaled heavily. He couldn’t force her to be cheerful and he didn’t really blame her for not being so. She seemed to lack conviction when it came to John’s impending rescue mission. Somehow, she seemed to be missing the vital spark. Ted wondered if the problem lay in her sudden inactivity after a period of fraught and frenzied struggle. Was it an acute sense of anti-climax?

‘What’s wrong?’

‘Nothing.’ Ted gave her a disbelieving look. ‘Okay. I have a sense of foreboding.’

‘Foreboding? As in, you think something bad is going to happen?’

‘I suppose so. I don’t know what – probably nothing. I’m not a psychic or anything.’ She smiled sadly. ‘Just ignore me Ted.’ As she spoke, they both glanced over at the road, their attention drawn to a distant noise. It was an imperceptible buzz, unthreatening and yet out of place. Not one vehicle had been on that road all day long. No-one was going to Belloire. News, particularly bad news, obviously travelled fast. An outbreak of the plague could hardly have guaranteed the town’s isolation better. The noise continued to grow, from a buzz to a rumble, a rumble to a roar, albeit a muted one.

The truck pulled to a halt adjacent to their hiding place in the field. Ted and Veronica crouched down and then slid to the ground, their bellies tight to the grass.

'Shit,' said Ted. Veronica's eyes were wide as if she was screaming inside. Ted was just as terrified but kept his features a mask. He had his limits too and he reached them more readily than anyone back in Britain suspected. His capacity for heroism was both finite and readily attainable.

The truck appeared monstrous in comparison to the other vehicles in German service, with three axles and a heavy box body. It was painted uniform grey, with German crosses on each door. Two soldiers sat in the cab and seemed reluctant to step down onto the road. One of them stifled a yawn.

'What are they doing?' hissed Veronica.

'God knows. Just get ready to scarper,' advised Ted. The vehicle's engine continued to run and Ted hoped that this indicated an impending move. There was no obvious reason for them to have stopped where they did and they certainly weren't caught up in the traffic. 'I wish they'd fuck off,' said Ted to himself as he peered through a tuft of grass. The driver looked bored, the passenger... well, he couldn't make him out too well. He was just a presence like a shadow, sitting in the passenger seat. As he watched, the window was wound down and the driver flicked a cigarette onto the road. He checked his watch and looked over at his passenger expectantly. Ted could just discern a nod from the other man and then both doors opened – Ted could see right through the truck to the hedge beyond.

Both men jumped heavily to the ground. Next to him, Ted felt Veronica tense and reach for the gun she had in her pockets. Her composure, it seemed, had returned. She was ready for a fight.

Ted held her arm gently and whispered to her. 'We don't want to shoot these two if we can avoid it. Having that truck stranded by the side of the road is going to attract the wrong sort of attention.'

She nodded her understanding. The two men were in no obvious hurry. They chatted and one of them kicked idly at a stone. Neither wore a helmet or cap. Their blond hair seemed to shine in the fading sunlight. Ted watched their every move, trying to glean some understanding of their purpose. They were waiting but for what? And why here? There was nothing obviously special about this spot. One of the men – they could actually have been twins from this distance – stretched his arms above his head. He lowered his arms again, let his head sink forward, then drew it back and wiggled it from side to side as if performing some sort of athletic warm-up. His companion spoke, the words carried as an indistinct mumble on the breeze. He nodded, reached into the cab and withdrew an MP38 submachine gun. For the first time Ted realised that the other soldier was armed with a pistol. Each of them now held what looked like a little white bag in their hands.

Veronica had moved next to Ted and was perplexedly watching this strange, almost ritualistic behaviour. She and Ted exchanged looks, the latter shrugging and pulling a face. The immediate threat seemed to have receded as far as they were concerned; the German soldiers were more interested in whatever they had brought with them in the vehicle. They paced slowly to the rear of the truck and then placed the little bags over their faces. Now Ted and Veronica could see that they were face masks, perhaps of the type that a surgeon might wear.

Ted was intrigued. There was another pause. The soldiers spoke again and this time one stepped back as the other stepped forwards. The first soldier cocked his MP38 and stood ready as the second reached for a door on the box body. He spent a moment unfastening a lock, then swung the door open and jumped clear. A cloud of grey-black smoke belched from the doorway, coils of sooty gas emerging in a puffy explosion. Both soldiers backed off now, ten yards clear of the truck and almost out of Ted's line of sight. Again, they waited.

Ted diverted his attention from the little drama being played out before him. He scanned the skies, looked at the clouds, the position of the sun and then stole a glance at his watch. He wasn't expecting John yet but soon. *How precise would his timings be*, he wondered? *What variables impacted upon a flight of this type?* If he did show up now, they were trapped; he wasn't going to land in a field next to a small detachment of the Wehrmacht.

The skies were clear. Nothing moved and nothing could be heard above the noise of the truck's engine. Ted brought his gaze back to the vehicle once more. Both soldiers still stood back and both retained their masks, clamped protectively over their faces. Gas poured from the box body in a steady stream. Ted and Veronica both picked up the scent in the air, petrol fumes.

Veronica wrinkled her nose distastefully. Then one of the soldiers walked back to the cab, giving the truck a wide berth as he did so. Upon reaching the cab he climbed in and switched off the engine, which shuddered to a halt. The ensuing silence was profound.

Switching off the engine was an emphatic gesture. It signified the beginning of the next stage of whatever little operation these two men were engaged in. Ted shook his head again in complete bafflement. Maybe two minutes passed and the smoke issuing forth from the truck began to thin, then subside. Straggly remnants of the dirty-looking gas drifted away on the warm breeze and then the soldiers approached the truck once again. The soldier with the pistol climbed warily into the box body and was out of sight for a minute. The other soldier craned his neck to see inside but kept his distance. Moments later the other soldier re-appeared, backing out of the truck and dragging something heavy behind him. He left the object on the edge of the doorway, gingerly climbed over it and jumped down to the road. The soldiers finally removed their masks. The first soldier began to drag the object again, sharp forceful tugs requiring some effort, until it fell onto the road with a sickening thud.

'Oh, my good God,' said Ted in disbelief.

Chapter Thirty-two

John took a last look around before he started up the Lysander's engine. He hoped that his movements hadn't been too furtive… not that it would matter soon. He knew he was doing the right thing, which didn't necessarily mean that his bosses would concur. He didn't care. If they could be bothered to court-martial him then he would be grounded. *Fine*, he thought; grounded pilots didn't get shot down. He checked all the instruments arrayed before him. The story they told was of a perfectly functioning aeroplane.

He moved the controls and visually checked that flaps and rudder responded as they should, just another clean bill of health. He increased the revs and taxied forward, watched by a small sending-off committee of groundcrew, none of whom had any idea about the nature of this flight, or of his surprising destination. Moments later, he lifted into the air and eased the Lysander up to two thousand feet. John had the sky to himself as the sun began to drop below the horizon. Altitude gave him a few more minutes of light and he knew he'd be at his landing zone in twenty minutes. It was quite straightforward really.

He cruised at one hundred and eighty knots for several minutes, scanning the skies for night fighters until the coast of Dover fell away far beneath. John scanned the skies one last time before pulling the canopy closed. A flotilla of MTBs sped for Britain leaving long white trails in the sea, each one a watery scar that would heal in minutes. John imagined their gunners straining in the gloom for a proper look at his aircraft and wondering whether or not to send a few shells his way. He was a target of opportunity for bored AA gunners.

John steered a course that took him round the channel ports of Dunkirk, Calais and Boulogne. These were the embarkation areas for the anticipated invasion of Britain and would be well defended against air attack. He didn't expect to encounter any single-seat fighters at this hour; they flew in daylight as a rule. He was minutes away now and began his descent.

John matched up the ground with the folded map on his knee, picking out the hills near the border with Belgium. The city of Lille soon came into view, two dimensions laid out in a random configuration of streets and squares, church steeples reaching forlornly for a salvation that had already slipped through their grasp. The lower his approach the more defined the city became, until it took on its third dimension with a haphazard array of roofs and spires giving shape to the roads and avenues. Soon he was able to pick up the hamlet of Belloire. From the air it looked like a piece of the city, broken off and forgotten about, having floated away on a grass-green sea.

He looked for landmarks and then his doubts came crashing in. A deluge of doubt and self-recrimination assailed his being and with sudden clarity he knew he'd made a mistake. This was a fool's errand and he suddenly doubted his ability to recover or to undo the mistake he had made. The Germans had let him stray into what was now their airspace using the last vestiges of daylight but he didn't expect them to let him back out with such ease. *What sort of arrogance had taken hold of him? What made him think he knew better than his superiors?*

But since he was here, he decided to make a sweep of the field. Then he could return. He'd touch down at Middle Wallop and no-one would know the difference.

The field was there were he'd left it and he fancied that he could see the long indentations from his previous landing. What he couldn't see was any trace of Ted. The matter was decided. On the road, he spotted the truck and saw two figures running for cover. Both men dived into the roadside ditch just as John swept over the road. He pulled the aircraft up and began a banking turn, hoping that the soldiers didn't regain their composure sufficiently to open fire. He kicked the rudder round and the Lysander pulled a tight turn, maybe two hundred feet above the ground. The fence and the road blurred and merged for a moment and then he straightened out, climbing and heading back to Britain.

***

Ted watched as the Germans kicked the body into the ditch. They seemed to debate a further course of action for a few seconds, one of them pointing to the field. Ted imagined they were discussing how to conceal a body in the way which required the least effort. The laziest option seemed to prevail; they left it there, barely hidden at all. He caught sight of Veronica's face in the encroaching gloom, her horror undisguised. He squeezed her shoulder reassuringly and she smiled weakly, tears rolling from the corners of her eyes. She kept her gaze fixed on the scene, as if she had resolved to become the best possible witness to this crime. Perhaps she had some future retribution in mind.

Ted looked back to the truck, hoping that they had finished and would now return to camp to wash the blood from their hands… but to his horror the same soldier began to pull another body from the back. This corpse, recognisably that of a man in a suit, suffered the same unceremonious treatment as the first. This macabre cameo was played out one last time and then the soldiers closed the box body up and strolled to the cab. Simultaneously Ted heard the sound of an aircraft and grimaced. *Not now*, he thought, desperately. The Germans heard it too and ran, diving into the ditch just a few feet away from their recently abandoned victims. Ted turned to lie on his back and saw the peculiar shape of John's aircraft sweep overhead. The Lysander's wings in outline resembled two huge coffins.

He tried to plan his response to this development. How did he make his presence known to John without also alerting the German soldiers?

He glanced in their direction but they were keeping their heads low. As he watched, the Lysander banked, turned and was clearly now beating a path for home. With salvation slipping from his grasp he knew he had to act, to take the chance. The big plane was a hundred and fifty yards away, climbing, its engine working hard. He stood and waved but John swept overhead. Ted rocked slightly in the aircraft's wake and cursed for he knew that his friend had missed him. One of the German soldiers stood and even in the fading greys of the day he could see his mouth agape. The soldier fumbled with his holster and withdrew a Luger.

He seemed to pause as if willing himself to believe that his crime had been discovered and that he needed to react. He pulled on the pistol's complex slide mechanism and took rough aim. Ted fell to the ground, out of sight and reached for his own weapon. Veronica had the other Walther in her hand and a look that said she was ready for a fight.

The first nine-millimetre bullet cracked somewhere above their heads. A moment later it was followed by another. The shooting was hopeful-hopeless in nature; a warning or practice. Most soldiers were poor pistol shots and Ted was thankful for that fact. Thankful too that he wasn't. The second soldier began to open fire now, a ragged stream of machine gun bullets slicing the air but hitting nothing. Ted pressed himself into the ground, an arm around Veronica. Inside he was crushed but he found the strength to maintain some aspect of the struggle. If he could even help Veronica to escape, then the equation of this fruitless expedition would be balanced, except for the three dead Frenchmen gassed and dumped at the side of the road. How much horror did one man have to witness before his debts were paid, he wondered?

There was no need for stealth now. 'You start crawling out of here,' he said. For a moment he felt like a proper soldier again, giving orders and expecting them to be carried out. 'I'll take care of these two. You'll have to find somewhere to live and just keep your head down,' he added. He was aware of the fact that his advice was vague, obvious in nature and essentially pointless, both in the giving and the receipt. There were so few options available to either of them that they would take whatever path presented itself.

'What about you, Ted?' she said desperately. Another bullet cracked. Ted thought he heard heavy footfalls resonating through the clay. He lifted his head but saw nothing to indicate this being the case. The two German soldiers seemed to be staying put.

'I'll be fine. You get…'

'Ted!' She looked in his direction. He was lining up the sights on the pistol, aiming for their adversaries. 'Ted!' she shouted again.

'What?' he snapped. 'You should be…'

'He's coming back. The plane is coming back.'

He fired his shot and rolled onto his back in one swift movement. Exactly as Veronica had said, the Lysander was closing in.

'He saw us!' he yelled above the noise.

***

John only had a rough aim with the two machine guns mounted in the wheel spats; more than that, he had no practice at ground strafing. He'd ordered the armourers to load the guns almost as an afterthought but was glad of his unintentional foresight. Twin lines of grit seemed to spring from the ground as his bullets struck, as if two lines of buried cord were being ripped from the soil. He released the fire button too soon to hit his target and climbed for another pass. The Germans took advantage of the interval in John's assault, regaining their feet and running for the truck.

***

Ted snapped off an opportunist shot which plucked the grass behind one of the soldier's heels and followed this up with another. The second shot was a hopeless effort, released with the precision of a Hollywood gangster but the bullet hit the soldier in the small of the back, nevertheless. He collapsed with his arms thrown in the air, dead before he hit the deck. His mate paused, undecided, torn between the illusory safety of the truck and the rather more substantial safety of the ditch. He began to re-trace his steps, his face etched with panic and indecision.

Ted watched as the Lysander grew in size, closing in on the hapless soldier like an immense owl sweeping down to pluck a field mouse from the security of the grass. The first volley hit the truck, the next spewed up the ground as before, tearing it open with precise pinpoints of metal. The German turned to see his avian tormentor and looked set to throw himself to the ground until a bullet ruptured his right thigh and another caught his ribs. In a violent spray of blood, he fell to the ground. Ted watched him lift his head as if looking for help. Slowly it sank back down until he was face first in the grass and quite dead.

'C'mon,' said Ted, pulling Veronica to her feet. She was next to him in an instant but dazed by the violence of those few seconds; too dazed to be horrified yet. They watched in silence as the plane wheeled round and came in low, seeming to hop over the hedge that marked the field's boundary. Clear of that obstacle the bulky aircraft appeared to sink onto the ground, the wheels throwing up twin jets of soil, the engine note changing. The tail swung from side to side as John slowed the heavy machine with huge flaps that defiled its aerodynamic characteristics. He trundled along until he was next to Ted, the plane towering over his passengers.

The canopy swept back. 'Taxi for Dexter?' he shouted before reaching into the back and throwing down a rope ladder. Ted shouted up, 'room for another passenger? Said I'd drop her off on the way.'

'Bit of a squeeze in there, but she's more than welcome.' Ted assisted Veronica up the ladder, the draught from the aircraft's huge prop blowing their hair and jacket tails about as if they were caught in a gale. Unavoidably and ungallantly he pushed her upwards, a hand on each buttock and she scrambled almost headfirst into the cabin. Ted gave France a last look and followed her, pulling the rope ladder in after him. Immediately, they lurched away. John could feel the extra weight affecting the dynamics of the Lysander. The ballast of his two passengers made the plane feel sluggish.

He taxied hastily to the furthest extent of the field for his take-off run. The Lysander swung round as if propelled by unseen hands and then drove forwards with a roar, the propeller dragging them into the air. Ted glanced at Veronica in the sparse remaining light. Her eyes glistened with excitement and relief. She reached out and clasped his hand in hers.

Chapter Thirty-three

Churchill was glum. He was tired too. There were times when he doubted his capacity for prosecuting this war. He certainly didn't have youth on his side and there were plenty of occasions when this fact manifested itself all too clearly: aches, pains, doubts, weariness… they all played their part.

Determination was one thing, but without the energy to translate determination into action, all was lost. The one thing about which he had no doubts was that he was still the right man to lead the country. He had been born for this struggle. In a battle of good versus evil, he was happy to lead the side of virtue, to be its figurehead. History would judge him favourably, regardless of this war's outcome. Everything that had gone before, the mistakes, the errors of judgement, the criticism, as well as the moments of triumph, were simply preparation for this, the greatest conflict of them all. He had made mistakes but learnt from them.

They – the British people – had faced these same foes just a generation ago, of course, but in the Great War the German regime was not in the thrall of such unadulterated evil as it was now. His job had never been more vital. The disparity between good and evil had never been greater. Winston Churchill represented many things: Britishness, honesty, martial spirit but more than that he represented freedom. This was his destiny but it was also a tremendous burden and never more so than now.

He had turned the disaster of Dunkirk into the 'miracle of Dunkirk,' using his greatest gift, his greatest weapon – the spoken word. He had united the nation in its determination to prevail, again using rhetoric, the one thing he had in great supply. He was urging the air force on to ever greater efforts – and sacrifices – to defeat the Luftwaffe. Time would tell if their epic stand was a prelude to defeat, or a springboard to victory. Valour was useless without the actual weapons needed to fight. Pilots, the most complex component in the fighter plane, were running out. The RAF was being bled dry and yet hope was not lost.

But what really discouraged the PM was the loss of Ted Dexter. Ted, that ordinary man, was responsible for taking the fight to the Nazis. There would be other men, following in his wake but he was the original, the blueprint. For the PM he had a talismanic property, as if he had gained strength from being able to invest so much in a man so ordinary. Ted was special, simply because he was nothing special. He was born with one great gift – that of being British. If Ted could fight the Germans single-handedly then there was no stopping the British people collectively. He symbolised the struggle between good and evil.

Ted was good but not perfect and that somehow made his part in the conflict all the more effective.

The hairs on the back of his neck stood as he thought about his secret hero. But now he was gone and his secret with him.

He felt bereft. He had pinned so many hopes on Ted Dexter, unrealistic hopes. He was the man sent to do the things that Churchill himself would have done had he been much younger. His mission to kill the German officer who had ordered the murder of a platoon of British soldiers was a challenge to the forces of evil, the throwing down of a gauntlet. He was telling Herr Hitler that actions like this wouldn't be tolerated, that good would prevail as night follows day. And yet what was he to read into the message he had been sent in return? He couldn't afford to be superstitious and yet this was a bad omen. The country needed victories, no matter how small. He had summoned Hugh Dalton, General Brooke and Brigadier Murray. They needed to bring him ideas, good news and hope.

Brooke was the first to appear and was shown into the PM's study by a butler. Brooke was entrusted with the task of defending Britain against the forthcoming invasion. He was one of the few generals who inspired confidence in the PM but his duties were undoubtedly onerous. Churchill dispensed with preamble. Niceties could wait.

'The black dog of depression, General. It is the cross which I must bear,' he began. He pointed to a chair and Brooke sat. The PM's glass was empty and there was just the faintest whiff of cigar smoke. It was as if he had decided that even those comforts couldn't hit the mark such was the quality of his despondency. 'I expect that you will have heard the fate of young Corporal Dexter?'

'I have sir. You must be disappointed.'

'And saddened. I believe he had a girlfriend. We're not supposed to know that,' he said and chuckled. 'I pinned a lot of hopes on that young man. Silly of me really.' Brooke looked at the PM. At times like this he seemed old. The public never saw him being anything other than defiant. They never heard talk about anything other than his belief in eventual victory. Brooke knew that in part it was an act; but only in part. He would get over it.

'I think that you are something of a traditionalist, General,' continued the PM. Brooke smiled affably. 'I don't suppose you totally approved of Corporal Dexter.'

'Well, I... I'm not sure about this type of thing, sir.' He paused. The PM didn't look up. 'There's a theory about the Irish. Maybe it's a joke really. It's that for an entertaining night out, drinking and carousing you would be wise to choose a Southern Irishman for company. But for someone to watch your house while you were out, you should choose a Northern Irishman.'

Churchill nodded and then chuckled again. He couldn't quite picture the rather stern Brooke being an expert on the subject of carousing.

'And your point is?' asked the PM.

For a moment Brooke had lost his train of thought. *What was his point?* He felt like he was about to contradict himself.

'My point is that it is a grave over-simplification.'

'So, I would be unwise to trust Dexter to guard my home?'

'You put a lot of faith in him. He was just a junior NCO. We dragged him out of a cell to bring him to you, if you recall. He'd assaulted a civilian.'

'I was under the impression that the civilian in question rather deserved it.' Brooke was about to reply when Dalton and Murray were shown in. They sat next to the General and were welcomed by Churchill.

***

The Lysander taxied to a halt and John shut off the engine, leaving a disturbing silence. The airfield was dark and to all intents and purposes, lifeless. It was difficult to reconcile this huge patch of nothingness with its function as a busy fighter base in the front line of a battle which would determine the future of Europe or possibly even the world. John helped his passengers clamber down onto the spongy grass.

'You're home, Ted,' he said.

'You're sure this isn't France?' said Ted from the darkness. Both men laughed having shared this concern the last time they had returned from that country; *what if John flew in the wrong direction and merely landed elsewhere in Hitler's empire? What if they were, in fact, further from safety?*

'Definitely England. Middle Wallop, to be precise,' assured John. 'Who is our guest?' They began to climb down from the lofty plane.

'I'm Veronica,' came the reply from the darkness. John could only see an indistinct outline of the woman who spoke. 'I helped Ted escape,' she continued without any attempt at modesty.

'It's true. She did. Shall we try to find signs of life?' They began walking to a series of hangars that boxed in one corner of the airfield but paused as they saw the shielded headlights of a truck approaching them. Overhead, a single-engine aeroplane flew through the low cloud. John thought he recognised a Boulton Paul Defiant fighter. It might even have been sent up to intercept them. The three of them instinctively drew together as the Morris truck halted. An officer stepped from the cab and four RAF airmen jumped from the back.

***

'Gentlemen, I need to know how we proceed. The loss of Corporal Dexter is a rather bad portent. In part I think we saw his deployment as an experiment to see what was possible and what was not. Although we have no knowledge of what went wrong exactly, this is hardly an encouraging start. I want us to set Europe ablaze. I want us to fight back, not to sit impotently like tired victims of misfortune. Hitler must see us being strong.' He seemed to run out of words at that point as if he had lost the next page of a scripted speech.

'With respect Prime Minister, there will be plenty of opportunities for us to engage the Germans at land and sea, regardless of the outcome of our current air battle with them. As you intimated earlier, I am not a proponent of private armies and cloak and dagger work. We can excel by using conventional methods. We are building a powerful army and we still have the most powerful navy in the world.'

'We have our strengths indeed but we don't seem to be on the offensive yet. We're like a boxer on the ropes,' added the PM.

Murray spoke now. 'I do think that these alternative forms of warfare are still worth pursuing. With a small number of men, we can potentially wreak enormous damage on the enemy.'

Dalton spoke next. 'I have to agree with the brigadier. We can't let one failure dissuade us from continuing. His loss is sad and we lose the experience he would have brought us but we have other people of the quality required for this type of work. Their impact could be out of all proportion to their numbers. Talking in economic terms they could represent very good value.' He looked at the other men. 'I don't really like to talk about human beings in that way – as if they are a commodity – nevertheless small groups of men or individuals may well have their uses.' He was a recent but enthusiastic convert to the idea of covert warfare.

'And have you recruited them yet?' asked Churchill. 'These other men?' He stood. Dalton, Brooke and Murray watched as he poured himself a whiskey. He indicated that they could help themselves but they remained seated, deferential. Murray and Dalton exchanged glances.

'We're in the process of refining our selection processes, Prime Minister,' said Murray. 'Not all of our candidates were suitable.' Dalton nodded his assent. Murray continued. He felt quite defensive when it came to the new organisation. 'We need more rigour to weed out the weaker men. We need to find men who can apply themselves to the training they need with self-discipline and resolve, men who can think in their feet, react to changing situations. Soldiers aren't always ideal material because they are used to being told what to do and may, in some cases, lack initiative.'

'Some soldiers may seek the easiest means of achieving a purpose rather than the best,' agreed Brooke. 'And what we don't want – what *I* don't want,' he corrected, 'is to take the cream of the armed forces away from conventional units.'

There was silence for a few moments as if the other men had decided to join the Prime Minister in his despond. Brooke risked a glance at his watch and wished that Churchill would let them all retire for the night. He'd been inspecting beach defences all day. They were a shambles.

He had enough despondency of his own without taking a share of the PM's. He wondered if Churchill knew how bad things were. It was probably better that he didn't. The country was hanging on his every word, taking hope from every nuanced sentence that he uttered. No-one else could have done it so well he had to admit.

'Dexter was only one man, Prime Minister,' reminded Brooke. 'We have lost thousands and will lose thousands more but that doesn't mean that we can't defeat Hitler.'

Churchill gave a tired smile and sipped from his glass as if it contained a potion that would energise him. He said to Brooke, 'That is a heartless point of view, but quite true of course.'

'I'm a general. There is little room for sentiment in my job. Generals must accept losses, plan for them in fact. They are regrettable – now that is a heartless word – 'plan', but I can't allow my thinking to be clouded by the loss of soldier's lives. Certainly not one soldier.'

Churchill nodded as if he had received a gentle reprimand from Brooke. Murray and Dalton looked on, waiting for his response. Churchill swilled the remains of his whiskey around his glass. 'Our perspectives are quite different General Brooke but you are correct, of course. The fight goes on.' He looked at each of them in turn. Dalton smiled. 'I'll fight myself if I have to,' he added. None of them were in any doubt that he would. Give him a revolver and he'd take on the Germans as they landed on the beaches. Give him a squadron of cavalry and he'd probably drive them back into the sea.

Brooke found himself constantly taken aback at the complexity of the man in charge.

There was a knock at the door which curtailed any further discussion. A captain in the uniform of the Grenadier Guards stepped into the room.

'Excuse me Prime Minister. I've just received a phone call from RAF Middle Wallop.'

'How peculiar,' said Churchill. 'What is the message?'

'I don't know if this will make any sense to you but I was asked to inform you that…' he referred to a piece of note paper, 'that Corporal Dexter has just returned.'

Churchill gave an uncharacteristic guffaw and slapped his thighs with the palms of his hands. 'As I said gentlemen – the fight goes on!'

Chapter Thirty-four

'Who are you?,' shouted the officer. His men had fanned out behind him, rifles in the low port.

'Flight Sergeant John Guy. This is Corporal Ted Dexter and this is…'

'What are you doing here? Where have you come from?'

'Well, we have just…'

'Are you expected?'

'Not exactly. *I'm* expected I suppose but…'

'Follow me. Get into the truck and don't try anything,' said the officer. A corporal spoke in his ear. 'Are any of you armed?' asked the officer.

Ted tried to reply. 'We have…'

'If you have any weapons, I want you to pass them on to Corporal Blackburn,' said the officer. He seemed to be only a few short mental steps away from hysteria. Blackburn was altogether calmer. He stepped forwards and held out his hand. Ted and Veronica handed their Walthers over.

***

The RAF officer posted a guard next to his three prisoners but had decided against detaining them in a secure room. Logically they posed no threat for a number of reasons. Firstly, they had landed by aeroplane on a British airfield, which was hardly the stealthiest means of arriving in the country. Secondly, they had made no attempt to run or to resist. Thirdly, they had meekly handed over their weapons. Against that, of course, was the fact that Corporal Blackburn had reported to him that the pistols he had taken from them and subsequently unloaded, were German in origin. But other than that, they themselves didn't seem to be… German.

As requested, he rang through to the Group Captain on duty that night and passed on their unlikely message. Group Captain Archer was both dismayed and dismissive but said that he would 'see what he could do.'

Eventually, an orderly brought in a tray of hot drinks and toast, produced at short notice and with much complaint by the officer's mess cook. Two more airmen appeared with blankets and pillows and dumped these without ceremony on the floor. They barely looked at John, Ted and Veronica as if total strangers landed in their midst all the time. Perhaps they did.

'Great to be back,' observed Ted, facetiously.

'Do they always make such a fuss of you?' asked Veronica.

'This is star treatment,' said John. 'Usually they lock us up.'

Veronica looked at the pilot unsure if he was joking or not. She said, 'do you think they'll pass on your message?'

John nodded. 'Put it this way, they'll be in deep trouble if they don't.'

'But Churchill? Really?' she said, unable to comprehend the enormity of what she had heard.

'Churchill, really,' confirmed Ted.

'Who are you, Ted?'

'I told you – Ted.' Beside him John nodded.

'He's Ted all right.'

'Yes, but who's that? I know you are Ted, but Ted who? What are you?' She shook her head in puzzlement. 'Have you met Churchill?'

'Yes,' confirmed Ted. 'We both have. We've met the King too.'

'The King? My God. I'm very impressed.'

'You should be.'

***

Gradually their conversation died down and they began the task of making beds. John and Ted collected cushions to produce a makeshift mattress for Veronica. John then pulled two chairs together to make a bed for himself but discovered that he was much too tall to every get comfortable in such a way. Ted threw a blanket on the rug and curled up. He was the first one of them to get to sleep.

Their sentry changed every couple of hours, clanking about the in the attached kitchen area, making tea and smoking heavily. The three prisoners looked decidedly unlikely to make a break for freedom.

In the morning they were given a change of clothes and the opportunity to wash. At such short notice the only suitable clothes which could be found for Veronica was a WAAF uniform.

'How do I look?' she asked giving a self-conscious twirl. She wasn't sure if she should feel silly or not.

'You look good. Very smart,' said Ted.

She smiled appreciatively. 'I could get used to this,' she said.

'You might have to,' warned John. He looked at her earnestly.

'What do you mean?'

'Nothing. Just ignore me.'

'No, really, I want to know what you mean.'

Ted took over the conversation. 'You're likely to be asked to do this sort of thing full-time. Espionage, or whatever you want to call it. You're better off knowing that before you meet any of these people.'

'What people?' she asked. Veronica looked alarmed.

'Just people.' Ted tried to sound dismissive. 'If they ask and you don't want to do it then just say no. But you will be asked.'

'What do you think?'

'About what?'

'I mean what should I say?'

'I can't help you with that. They might have dangerous work in mind for you. As far as they're concerned you've already proved yourself. You are the type of person they want but it's the sort of thing you volunteer for. They can't make you do it.'

'And did you volunteer for it?'

'I suppose so.'

'Why?'

Ted took a deep breath. He asked himself the same question often. 'I don't really know. Maybe I just fell for the flattery.'

***

At 09:30 a black Wolseley drove through the gates at Middle Wallop. At 09:45 it drove out again with Ted, John and Veronica inside. Their destination was London. They had just watched a scramble take place as a huge formation of Heinkel bombers was detected coming in over the Channel. John in particular watched closely – this base was his new posting and what he had just witnessed his new job, for now, being carried out by others.

What seemed like scores of pilots had charged headlong for their aircraft, shrugging on life vests, their heavy boots and Irvin jackets making them clumsy figures. They looked eager to embrace combat but John knew better. All but a few would be experiencing gut-wrenching fear – spiked with adrenaline – but fear nonetheless. Their waiting Spitfires were tended by small teams of erks, each one a master of his job. The aircraft had taken to the air and vanished in an impossibly brief time and they were left to marvel at the efficiency with which these young men were sent into combat. Where there had been frenzied but purposeful activity, there was stillness. Birdsong had replaced the hot roar of aero engines. Their thoughts mirrored those of the groundcrew left behind; *how many would return?*

***

Their journey took about an hour. The London streets teemed with activity as if a display of normality was being staged for Hitler's personal consumption. Here he could witness first-hand the British spirit that would see ordinary people through the war. *If only we could bottle it and drop it on Berlin, the war would be won.*

Red double-decker buses and black cabs plied their trade. The shops were open for business, even if business wasn't good. Here and there, artfully arranged sandbags gave clues as to the times these people lived in. High above them, tethered barrage balloons added a surreal touch to the city's shape. A visitor from another world might have thought that they were there to stop London sinking into the Thames. The dome of Saint Pauls, Tower Bridge, Big Ben all served as reminders of something essentially decent still in existence. They were reassuring symbols of a great nation battered but unbowed. Perhaps, mused Ted, it was just as well that the nation's capital was based in a city of such grandeur. Things that were worth fighting for were grouped together, concentrated in one area that served to define the empire for which he fought. Perhaps lesser nations had given up the fight because they lacked these things, these markers of history and tradition.

A smart-looking, but slightly older-than-usual policeman stopped their car at the entrance to Downing Street. Ted noticed the two rows of medal ribbons on his tunic, another Great War veteran. He too symbolised a defiant nation. A guardsman stood nearby eying them suspiciously. He looked as if he was itching to shoot someone. Ted guessed that he hadn't been in France. He didn't seem to have lost the pre-war soldier's enthusiasm for bloodletting.

The driver's ID was sufficient to guarantee only a short delay and the car pulled down the street to the door of No.10, which was guarded by another constable. The driver, who hadn't spoken for the entire journey got out and opened each door in turn so that the PM's guests could exit in a suitably dignified way. He led them to the door which opened as if magically and then departed.

'Please come in. The Prime Minister will be with you shortly,' said a man in a suit. Veronica's mind was swamped with detail: the shine on the man's shoes and his pencil moustache, the array of paintings in the hall of 10 Downing Street. The carpet was soft underfoot as if they were treading on sponges. The man led them into a high-ceilinged room and indicated a clutch of stiff-backed chairs in which they could attempt, but ultimately fail, to make themselves comfortable. The house smelt of some indefinable cleanliness, a mixture of disinfectant, wax polish and scent.

'It's very grand,' said Veronica in awe. She turned round and began to stroke the soft leather of her seat. The Prime Minister entered the room at that point.

'I see you've met the furniture,' he said, mischievously. She turned so quickly that she almost fell from her chair. Churchill seemed highly amused. Veronica was mortified. 'Corporal Dexter and Flight Sergeant Guy, it is great to see you again,' he said warmly. 'There was a degree of concern surrounding you, Corporal Dexter.' Churchill shook their hands, his delight obvious.

'Yes, sir. Flight Sergeant Guy told me I ended up in the bag.'

'You obviously didn't. You are a cat with nine lives, perhaps? And who is your friend? You always bring something back from your trips to the continent.'

Ted laughed. 'This is Veronica.'

'Veronica? Does she have a second name, Corporal Dexter?'

'Presumably she does, sir. I don't know it.'

Veronica stood. 'Veronica Hamill,' she said.

'I am both charmed and intrigued Veronica. I wonder how you came to be in a Royal Air Force aeroplane along with these two gentlemen.'

'It's a long story.'

'Carry on. I have arranged for some food to be brought to us anon.'

Veronica began the story from her perspective, being accosted by a strange man in the main street of Belloire, luring Ebbinghaus to her flat, the search, their escape to the roof and their next escape to the countryside. She made no mention of how she had come to be in France in the first place. Churchill sat in silence, seemingly transfixed. Only when she had finished did he put a question to her.

'So, you say the truck was used to *gas* these men?' he asked. The words were tinged with disbelief.

'It certainly looked that way. And we could smell the petrol fumes coming from the back of it.'

'I see. What a disturbing tale.' He turned to Ted. 'You shall have to include this in as much detail as you can when you are debriefed by the brigadier.

'I will, sir,' said Ted.

'It seems like we are in your debt, Veronica. You have helped rescue one of our top men. More than that you helped him to carry out his mission.'

'But we weren't successful, sir,' reminded Ted.

'Perhaps that is the fault of the mission rather than you. I am sure there are many things you would do differently if you were given a similar task again.'

Ted saw the glint of excitement in the old man's eyes and knew that this was not the time to ask for a return to his regiment. Churchill undoubtedly had big plans for his personal secret agent. His relief at having made it home began to dissipate as the PM's enthusiasm gained its own momentum. Furthermore, if Churchill's assertion that he had the nine lives of a cat was correct then he, by any measure, had used up several of them by now. At this rate he would need ninety-nine lives just to see out the year.

John spoke now. 'One thing which I don't understand is why I was told that Corporal Dexter had been captured. The planned sortie to collect him was actually cancelled.'

'Yes. I believe so. Simply not good enough. I wouldn't normally commend anyone for refusing to obey their orders but in this instance I'm very glad that you did. Brigadier Murray will have to take a long look at his sources of intelligence. We need to establish whether or not this was a deliberate case of misinformation or a simple mistake.'

Chapter Thirty-five

The following day John reported to his new squadron leader.

'I haven't got the faintest idea why you've been sent here, why you have arrived late, why you were taken to London or why you are not locked up awaiting a court-martial. But here you are, so welcome to 601 Squadron. Ever flown a Spitfire?'

'No, sir,' answered John as if this omission was a crime.

'Great,' said the officer with a weary sigh. 'You *are* a pilot?' he asked. His tone was curt, unfriendly. John guessed that he had recently been promoted to a position once held by a much older man. The air war offered mixed prospects; great for promotion, but correspondingly poor for survival.

'Yes, sir. I flew Battles in France and recently I've been flying Lysanders.'

'So that is your aircraft parked outside? Well, you can pick up your equipment from the QM. You need to see one of the flight commanders for an aircraft and a familiarisation flight.'

John saluted and with that less than ringing endorsement he left the office. He stood outside in the morning sun and watched as a flight of Spitfires took off on a routine patrol. He admired their clean lines – there could hardly be a better looking, more purposeful aeroplane in existence. Nevertheless, he felt no compunction to climb into the cockpit and fly one.

***

Veronica and Ted were taken to see Brigadier Murray. Ted could scarcely think about anything other than seeing Jean again and hadn't been able to get a message to her to tell of his safe return.

'Remember what I said,' reminded Ted as the Wolseley pulled into camp.

'About volunteering?'

'About *not* volunteering.' Their driver paused next to a sentry and wound down his window so that ID could be checked. 'It's the flattery that gets you,' he warned. 'That's how come I'm doing all this stuff.'

'But I might *want* to do it – that's if I'm offered, of course.'

'Oh, I think you'll be offered all right. It's dangerous. You'll almost certainly get sent back to France after your training. If you're caught by the Germans, they won't treat you as a prisoner of war.' The car had just stopped outside the block containing Murray's office. Once again, the driver opened their doors and led them to a waiting room, much less plush this time.

The brigadier came out to them almost at once and shook Ted warmly by the hand.

'And you must be Miss Hamill?,' he said gallantly. 'Please come in. We need to talk.'

They made a stab at some pleasantries but both men knew that they were here for an official debrief. Eventually Murray got things underway.

‘So how did you get on, then?’ he asked, although he must have known the answer. Ted told him about the mission. He spoke dispassionately, his earlier reservations and dissatisfaction tempered somewhat by the fact that he had escaped from France. He told the brigadier about the need for a torch and a map and safe houses and contacts and the multitude of details that might turn failure into success. He spoke candidly about the purpose of the mission and that it was not sufficiently important to risk a man’s life over. The brigadier nodded and made occasional notes but his face betrayed no emotion. If he was disturbed by Ted’s revelation about the purge on the town of Belloire following the German’s discovery of their dead soldier, then it didn’t show.

‘I just don’t think it was worth it, sir,’ stated Ted baldly. ‘I killed one German – the wrong one and just a private soldier – and they killed at least three French in return. They may have killed more.’

‘The manner in which they killed them also puzzles me. Are they experimenting with ways to dispose of their enemies?’ asked Murray. He seemed to be putting the question to himself. Ted shrugged.

The brigadier continued. ‘Well no matter. That is something for us to think about but it is certainly a beastly thing to do.’

Ted pursed his lips. *Beastly?* He wasn’t finished in his appraisal. ‘There are a couple of things I have been thinking about, sir. Things I don’t understand.’

‘Okay.’

‘How did you know that Feldhus was there?’

Murray raised an eyebrow. Then he asked, 'and the second thing?'

'Who told you that I'd been captured?'

'The answer to both lies in the machine you brought us from France. Using it, and a few frightfully clever chaps – mathematicians and so on – we have been able to decrypt German radio traffic. The actions of Feldhus's men in killing our soldiers caused quite a furore and generated a great deal of radio traffic between Northern France and Berlin. That's how we located him. As for your supposed capture that is from the same source but we think we have a contact within German high command who is feeding us information.'

'But the information was wrong, sir.'

'It was but that may have been a mistake. They did capture someone they thought was involved, this contact – if that's what he is – might have put two and two together.'

'Or they're deliberately leading you up the garden path?'

'That's possible. We just don't know.'

'And how could they know that we were intercepting their radio transmissions? If they didn't know then there would be no point in passing information that way.'

Brigadier Murray gave a great sigh and then laughed. 'There are some things I am not ready to tell you yet. If at some future date you are captured then it is better all-round if you know the bare minimum. I'm sorry.'

Ted nodded.

‘Well, I think we are finished for the meantime. There is someone downstairs who’d like to see you while I chat with Miss Hamill.’

***

‘Thank God,’ said Jean running to him. They embraced and neither spoke. Ted had allowed himself to dream of this moment, never being sure that it would happen. Every detail of her face, the curve of her hips, the flow of her hair was etched in his memory but the reality was so much better than his imaginings. She didn’t ask him any questions, preferring the bliss of ignorance. She didn’t ask where he’d been, what he’d done or when he would return to France… as she knew he would.

‘I don’t have to be back on station until tomorrow afternoon,’ she said.

‘Are you dropping a hint?’

‘Yes, Ted, I am.’

‘Well that’s settled then,’ he said happily.

***

‘We are very grateful to you for helping our man escape from France,’ said Murray.

Veronica smiled warily. She looked around the room to establish who else might be present with them, thus qualifying his use of the word ‘we.’ They were alone.

‘You displayed great resolve and bravery.’

Veronica gave a little shrug to convey her modesty. She stopped herself from saying, *it was nothing really.*

'Not to mention resourcefulness. We are very impressed.'

We?

'It made us think…' He paused for effect.

Veronica braced herself. *Here it comes*, she thought. Forewarned and thus forearmed, she'd prepared her answer. It was concise, terse even, easy to remember, easy to understand and unambiguous – *no*. She smiled warmly with all the fake sincerity she could muster.

'Yes, we thought that you might be interested in doing some work for us. We could make use of your skills. Mr Churchill is very keen for us to send people abroad to cause merry hell with the Germans…' He left the sentence sounding unfinished, as if giving her the opportunity to dive straight in with her acceptance. She remained tight-lipped.

'It's a new venture which we are calling the Special Operations Executive. SOE for short. I think that you'd be ideal.'

'Sounds dangerous,' she quipped, nervously.

It was Murray's turn to smile.

'You'd be fully trained,' he said, evasively.

She knew that training might give her a means to lessen the risk but did nothing to obviate the danger itself. The time for using her carefully prepared answer was drawing near and yet the flattery had had some effect. A flat refusal sounded ungrateful somehow, after all, she had been rescued from France. Maybe she could break the news in easy to accept little parcels.

‘I’ll certainly think about it,’ she said. ‘It does sound very interesting.’

‘I was hoping for something a little more definite. There’s no time like the present. You know that you could do it. We certainly need to recruit women and when we find someone so well-suited…’

‘No,’ she said, flatly.

‘No?’ He feigned surprise. In truth it wasn’t much of an offer and he knew it. It hadn’t even been decided how much these new people would be paid but it wouldn’t be much. It wasn’t worth it by any measure.

‘No. It’s not for me.’

‘I had hoped…’

‘No.’

‘I had hoped to avoid using any form of coercion,’ he said apologetically. Veronica’s blood ran cold.

‘Coercion?’

‘I’m afraid so. Would you like to reconsider?’ Now he feigned fairness. He was an expert feigner. There was a tense silence. Veronica looked down at her feet, crossed her legs and then uncrossed them. It was hard to ditch the past.

‘I really don’t think I’m suitable material,’ she argued at last.

‘When I talked before about your talents, I really only touched on them didn’t I?’

‘Oh?’

'Your move to France wasn't strictly for finding work and it certainly wasn't a holiday. Deception and fraud according to the police. A bit of smuggling too. You've even had a bit of practice with firearms, haven't you?'

'You've done your homework.'

'It wasn't difficult, believe me. This is the chance to wipe the slate clean. Work for us and you could be pardoned. There would be no courts, no prison, no ruination.'

'You'd have to prove it,' she said, defensively.

'We can do that. Even if we have to invent the evidence – we can do it. We can do anything. We know all about your sexual tendencies too. We can put you in jail just for that. We can do worse than that in fact. I believe that it might be possible to castrate you using chemicals.'

Veronica winced at the thought.

'Fine. I was just playing hard to get. I'd love to work for you,' she replied through gritted teeth.

'Oh good,' said Murray, with delight. Genuine delight, this time. 'It's great to have you on board.'

'Great to be on board!' she agreed. *Her* delight was not genuine. She could feign with the best of them.

Chapter Thirty-six

Ted reported to Murray's office after a breakfast prepared by Mrs Torrance. She had smiled sadly at his return, perhaps thinking of her husband. Ted had learned that there was still no news. No news in this case was unlikely to be good news. Mrs Torrance had given Ted and Veronica a wry look at breakfast but she had set two places and there was evidently enough food to go round.

'Some good news, Corporal Dexter.' Ted saluted and sat down at Murray's invitation. In Ted's mind the phrase 'good news' equated to 'leave.' 'No medals this time, I'm afraid but you do get a promotion.' Ted smiled weakly. 'Congratulations *Sergeant* Dexter.' Ted mumbled his thanks. Murray noticed his customary lack of enthusiasm.

'We've also managed to secure the services of your friend Veronica. I think she'll be a great asset. You look surprised.'

'Em, I am a bit, sir.'

'Yes well, I talked her round after her initial reluctance.' Ted nodded. He had been sure she'd refuse. She'd said as much. 'And the other good news is that we have some more work for you.'

'Oh,' said Ted. He did not say it in the way one might say, 'oh that *is* good news.' There was no lilt to his voice, no indication that it was anything other than bad news. Leave hadn't been mentioned and nor was there any discussion about whether or not Ted actually wanted to continue with his new vocation.

'Yes, we have been compiling a list of people who… D'you know I've been wracking my brains to come up with a phrase that encapsulates what I'm trying to say. Very difficult. Anyway, these people are perhaps not entirely beneficial to the war effort. I think that's what I'm trying to say. They are people who would be serving their country well by, er… ceasing to exist.

'Ceasing to exist, sir?'

'Yes. You know the sort of thing.'

'A blacklist?'

'Yes exactly. Well more of a *grey list* perhaps.'

'And how many people are on the list, sir?'

'It's early days so we've only really made a start,' havered the officer. Ted maintained his gaze until Murray capitulated. 'About sixty so far.'

'Sixty! My God, sir. You want me to kill sixty people?'

'I never said *kill.*'

'No, but that's what you meant.'

'Yes.' There was a brief hiatus during which Ted's incredulity settled down into mere stunned disbelief. 'We're not expecting you to get rid of them all but you can certainly make a start. Some of these people might simply be arrested, charged, tried and so on. That sort of thing.'

'If I don't kill them first.'

'Yes.'

'And the Prime Minister knows about this?

'Naturally.' Another silence followed. Ted did not for one minute believe that Churchill was complicit in this operation.

Then he said, 'can I have some leave, sir?'

'Of course. We'll see how you get on and then we'll sort something out.'

So, there it was; *do it or you get no leave.*

'Now there is a chap in County Londonderry who has been creating a spot of bother. I rather thought that you might pay him a visit and see what the craic is. Craic, that's what you say isn't it?'

Ted looked at the brigadier. He fought the urge to shake his head in dismay.

'Yes sir. Craic is what we say.'

Thank you for reading this book. If you enjoyed it, a review on Amazon would be very helpful for me.

Printed in Dunstable, United Kingdom

72264896R00170